LIGHTS!
CAMERA!
<u>HELLSPAWN!</u>

The necromancer brought both arms down in a sharp, sweeping gesture. With a sizzling blue-violet flash and a deafening, bloodcurdling howl, the demon materialized.

Jessica Blaine let out an ear-piercing scream. She strained in terror against the chain that held her, scrambling like a scalded cat as she tried to pull herself loose. The apparition looming over her was huge, with stumpy legs that ended in shaggy, cloven hooves, and powerful, ape-like arms. Its long hawk-like talons raked the air. Its fanged jaws were open wide enough to swallow Jessica whole. Currents of energy ran through the creature, sparking in multicolored discharges.

"Oh, my God . . ." said the cameraman.

"Keep rolling! Keep rolling!" shouted director Johnny Landau. *"Whatever you do, keep rolling!"*

Jessica thrashed upon the altar, screaming herself hoarse. As Jessica tore frantically at the chain, the demon leaped, arms extended, talons glistening . . .

"Annd . . . *cut!* Print it!"

Also by Simon Hawke

THE WIZARD OF 4TH STREET
THE WIZARD OF WHITECHAPEL

Published by
POPULAR LIBRARY

THE WIZARD OF SUNSET STRIP

SIMON HAWKE

POPULAR LIBRARY

An Imprint of Warner Books, Inc.

A Warner Communications Company

POPULAR LIBRARY EDITION

Popular Library®, the fanciful P design, and Questar®
are registered trademarks of Warner Books, Inc.

Cover design by Don Puckey
Cover illustration by Dave Mattingly

Popular Library books are published by
Warner Books, Inc.
666 Fifth Avenue
New York, N.Y. 10103

 A Warner Communications Company

Printed in the United States of America

First Printing: October, 1989

10 9 8 7 6 5 4 3 2 1

For Marge

CHAPTER
One

"*Meshugge*!" said the broom, craning around to look out the windows of the chauffeured limousine. "These people are all *meshugge*!"

All around them, scantily clad young people were shussing past them on the Ventura Freeway, skimming several feet above the surface of the road on flying carpets and street-boards, four-foot-long air surfers that darted in and out of traffic like dragonflies flitting among wildflowers. Aside from the carpets and the streetboards, there was the usual crush of taxicabs and buses and chauffeured limousines, all levitated and impelled by low-grade certified adepts, as well as expensive private vehicles, sleek status symbols powered by thaumaturgic batteries. But the most numerous of all were the wild streetboarders, balancing precariously on enchanted air surfers attached by thongs to leather straps around their ankles as they slalomed through the traffic like banshees whistling on the wind. Two of them suddenly collided and their bodies went flailing end over end through the air, one landing somewhere on the other side of the guard rail and the other slamming into the hood of an oncoming bus with a wet, slapping sound. It was an ugly sight.

Exactly how the broom could *see* all this was something of a mystery, since it had no eyes. It didn't even have a face, which also rendered its powers of speech completely inexplicable. And yet, the broom *did* speak, in a matronly, New York Jewish accent no less, punctuating its remarks with elaborate gestures of its spindly arms. The chauffeur glanced up at his rearview mirror, licked his lips nervously, and tried to concentrate on his levitation and impulsion spells. As a certified lower grade adept driving for a private limousine service in Los Angeles, he had seen a lot of strange, unusual things, but a walking, talking sweep broom was a first. But then, from the moment he'd picked these people up at LAX, he knew that these were no ordinary tourists.

They didn't even look like people who could afford a taxicab, much less a limousine, but in L.A., that didn't mean a thing. Some of the wealthiest people in town dressed like bums and they often spent a fortune doing so. Still, he didn't quite know what to make of these three—four, if he was going to count the broom.

The young man was in his mid to late twenties, with shoulder-length, curly blond hair cascading down from beneath a dark brown felt fedora that was pulled low over his eyes. He wore a short, hooded warlock's cassock made from coarse brown monk's cloth, loose, multipocketed brown moleskin trousers, and hightop, red leather athletic shoes with blue lightning stripes on them. The warlock's cassock and long, flowing hair were a dead giveaway. The broom clinched it. The young man was an adept. And the girl beside him referred to him as "warlock," as if it were a pet name.

Her name was Kira and she was a striking young woman in her late teens or early twenties, fit, foxlike, feral-pretty, with coal black hair cut in a renaissance punk style—swept back sharply on the sides and angled down over her forehead in a thick fall. She wore a chain mail and black leather jacket with a stand-up collar, skin-tight, dark red breeches, short black leather boots, and a soft black glove on her right hand. Her speech and streetwise manner clearly identified her as a New Yorker.

The boy was perhaps the most striking of the bunch—again, if one didn't count the broom. He was small and wiry, with delicate features that gave him a slightly androgynous aspect. His lips were thin and had a tendency to drop down slightly at the corners of his mouth. His nose was straight and blade-edged, his cheekbones high and pronounced. His eyes were dark and almond-shaped and his eyebrows had a thin and graceful arch. His ethnic origin was impossible to pinpoint. He could have been Eurasian, a light-skinned black, Hispanic or Creole or Indian, but his accent was thick, London cockney. He couldn't have been more than thirteen or fourteen years old, yet except for his size, there was nothing childish about him. His dark hair was worn short on the sides and luxuriantly thick and long in the center, like a horse's mane, descending in a ponytail down the middle of his back to his waist. His tatterdemalion ensemble included a patchwork leather-fringed jacket and surplus military trousers and combat boots. He wore thin black leather gloves with the fingers cut off and studded leather bracelets. The others called him Billy.

As for the sweep broom, well, they just referred to it as "Broom" and it seemed to be the young warlock's familiar. A bit overly familiar, thought the chauffeur. It kept telling him how to drive. He sighed with weary resignation. Hell, you could always tell these New Yorkers, he thought. Loud, obnoxious, wired, and intrusive. All they ever did was complain about how everything was so much better in New York. If everything was so much better in New York, he thought, why the hell didn't they just stay there?

"You, *schmendrick*, pay attention!" cried the broom, tapping the chauffeur on the shoulder with a rubbery finger. "Slow down already! You think this is some demolition derby here? You're going to hit somebody! I would like to survive this drive if you don't mind!"

The chauffeur shook his head, touched a button on his console and the window separating the driver's compartment from the passenger seats slid up. He sighed with exasperation. Another few minutes and they'd be at the hotel and he'd be rid of them.

"Well, I never!" said the broom. "Will you look at this? Did you see what he just did? The nerve!"

"Put a lid on it, Broom, will you?" Wyrdrune said wearily.

"'Ere, does she always go on like that?" asked Billy Slade.

"*She?*" said Kira. "Billy, you're talking about a stick, for God's sake."

"A stick?" the broom said. "A *stick*? That does it! I don't have to take this! Stop the car, I'm getting out. Stop the car this instant!"

The broom started to bang on the window between them and the chauffeur.

"Stop that!" Wyrdrune said.

"California! *Feh*!" the broom said, sitting back with a contemptuous sniff, which was rather curious, since it had no nose. "I don't know why we ever had to leave New York. What was so terrible? We had a nice apartment—"

"We lost our nice apartment," Wyrdrune said impatiently. "I was subletting, in case you don't remember. We've already gone through all this half a dozen times and why am I explaining to a piece of wood, for heaven's sake?"

Kira giggled.

"What's so funny?" Wyrdrune said irately.

"You two," she said. "You sound like a couple of *yentas* at the automat when you get going."

"*Yentas*?" said the broom. "Will you listen to this, the *shiksa* is calling me a *yenta*. A stick, a piece of wood, and now a *yenta*."

"And she'll be calling you sawdust if you don't keep silent!"

The voice came out of Billy, but it was not the voice of a thirteen-year-old cockney lad. Had the chauffeur not rolled up his window, he would have been surprised to hear the deep, resonant, and mature voice that had suddenly issued forth from that adolescent body. The cultured voice had a peculiar accent that was somewhere between Welsh and Celtic. The chauffeur would have been even more surprised to learn whose voice it was—not Billy's, but the entity that shared his body with him, the spirit of the legendary archmage, Merlin Ambrosius, court wizard to King Arthur Pendragon and father of the modern age of thaumaturgy.

Centuries ago, after falling victim to the spell of his apprentice, the sorceress, Morgan Le Fay, Merlin had been immured within the cleft of a large oak, which was kept alive for ages by the same spell that kept him prisoner. The age of chivalry and magic disappeared into the mists of time and new ages came and passed. With the rise of technology, the discipline of magic was totally forgotten, thought to be nothing more than myth and fantasy, yet all the while, Merlin slept . . . and deep beneath the earth, in a hidden, long forgotten tomb in the Euphrates Valley, others slept as well; powerful, inhuman beings of an ancient race from whom Merlin was descended. The Dark Ones, immortal necromancers entombed by the white wizards after the Great Mage War before the dawn of history. Entombed . . . and waiting.

When the age of technology ended at the close of the twenty-second century in the dark period known as The Collapse, what was left of civilization teetered on the brink. The world descended into anarchy. Cities became war zones. Rural areas became the wilderness again. One man, a retired soldier, driven to desperation by his desire to provide some warmth for his starving, freezing children, sneaked past perimeter guards and barbed wire fences into a protected area, all that was left of the denuded Sherwood Forest—a tiny grove of trees. One tree stood out among the rest, a gnarled and ancient oak that was at least ten times the size of all the others. Later on, he could not say why he picked that tree, but something in him snapped. With a cry, he attacked it with his ax and suddenly, the moment the ax blade bit into the trunk, a flash of lightning split the tree in half and Merlin was released.

That was the beginning of the end of The Collapse. The start of the second thaumaturgic age. Merlin brought back the forgotten discipline of magic. He founded schools and put the world on a thaumaturgic energy standard. The remnants of the old technology were revitalized by magic-users trained in Merlin's schools. From lower grade adepts who knew only simple spells to warlocks to wizards and still more powerful sorcerers to the mere handful of adepts who had reached the vaunted rank of mage, universities with postgraduate schools of thaumaturgy turned out magic-users to support the energy base that powered the second thaumaturgic age. Spells kept public transportation running; enchantments powered the old turbines and generators, providing clean, nonpolluting energy. Slowly, the cities came back to their former glory, but in a different and more natural way, a union of the dead technology and reborn magic.

Old, damaged asphalt was gradually replaced with grassy causeways. Acid-free rain slowly washed the ancient buildings clean. City streets became park rambles with shade trees and flowering gardens filled with birds bred by thaumagenetic engineering, creatures that not only sang sweetly, but also spoke and helped to keep the cities free from litter.

Yet not everything was rosy in this new thaumaturgic dawn. Human nature was nevertheless still human nature. There was still crime. There was still violence. There were still greed and jealousy and envy and all the spiteful, hateful feelings that went with them. And with magic in the air once more, the Dark Ones awoke within their tomb. They broke free of their eons-old confinement and now they were loose upon the unsuspecting world once more. And only four people possessed the power to stop them—a dropout warlock, a thief, a street urchin, and a mysterious professional assassin who was known by many names.

The authorities knew him only as Morpheus, named after the mythic God of Dreams, because he put people to sleep. Forever. Some knew him as Michael Cornwall. Others knew him as Mikhail Kutuzov or Phillipe de Bracy or Antonio Modesti or Maurice Le Fay, the list went on and on. Yet only a handful of people knew him by his truename— Modred, the immortal bastard son of King Arthur Pendragon and his half sister, the sorceress, Morgan Le Fay.

All were brought together by a spell that was embodied in three living runestones, enchanted talismans imbued with the life force of the Council of the White, the Old Ones who had defeated and entombed those among their kind who had been seduced by necromancy. They had given their lives to empower the spell that held the Dark Ones prisoner:

"Three stones, three keys to lock the spell,
Three jewels to guard the Gates of Hell.
Three to bind them, three in one,
Three to hide them from the sun.
Three to hold them, three to keep,
Three to watch the sleepless sleep."

Only one among the Council of the White was left alive after the others fused their life force with the runestones. His name was Gorlois and he was the youngest of the immortal white archmages. He went out into the world and lived among the humans. With a girl of the De Dannan tribe, he had a son whom he named Merlin. Years later, with a Welsh maid named Igraine, he had three daughters named Morgause, Elaine, and young Morgana, who became Morgan Le Fay. And now, two thousand years later, their descendants had been reunited. Kira, the orphaned thief, was descended from Elaine. Wyrdrune, the bumbling warlock, descended from Morgause. And descended from Nimue, the De Dannan witch who had been Merlin's lover, was young Billy Slade—now possessed by the spirit and the powers of his legendary ancestor.

Hidden by the glove on Kira's right hand, embedded in the flesh of her palm, was a shining sapphire runestone, a living gem animated by the souls of the immortal archmages who had lived before the dawn of time. Beneath his hat, embedded in his forehead over his "third eye," Wyrdrune wore a gleaming emerald runestone that gave him powers far beyond those of a bumbling warlock who had never finished thaumaturgy school. And set into the flesh of his chest, over his heart, Modred wore the third runestone, a darkly glistening blood ruby, uniting him with the spirits of his inhuman ancestors. Together, they formed the living triangle, the ancient spell made real, and Merlin—who had died in their first encounter with the Dark Ones—had returned once more, his spirit living on in Billy Slade, the scrappy little cockney street urchin from Whitechapel.

The limousine pulled up in front of the Beverly Hills Hotel and the chauffeur got out and held the door open for his unusual passengers, never suspecting how truly unusual they really were. Nor did they suspect what awaited them in the City of the Angels, a town which they would soon discover had been ironically misnamed.

She was very, very beautiful and very, very dead. Her sightless eyes were wide open and bright red from blood vessels that had burst. A trickle of coagulating blood ran down from the corner of her mouth, which was open in a never-ending, silent scream.

Ben Slater stared down at her nude body and slowly shook

his head. "My God," he said. "Twenty years on the police beat and I never saw anything that looked like that."

The look on the dead girl's face was unforgettable. It was as if she had seen the most horrifying thing imaginable at the moment of her death. But as unsettling as the expression on her face was, that was not what Slater meant. He was referring to her wounds.

"I've never seen anything like it, either," said Detective Sergeant Harlan Bates, standing beside him. "I don't know what to make of it."

Both men stared down at the body with a grim, uneasy fascination as the police photographer methodically snapped it from a variety of angles. The victim's name was Sarah Tracy. She was an actress. Neither Bates nor Slater had ever heard of her, but that was not surprising in a town where every waiter was really an actor and every exotic dancer read the trades. She had been discovered by Victor Cameron, who described himself as her "agent/manager," a title which both Bates and Slater took to be merely a euphemism for boyfriend. Cameron had been so distraught that he'd been taken to the hospital. Which did not, as far as Bates was concerned, serve to eliminate him as a suspect.

The nude body of Sarah Tracy was lying on its side, close against the wall. Slater noticed that it was almost directly opposite the rumpled bed on the other side of the studio apartment. There were some peculiar marks around the dead girl's narrow waist, above her hips. The entire area between her hips and breasts was heavily bruised, the discolorations running in three narrow bands, like horizontal stripes, almost all the way around her torso. And then there were the wounds. Three deep holes in the approximate center of her abdomen, one above the other, at the point where each discolored band ended. It was as if someone had taken three large railroad spikes and driven them into her body, almost clear through to the spine. Midway up the wall, there was a large splatter mark of blood, as if she had been picked up and *hurled* all the way across the room.

Bates had been a Los Angeles police officer for about ten years and Slater had spent the better part of two decades covering crime and corruption in the city before he went on to write a hard-hitting, streetwise opinion column, yet each time they saw a dead body, there was always that peculiar moment, that strange, indefinable sensation when for an instant, everything just stopped. Slater, who thought about such things more deeply than most people, called it "the moment of involuntary silence."

"You want to say something," he'd explain over a shot of whiskey and a beer at Flannagan's, "or even if you don't, you *feel* as if you should. You feel like you oughta shake your head and groan or something, *anything*, but you just can't. You stand there, maybe you swallow if your mouth hasn't gone dry, and for a minute you simply stare at this thing that used to be a person. It doesn't look real, somehow. It's like a mannequin. Not only is the spark gone, but it looks as if it was never there at all. And there it is, the mystery, staring you right in the face. The only thing that makes you different from that body is that spark and you could lose it anytime. Sooner or later, you're going to look like that. Maybe sooner than you think. And there's nothing you can do about it. Most people never have to confront their fate that way, but cops do it every day. Cops, pathologists, and a few reporters. They all share that moment of involuntary silence. Then they start cracking sick jokes."

It was one of the reasons why cops like Harlan Bates liked and respected Benjamin J. Slater. He was the barometer of their reality. He was their poet. He gave voice to their feelings in a way that most of them could not express themselves. Most of them would never, even in the direst of circumstances, consider seeing a shrink, but they would gladly stand Ben Slater to several rounds at Flannagan's and moodily unburden themselves, because the rough-hewn, dark-haired, plain-spoken reporter understood and, what was even more important, he was "all right." Those two simple words encompassed an entire litany of codes, both written and unwritten, and what it all came down to was the simple fact that Ben Slater could be trusted. If it was personal, it stayed that way. If he agreed that something said was off the record, Ben Slater never printed it. He protected his sources with the fierce tenacity of a junkyard dog and he had done the jail time to prove it.

However, Ben Slater was not universally liked by the men and women on the force. In particular, he was disliked by many of their senior officers, especially those with political aspirations. This was because Ben Slater had a nasty tendency to write the truth and, as the city's most popular columnist, he often flavored it with strongly held opinions. He did not, in the parlance of the upper echelons, "play ball." And those members of the force who cared more about moving up into administration than they did about fighting crime regarded Ben Slater as anathema. Therefore, Slater was not at all surprised when he heard the tone with which Captain Farrell addressed him when she came into the room. What surprised him was that the redoubtable Rebecca Farrell was even on the scene.

"Slater! What the hell are *you* doing here?"

Rebecca Farrell's personality was as fiery as her bright red hair, which she wore short in a shaggy, feathered geometric cut. She had a thick forelock that always had a tendency to dangle down over her eyes, lending her the aspect of a cocky bantam rooster. She was slim, leggy, and pretty to the point of almost unbearable cuteness, which had led her to develop an extremely aggressive and often abrasive demeanor in compensation for an appearance that she felt kept people from taking her seriously. However, as Slater knew only too well, anyone who did not take Rebecca Farrell seriously was making a serious mistake. She was the youngest police captain on the force, with the most ambition and the most to prove. Rebecca Farrell had been promoted through the ranks and she had built a reputation for being hard as nails, but she was far tougher on herself than on any of the people under her command.

"I'm just doing my job, Becky," Slater replied, in an offhand tone. "What about you? What brings you out from behind the desk?"

"The name is Rebecca," she said tersely. "And I'll thank you to address me as *Captain* Farrell."

"Sure. Just as soon as you start addressing me as *Mr*. Slater."

There had been a time, not very long ago, when it had

been Ben and Becky—a close and intimate relationship, despite the twenty-year difference in their ages, but that had changed when Becky was made captain. Slater had always thought that Becky Farrell was one of the best street cops he'd ever known. He had a high professional regard for her and a very warm, personal regard, as well. But he thought that her being mired in administration was a waste of her considerable abilities. She thought of it as career advancement, although she missed the streets, which made Slater's intolerance rankle that much more. And then there was the added complication of Slater's natural antagonism toward what he referred to as "the high command," a hierarchy of which she was now a part.

She took a deep breath and then turned on Bates. "Who authorized *Mr.* Slater's presence at this crime scene?"

Bates shrugged apologetically. "I'm sorry, Captain, I didn't know there was any order barring the press."

"Don't give me that," she said. "I don't see the press here. I see only Mr. Slater. Now where do you suppose the rest of them are?"

"I don't know. Maybe they didn't get the word yet," Bates said innocently.

"And maybe somebody tipped Slater in advance and let him slip past the police line?" she said.

Bates looked uncomfortable.

"Now, take it easy, Becky. . . ." Slater said.

"Look, don't you condescend to *me*, Ben Slater!" she said, spinning around to face him, though condescension was the farthest thing from his mind. Slater flinched and backed away and, for the first time, Rebecca Farrell's gaze fell on the corpse.

The moment of involuntary silence struck.

"Oh, my God . . ." she said softly after the initial shock.

"What do you figure made those wounds, Rebecca?" Slater said. "And those marks around her waist?"

Rebecca Farrell knelt down by the body for a closer look. Her entire demeanor seemed to undergo a drastic change. Little frown lines of concentration appeared over the bridge of her nose and her jaw muscles tensed as she examined the wounds. For a long moment, she said nothing, then, as if suddenly remembering that Slater had spoken, she said, "I don't know. I've never seen anything like this before."

It was almost exactly the same thing Bates had said. Almost exactly the same thing Slater himself had said, but something about the way Rebecca Farrell said it didn't quite ring true.

Slater watched her carefully. "You know, I think you have," he said.

She glanced up at him sharply.

"You always were a rotten liar, Becky," Slater said. "Maybe that's because you always were an honest cop. You used to be a hell of a fine detective before you tied yourself down behind a desk."

She stood and turned to face him. "I'm *still* a hell of a fine detective, Slater."

"I know," he said. "But the trouble is you don't work at it anymore. You've seen this sort of thing before, Becky. I can tell. I saw your face. I know you."

"What are you trying to say, Ben?" she said in a level tone.

He chose not to respond directly. Instead, he asked a question.

"What do these wounds look like to you?" he said. "Speculating, purely off the record?"

"I don't know. I told you, I've never seen anything like it."

"You're are a liar," he said.

She flushed and the corner of her mouth twitched slightly. Bates watched them both uneasily. No one spoke to Captain Farrell that way. No one.

"Suppose I tell you what it looks like to me," said Slater quickly, before she could reply. "It looks as if something grabbed her and threw her clear across the room. Something huge and incredibly strong. Something with three large claws . . . or maybe talons."

Farrell stared at him long and hard. "That's your considered opinion, is it?" she said. "Are you going to print that?"

"I don't know, Rebecca," he said. "What do *you* think?

You think maybe there's a story here? I mean, something more than just another L.A. murder? What do you think the coroner's going to say about those bruises and those wounds? And just supposing that you *have* seen something similar to this before, but you've kept it quiet, you think maybe *that* would be a story? You think if I hung around here long enough, I might even see an investigator from the B.O.T. show up?"

"Why should the Bureau of Thaumaturgy be interested in this case?" Rebecca said, a touch too nonchalantly.

"You tell me, Rebecca. Did somebody just kill this girl, or did someone summon up some*thing* to do it?"

"What are you getting at?" she said tensely. "What are you going to say in your column, Ben?"

"What do you think the rest of the media will say when they learn the particulars of this case?" countered Slater.

"The particulars?" said Rebecca, pursuing her lips and trying to look innocent. "I'm really not sure what you mean, Ben. What we have here is a young woman who's been stabbed to death and we've got a suspect in custody, under observation at L.A. County Hospital."

Slater frowned. "You know damn well that's not what happened."

"Do I? Then you tell *me*, Ben. What *did* happen? What forensic evidence have *you* got? This is hardly the time for wild speculation that could cause a panic in this city. I want to know what you're going to write, Ben."

"Well, if you're going to insist on following this tack, Rebecca, I think I may just write about a cover-up," said Salter flatly. "About the L.A.P.D. trying to keep from the public certain facts that indicate that someone in this city is practicing necromancy. That's black magic, Becky. The kind that kills people."

"Sergeant Bates, I want you to place Mr. Slater under arrest," Rebecca Farrell said.

"*What?*" said Bates.

"*What?*" echoed Slater with astonishment. "*On what charge?*"

"Interfering with a homicide investigation," said Rebecca curtly. "That'll do for starters."

"You can't be serious," said Slater, staring at her with disbelief.

"Cuff him, Bates," Rebecca said. "Read him his rights."

"Becky!"

"Bates! I gave you an order!"

"I'm sorry, Ben," said Bates awkwardly, putting the cuffs on him. "You have the right to remain silent. . . ."

"Becky!"

She turned and walked away.

"Rebecca!"

"Anything you say could be held against you in a court of law—"

"Oh, shut up, Harlan!"

"I'm sorry, Ben, I've got to read you your rights—"

"Oh, for cryin' out loud, I understand my rights!" snapped Slater. "Just book me and get me to a goddamn phone!"

CHAPTER
Two

"And . . . *action*!"

As the cameras started rolling, the necromancer raised his arms high above his head and blue fire crackled around his fingers. The effects team went to work as simulated lightning lit up the cyclorama behind him and wind machines made his long white hair and star-bedazzled robes billow dramatically as he stood on a reinforced papier-mâché rock promontory in a howling storm.

"All right, tilt down to Jessica! Cue Jessica. . . ."

As the camera framed the leading lady, she started to writhe upon the carved stone altar as if with terror. It was a blatantly sexual display. She was strategically garbed in a clinging, white off-the-shoulder shift that was slashed to her hips, the better to show off her admirably well-shaped legs as she lay on her side in an attitude calculated to display them to best advantage. With her loosely closed fist held up to her open mouth in that timeless and entirely artificial gesture of screen heroines showing great alarm, she pulled her shoulders back so that her breasts were thrust against the thin, sheer fabric of her dress. To facilitate all these gyrations and further add some spice to the scene, instead of being bound to the altar hand and foot, Jessica was held prisoner by an iron collar attached to a short length of chain embedded in the "rock."

"Yes, *yes*! Good, Jessica, *good*!" the director encouraged her as if he were praising a pet dog. "You're terrified! He's going to unleash all the powers of Hell at you! *Horror! Utter horror!* More! *More!* That's it, give it to me! *Give* it to me!"

What she gave him wasn't exactly horror, but it was eminently watchable, all the same. The camera crane pulled back, widening the shot so that the malevolently gesticulating necromancer could be seen standing atop the fake rock promontory above the fake carved stone altar, where Jessica faked it with everything she had.

"Annnnnd . . . *Cue demon!*"

The necromancer brought both arms down in a sharp, sweeping gesture and a sizzling, bright blue bolt of thaumaturgic energy lanced down toward the ground at the foot of the alter where Jessica was acting her little heart out. There was a bright, blue-violet flash, a lot of sparks, and clouds of billowing smoke shot through with heat lightning . . . and then a deafening, bloodcurdling howling filled the studio as the demon materialized.

"*Jee-zus* Christ!" whispered Johnny Landau, the director. He stood slack-jawed, rooted to the spot, momentarily forgetting to direct the scene as he stared wide-eyed at the fearsome apparition.

Jessica let out an ear-piercing scream and this time, she wasn't acting. She strained in genuine terror against the chain that held her, no longer writhing suggestively, but scrambling like a scalded cat as she tried to pull herself loose. The apparition looming over her was huge, with two stumpy, muscular legs that ended in shaggy, cloven hooves. It had a wide, V-shaped torso with a gigantic rib cage, massive shoulders, and long, powerful, apelike arms. Its three-fingered hands had long, curving, hawklike talons that raked the air as it howled like a runaway express train. Its face was mostly mouth, with fanged jaws open wide enough to swallow Jessica whole, and its eyes were catlike, burning orbs of green fire. The creature was semitransparent, with currents of energy running through it, sparking in bright, multicolored, thaumaturgic discharges.

"Oh, my God. . . ." said the cameraman.

"Keep rolling! Keep rolling!" shouted Landau, recovering from the shock of the demon's appearance. *"Whatever you do, keep rolling!"*

Jessica thrashed upon the altar and screamed herself hoarse as the creature howled and wailed, and then it gathered itself for a leap. As Jessica tore frantically at the chain, the demon leapt up into the air, arms extended, talons glistening, and an instant before it would have landed on the altar, the necromancer gestured sharply and the creature disappeared like smoke, leaving only the ecohes of its bone-chilling howls.

"Annnd . . . *cut*! Print it!" the director yelled jubilantly. *"God*, that was *incredible*! Amazing! *Un-be-lievable!* Jessica, darling, that was absolutely fabulous! Jessica?"

The leading lady was sprawled out on the altar, motionless. The director and several crew members rushed over to her.

"Jessica?" said Landau, standing over her and looking down with concern. "Jessica, honey, are you all right? Jessie—Jesus, somebody get a doctor!"

"She's all right," one of the crew members said. "I think she only fainted."

"Jessica? Jessie, come on, honey, snap out of it!" Landau slapped her lightly on the cheeks while one of the crewmembers held her propped up slightly. "Jessie?"

She opened her eyes, gave a violent start, and then sagged back down with a sigh when she saw that everything seemed to be under control. She closed her eyes, took a deep, ragged breath, then let it out slowly and opened her eyes once more.

"Hey, Jessie, honey," Landau said, "for a second there, you really had us worried!"

She sat up slowly and turned to one of the crew. "Get this damn thing off me," she said, indicating the collar. The moment it was removed, she suddenly lashed out and gave Landau a hard, stinging slap across the face.

"*Jessie!*"

"You miserable son of a bitch!"

"Jessie! What the hell?"

"I almost had a goddamn heart attack, you bastard! *Jesus!* It was so *real*! Why the hell didn't you *tell* me it was going to be like that?"

"I'm afraid that was entirely my fault, Miss Blaine."

The man playing the necromancer had climbed down from his promontory and stood behind them, holding his high, conical hat under his arm and looking contritely at Jessica Blaine. His long white hair hung lank and damp below his shoulders and his beard and whiskers obscured most of his deeply lined, pale face, which showed the strain of the scene he'd just completed.

His voice was young, however, soft and faintly accented. He passed his right hand over his face, as if pushing back a veil, and the years magically fell away from him. He suddenly stood revealed as a much younger man, in his late thirties or early forties, slim, darkly handsome, clean-shaven, with shoulder-length black hair and pale blue eyes. Beneath the ornate Hollywood version of a necromancer's robes, which he had unfastened, he wore a simple black tunic and trousers, the costume of a cleric or a monk.

"Please forgive me, Miss Blaine," he said, his voice sounding at the same time both soothing and compelling, "but not even Mr. Landau knew exactly what the effect would look like, so you see, there really was no way that he could have prepared you. And you must admit, having seen it, that it would have been rather difficult to explain what the effect would look like in advance."

Jessie Blaine expelled her breath in a sharp little gasp. "God, I should say so! But, dammit, you could have warned me just the same, Khasim! You might have given me at least *some* idea of what to expect! That . . . that horrible *thing*! It scared me half out of my mind! My God! I still can't believe how *real* it was!"

"Merely a magical illusion, Miss Blain," Khasim said. "You were in no danger whatsoever, I assure you. However, had I suspected that you were truly in such great distress, I would have canceled the illusion at once. I merely assumed that you were acting. Since your acting is always so utterly convincing, I fear that it simply never occurred to me that you were actually terrified. I don't know what to say. I feel terrible. Can you please forgive me?''

"Well . . . I wasn't exactly *terrified*, Brother Khasim," she said, warming somewhat now that her vanity had been appealed to. ''But of course I'll forgive you.''

"Jessie, you should have seen yourself!" Johnny Landau said. "Wait'll you see the rushes! You were incredible! Totally convincing! And Khasim, my man, that was truly spectacular! You even had *me* believing it was real! Incredible! Just incredible! Best special effect I've ever seen! You're a genius! A genius! Okay, people, that's a wrap! Strike the set! Nice job, everybody! See you all at the wrap party tonight!''

The effects team watched Brother Khasim as he walked away, the wardrobe department's star-bespangled costume billowing behind him like a cape. Their expressions were not very friendly.

"That guy's gonna cost us our jobs if this keeps up," one of them said.

"So what're you gonna do?" one of the others said with a shrug of resignation. "You can't hardly do a picture anymore without a special effects adept. It cuts costs and the audience expects it. Besides, you saw that effect illusion. How the hell can we compete with that?''

''Heck, Joe, we could've duplicated that effect.''

"*Live?* You want to tell me how, Mort?''

"Well . . . no, of course not *live*, but—"

"But nothing, Mort, that's just the point. No matter what we could come up with, an adept like Brother Khasim could do it in a fraction of the time and at a tenth the cost, even with the huge salary the studio pays him. It lets them bring the picture in quicker and with a smaller budget. Face it, he's good. The best I've ever seen. We just can't compete.''

"Yeah, but there's still things they need us for," Mort said. "Like today, with the lighting effects and the wind machines. We can still do that a lot cheaper than it would cost them to have Khasim whip up a thunderstorm.''

"Yeah? And how long before that turns into a conflict with the electrician's union?" the first man said. "You don't have to be a special effects man to flip a switch, Mort."

"Bert's right," said Joe with a heavy sign. "We're being squeezed out. Used to be wizards were too high-and-mighty for special effects work in films and all we got were lower grade adepts that weren't much of a threat. But now with sorcerers like Brother Khasim coming into the motion picture business, they just don't need us anymore."

"There must be something we can do," said Mort, looking worried.

"Maybe there is," said Bert thoughtfully. "There's been a lot of talk about this Brother Khasim character. Story is he's only doing this to help his mission, but he's cutting into a lot of people's territory. I think maybe I'll call in a few favors and find out what the deal is with this mission of his. Talk to some people I know and see what I can pick up about our mysterious adept."

"Want us to ask around as well, Bert?" Mort said.

"Yeah, why not? Let's see what we can learn about him. Find out where he came from; where he studied; who his teachers were and how come he can do things none of the other effects adepts can do."

"Like that demon, for instance?" Mort said.

"Yeah," Bert said, nodding. "Like that demon."

"Hey, Bert? Come here for a second."

Joe stood next to the fake stone altar in the spot where Khasim had made the demon effect materialize.

"Take a look at this," he said.

He pointed down at a several large scuff marks and indentations in the floor.

"So? What is it?" said Bert.

Joe glanced up at him with a strange expression. "Looks like hoofprints," he said.

Good God," Rydell said softly. "Morpheus."

"Please, the name is Michael Cornwall, if you don't mind. It would be safer for both of us if you didn't use that other name," said the well-built man with the dusty blond hair and neatly trimmed beard. His eyes were hazel and he wore tinted

gold-rimmed glasses, an archaic affectation. His dark, cus-
tom-made suit was elegantly cut in the latest neo-Edwardian
style, showing a touch of lace at the throat and cuffs. His
voice was crisp, with a slight accent that sounded faintly
British.

Ron Rydell was not happy to see him. Ten years earlier,
the young producer/director had been on his way to becoming
one of the fastest rising stars in the film industry, the hottest
wunderkind in the business. But he was also way over his
head in debt to some savage loan sharks. His first two films,
independently produced and directed by himself, had been
critical successes, but financial flops. He had overextended
himself and his nervous backers had stopped answering his
calls. Bankers were polite, as bankers always are, but equally
intractable, especially when it came to a relative newcomer
to the business with a less than impressive commercial track
record. Frustrated, Rydell had turned to less conventional
sources. And things had gone rapidly downhill from there.

He went over budget on the film and his new backers started
squeezing. Rydell soon found himself bone dry. He had managed to dance around creditors before and he had thought that
this would be no different. After they broke his leg, he got
scared. But when they brutally beat up his girlfriend in his
presence, his fear was driven out by stone-cold rage. He
burned every card he had to make contact with "the best man
in the business," a business that did not advertise through
normal channels. He incurred some obligations to people he
would rather not have been obligated to, but fury drove him
and he didn't care. It was pay-back time and he eventually
found just the man to do it. Ten years ago, Ron Rydell had
been very happy to see Modred, whom he knew only as
Morpheus, but he was not very happy to see him now. Not
now that he was a successful producer of slick action/adven-
ture films. And certainly not in his own living room, in the
middle of the night. He had just come home from a late night
at the studio, supervising the editing of his latest film. His
house was dark, and when he turned on the lights, he was
brought up short by the sight of Modred relaxing in the
leather-upholstered armchair and smoking a cigarette.

"It's been a long time . . . 'Mr. Cornwall.' Or should I call you Michael, since we're such old friends?'' Rydell said, staring at him uneasily. He licked his lips nervously. ''What's it been, about ten years?''

''About that. Michael will do, or Mike, if you prefer. I see you've done well in the meantime.''

''I've done all right.''

''Oh, I'd say you've done rather better than 'all right.' You've become an important man in this town. What is the old phrase . . . someone who pulls a lot of weight?''

Rydell gave a small snort. He compressed his lips into a tight grimace and nodded. ''I knew it,'' he said. ''I always knew it would come one day.''

''I assume you recall our arrangement?''

''Arrangement?'' said Rydell with an ironic smile. ''Oh, yeah, I recall our 'arrangement.' I remember like it was yesterday. How the hell could I ever forget? I asked you for a little time. I said the bastards squeezed me dry, but I swore that whatever it took and whatever it cost me, even if I had to sell my goddam soul to pay you, I'd do it somehow.'' He paused. ''And you said you'd take my soul. As collateral.''

''Almost word for word,'' said Modred, smiling. ''You have an excellent memory, Rydell.''

''Yeah, well, some things are more memorable than others,'' Rydell said wryly. He exhaled heavily and went over to the bar to pour himself a stiff drink. He still walked with a pronounced limp. ''You know, I read about what you did in the newspapers. And then I waited ten years for the other shoe to drop. Scotch?''

''Please.''

''You take it neat, right?''

''As I said, an excellent memory.''

Rydell smiled wryly. ''My friend, I've never forgotten *anything* about you.''

''Trouble sleeping nights?''

Rydell handed him the glass of whiskey. ''No, funny thing about that. I lose sleep over other things sometimes, but never that. It's funny. I had three people killed and, you know, it doesn't bother me a bit. I've often wondered about that. Truth is, those scum-bastards had it coming and I'm glad they're dead.'' He paused slightly. "I guess that makes me a pretty cold-blooded son of a bitch, doesn't it?''

"It makes you human,'' Modred said. "And you were right, they certainly had it coming. Which reminds me, whatever became of the young lady?''

"You're kidding,'' said Rydell, sitting down on the couch. "You really don't know?'' Then he nodded. "That's right, I remember. You read books. No movies, no TV, no theater. None of that lowbrow stuff for you, eh? Well, Jessie had to have her face worked on quite a bit, but she came out of it okay. More or less okay, anyway. She got her looks back, but she's been insecure about it ever since. Always out to prove she's still got it, if you know what I mean. And she's still jumpy as all hell. But I suppose she got what she wanted in the long run.''

Rydell stared down at his glass. "Funny thing. Only reason she ever went out with me was because she wanted to get into one of my films. Unfortunately, by the time I found that out, she was already in the hospital with her face all busted up and I felt like it was all my fault. So I paid for her new face, complete with improvements, had a thaumaturgic surgeon brought in to assist the team, first cabin all the way, deeper and deeper into debt, and then I gave her the lead in the first cheap quickie that came along. Hell, I was broke and I figured you'd come knocking pretty soon, wanting to be paid, and you were the one man I did *not* want to have financial problems with, believe me, so I grabbed the first film I was offered. I didn't give a damn what the hell it was.''

He smirked and swirled the ice around in his glass. "That was *Curse of the Necromancer*. Most godawful fucking script you ever saw. Made Jessica Blaine a star and me a multi-millionaire. I promptly hung up my artistic principles and made a sequel. The critics crucified me, but the picture earned out in the first week of release and I haven't looked back since.'' He tossed back the rest of his Scotch. "But you didn't come here to hear the story of my life, right? I'm sure you'd rather get down to business. I'll say one thing for you, when a guy asks you for some time, you sure as hell give him some time. What took you so long? Hell, forget it, I can't complain. I'm sure you had your reasons. Anyway, I can afford it now, but you'll have to give me 'til tomorrow to get the cash. I don't keep that much around.''

"I don't want your money, Rydell," Modred said.

"What?"

"I said, I don't want your money."

"What is this, a joke?"

"No joke. I'm absolutely serious."

Rydell stared at him apprehensively. "What, then?"

"A favor."

"I see," Rydell said nervously.

"No, I don't think you do," said Modred. "Ten years ago, you were in trouble and you needed me, but you could not afford my price. I told you then that I didn't work for just anyone. I took that contract because those people needed to be dead and I thought there was a chance that at some future time, you might be in a position to do something for me. I've done that on occasion, when I thought the situation—and the client—merited such consideration. You don't need to concern yourself, Rydell. I'm not trying to get my hooks into you. Think of it as a simple trade, a barter. I provided my professional services for you, and now I would like you to provide your professional services for me."

Rydell frowned. "I'm not sure I understand. What are you telling me, you want to make a *movie*?"

"No, I want *you* to make a movie," Modred said. He shrugged. "Or not make it, as the case may be. Simply going through the preliminary stages may be all that is required. I'm not quite sure how it works."

Rydell shook his head. "I'm confused. What exactly is it you want me to do?"

"I need access to the Hollywood community and to the social set surrounding it," said Modred. "The sort of access that only an insider could enjoy. And I need you to arrange it for me."

Rydell moistened his lips and went to pour himself another Scotch. "I think I'm beginning to understand," he said, his hand slightly unsteady as he poured the drink. "You've got a contract on somebody in the business and you want me to help you get next to him, is that it?"

"No," said Modred. "Although I can understand why you would come to that conclusion. I'm not in that particular line of work anymore, Rydell. I don't really need the money. I'm a very wealthy man. In fact, I could probably finance your next film out of pocket if I chose to. Come to think of it, that might not be a bad idea. It could be the best approach."

"Finance my next film?" Rydell said with a snort. "Look, I'll grant you that I don't make epics, far from it. I can do more with a low budget than anybody in this town, but with all due respect, I'm not sure you realize just what it costs to—"

"Would twenty-five million do?"

"Twenty-five mil—" Rydell had to clear his throat. *"Twenty-five million dollars?"*

"If that's not enough, you could have more. I could have it deposited to your account tomorrow."

Rydell tossed back the drink and poured himself another. "I think I'd better sit down," he said, coming back to the couch and bringing the bottle with him. He sat down, glanced at the bottle, then pushed it aside.

"On second thought, I'd better keep completely sober. Listen, what the hell is this about? You trying to run some kinda con on me?"

"If I was, I'd hardly admit it, now would I?" Modred said, smiling. "In any case, if you don't believe me, give me the name of your bank and wait until tomorrow. By close of business, you should have twenty-five million dollars more in your account."

Rydell shook his head in disbelief. "You're really not kidding? You've actually got *ready access* to that kind of money?"

Modred nodded once.

"Jesus. Your . . . uh . . . former business couldn't possibly pay *that* well, could it?"

"Let's just say that I've invested wisely over the years," said Modred, wondering what Rydell would have thought if he knew that he was referring to centuries rather than decades.

"All right, it's none of my business anyway," Rydell said. "And I suppose if I did ask any questions, you could tell me anything you wanted. Either way, I guess I'd just have to trust you.''

"I trusted you," said Modred.

Rydell grimaced and nodded. "Yeah, that's right, you did." He took a deep breath and let it out slowly. "That still doesn't make this any easier. I mean, I owe you, but—"

"I know. I quite understand," said Modred. "After all, I was a professional assassin. A 'hitter,' as you Americans say. For all you know, I still am. And I could have a contract on one of your friends. Perhaps a very close friend. However, ask yourself, if that were the case, then why would I need you? I could easily track down my quarry without your help. Besides, if I'd been hired to do away with someone in the business, then chances would be that it was someone in the business who had hired me and then, if necessary, I could easily use my client to introduce me to Hollywood society."

"Yeah, I suppose you could at that. Except chances are you'd wind up running into me," Rydell said.

"And what would you do?" said Modred with a smile. "Give me away? Tell them that I was an infamous international 'hit man' known as Morpheus, wanted by every nation from here to China? They'd be bound to wonder how you knew."

"I could make an anonymous phone call," said Rydell.

Modred smiled. "And the police might come and question me, but I have not remained at liberty for all these years without taking elaborate precautions. I promise you they'd find no reason to detain me. However, I would immediately know who'd called them. Honestly, Rydell, if I really believed you'd be a liability to me, do you suppose that I'd have let you live?"

Rydell swallowed hard. "No, I guess you wouldn't. But I still don't understand. Why the hell give me twenty-five million to make a movie?"

"You don't think it would be a good investment?"

"Come on, I'm serious, for God's sake."

"So am I," said Modred. "I'd hate to lose my money."

"Look, I've made films that lost money and I've made films that made money. Believe me, by now, I know the difference. I've made films for a lot less than twenty-five million and they've made a fortune. But it doesn't make any damned sense. What, you want to go to a few parties? Fine. I could introduce you around. No problem. You don't have to drop twenty-five million for that. So what's the angle?''

"Perhaps I simply want to become a successful film producer now that I've retired," Modred said. "And working with someone who's already an established name in the business is simpler than starting from scratch.''

"Uh-huh," Rydell said. "Sure." He took another deep breath. "Look, I owe you. If it wasn't for you, I'd probably have been anchored to a channel marker out at Santa Catalina. I figure if you waited ten years before you came to me, then whatever it is must be important. I'll do it, and not just because I'm afraid of what might happen if I don't. But I could help you better if I knew what you were after.''

"I'm not sure you would believe me if I told you," Modred said.

"Try me.''

"Very well," said Modred. "I'm out to trap a necromancer.''

"Come on, Ben," said Sergeant Bates, opening the cell door.

"It's about damn time," said Slater, furiously, as he stormed out of the cell. "I don't know what in God's name she was thinking of! If she thinks—''

"Uh . . . I'm afraid you're not getting out just yet, Ben," said Bates awkwardly.

Slater came to a dead stop in the corridor. *"What?"*

"I'm supposed to take you up to one of the interrogation rooms," said Bates. "Somebody wants to see you.''

"What somebody?''

"A guy from B.O.T.," said Bates.

"Damn, I *knew* it!" Slater said, hitting his palm with his fist. "I *knew* it! If the Bureau is involved, then it sure as hell isn't a routine murder case. So that's what this is all about, is it? They're trying to figure out a way to make me keep my mouth shut.''

"Look, Ben," said Bates, "for what it's worth, I'm not

sure how much Captain Farrell had to do with this. She's really being pressured. It's coming down hard on all of us. Real hard. Somebody upstairs has clamped down real tight on this.''

"You mean a cover-up."

"All I know is that this B.O.T. guy, Gorman, has practically taken over the precinct. We've got orders not to talk to anybody. Everyone's on edge. And there's some new V.I.P. who just showed up—''

"Harlan, you've got to make a call for me," said Slater. "Call the paper. Tell them I'm here and being denied due process. You don't have to give your name. Hell, half the precinct saw me brought in wearing handcuffs. I've got a lot of friends here. There's no way the brass will know who called."

"It's okay, Ben, the call's already been made."

"It has?"

"It's like you said, Ben, you've got a lot of friends here. Believe me, I don't like this any more than you do. Nobody does. This is not the way we work things."

"Yeah, I know," said Slater. "But it looks like the Bureau is really throwing its weight around. That means somebody's running scared. And I've got a pretty good idea why."

Bates escorted him upstairs to one of the interrogation rooms, then handed him over to the people inside. Before he turned to leave, he gave Slater a quick wink.

There were three people inside the interrogation room. One was Rebecca Farrell. She stood leaning against the wall, looking tense and drawn. The other two were men. Slater quickly sized them up. The man from the Bureau he spotted right away. He was the one on his feet, pacing back and forth, looking every inch the bureaucrat. Middle thirties, Slater figured, medium build, dressed well in a conservative, three-piece neo-Edwardian suit. No lace and only a hint of cuff showing. Not too stylish, just enough to present the proper corporate image. Most of the Bureau's personnel were former corporate wizards from the private sector. This guy had a high forehead, a neatly trimmed beard, and his light brown hair was thin on top and worn traditionally long in back, down to the shoulders. Just enough to socially sig-

nify he was a wizard, but not an inch longer or shorter than
it had to be. Everything about him was crisp and proper,
from his tailoring to his demeanor. Anal retentive, Slater
guessed. Just the sort to make a big production out of everything.

The other man sat quietly at the table with his hands clasped
in front of him. He was slightly older than Slater and ex-
ceedingly thin, almost to the point of emaciation. He was
clean-shaven and his cheekbones were very prominent. His
hair was gray and worn tied back in a loose ponytail. A
sorcerer. However, he was not wearing the formal, full-length
robes. His suit was impeccably tailored, light gray with a fine
dark stripe and a very stylish cut. The coat hung to mid-
thigh, with a full stand-up collar and lapels. He wore a silk
jabot at his throat and a generous amount of lace at his cuffs.
The large fire opal he wore on his ring finger must have cost
a fortune.

"Do you people have any idea what you're letting your-
selves in for?" Slater said. "Bad enough you—"

"Sit down and shut up, Slater," said the B.O.T. man.

"That's sit down and shut up, *Mr.* Slater. And it wouldn't
kill you to say please."

"Sit the hell down!"

Slater sat down at the table. The sorcerer cast a brief,
sidelong glance at Gorman, but said nothing.

"I want a lawyer," Slater said.

"There'll be plenty of time for that," said Gorman. "You
haven't been formally charged yet. What I—"

"I want a lawyer *right now*," said Slater.

"I think you'd better understand something, Slater," said
Gorman. "You're in no position to be making any demands
here. You're being charged with a very serious crime. Interfering with a homicide investigation and resisting arrest
is—"

"Look, son, I was working the crime beat in this city when
you were still playing with your first magic kit," said Slater.
"I forgot more about interrogation techniques than you'll ever
learn, so I'm not about to be intimidated, all right? Now if
you think you can really make those charges stick, then be
my guest and take your best shot. But if I were you, I'd

rethink my position pretty damn quick, because you're on very shaky ground already.''

He saw Rebecca Farrell give Gorman a look as if to say, "I told you so," and was surprised to notice a faint smile flicker across the sorcerer's face. He wondered who the man was. A senior B.O.T. official? He didn't look the part. Some independent that the department was consulting? Unlikely. He wouldn't be sitting in on an interrogation then. Someone from the mayor's office? No, there weren't any sorcerers in city politics. State? His train of thought was interrupted by a knock at the door of the interrogation room. A patrolman stuck his head in.

"Excuse me, Captain Farrell, but there's an attorney out here demanding to see Mr. Slater at once. And there's some media people outside, too.''

"I told you this was a dumb idea," said Rebecca Farrell to the B.O.T. man. "Now it's all going to blow up in your face, whether you like it or not.''

"Now you listen here, Farrell—" Gorman began, but the sorcerer interrupted him.

"No, I think you'd better listen, Gorman," he said, speaking with a British accent. "She's absolutely right. The way to achieve cooperation with the press is to work with them, not antagonize them. I suggest you release Mr. Slater immediately. I fear you've overstepped your bounds.''

Gorman's jaw muscles tensed visibly and he stiffened. "With all due respect, sir, I'm not sure that—"

The sorcerer casually glanced at him and raised his eyebrows. He didn't say a word, but Gorman shut up instantly. He licked his lips and looked away.

"Yes, sir. Captain Farrell, you may inform Mr. Slater that there's been a mistake. He's free to go.''

"Inform him yourself," she said. She turned and left the interrogation room.

"That's all right, I got the message," Slater said, standing up. "Gorman. How do you spell that, with one 'n' or two?''

Gorman was about to reply, but the sorcerer spoke first. "Mr. Slater, you are, of course, under no obligation to remain here a moment longer, but I would personally be very grateful for a few minutes of your time.''

Slater glanced at Gorman. "Sure," he said. "Why not?"
He sat back down.

"Mr. Gorman," said the sorcerer, "would you be so kind
as to inform Mr. Slater's attorney that no charges are being
filed against him and he will be out momentarily?"

Gorman left without a word.

The sorcerer shook his head. "Nervous chap, wouldn't
you say?"

"I think I'd use a stronger adjective," Slater said. "So,
between you, me, and whoever's on the other side of that
mirror, why should both the B.O.T. and the I.T.C. be interested in a so-called routine homicide?"

There was no doubt in his mind now that the sorcerer was
from the International Thaumaturgical Commission. Gorman's deference to him clinched it. Bureau adepts took a
backseat to no one—except agents of the I.T.C.

The sorcerer smiled. "Allowed me to introduce myself,
Mr. Slater." He held out his hand. "My name is Thanatos."

"Thanatos?" said Slater, taking his hand. "That's another
name for Death, isn't it? Somehow, I didn't think I'd be
meeting up with you so soon."

The sorcerer chuckled. "It is, of course, not my truename,
but my magename."

"I figured. But I thought most adepts didn't go in for
magenames anymore," said Slater.

"Oh, a few of us still do," said Thanatos. "Those whose
truenames have never quite pleased them for one reason or
another, or those with a flair for the dramatic or those who
simply like to see themselves as purists."

"Which one are you?"

"Oh, a bit of all three, I suppose," said the sorcerer, with
a smile. "The truth is I have a nostalgic fondness for that
name. I didn't choose it myself. It was bestowed upon me
by my old professor, whose patience I often tried back when
I was a graduate student. He often said I'd be the death of
him, and so he named me Thanatos. It was none other than
the late Merlin Ambrosius, himself."

"Nothing like learning from the best," said Slater admir-
ingly.

"Yes. He'll be sorely missed," said Thanatos. "Mr. Slater—"

"Ben."

Thanatos smiled. "Ben. I asked for but a few moments of your time, so I will get right to the point. I've only just arrived here, but I've already managed to get something of a handle on this situation, as you Americans say. It's my understanding that Captain Farrell had you placed under arrest only so that you would be brought here before you could communicate with anybody else. A bit irregular, perhaps, but apparently she hoped to explain the situation to you as a captive audience, if you'll excuse the pun, and prevail upon you to cooperate voluntarily, which is precisely what I now hope to do."

"I'm not making any promises," said Slater.

"I wouldn't ask you to," said Thanatos, "at least not until you've heard me out. You should know that it was agent Gorman, and not Captain Farrell, who decided to actually threaten you with those charges, apparently thinking that you could be intimidated. Captain Farrell insisted that it was a foolish idea, guaranteed to cause them trouble, but Gorman is young, ambitious, and rather impetuous. And, although he won't admit it, he's also genuinely frightened. When I learned of the situation, my inclination was to order you released at once. Even though, technically, I have no official standing here, Gorman would not have been able to refuse me."

"Yes, I know," said Slater. "As I understand it, the jurisdictional boundaries are a little vague in this area, but the police tend to defer to the Bureau when it expresses an interest in a case, mainly because it probably involves a magic-user and high grade adepts don't usually go in for police work. It doesn't pay enough. And the Bureau defers to the I.T.C. because if they don't, you guys can yank their registrations and there goes all that postgraduate training in hocus-pocus."

Thanatos shrugged. "A bit oversimplified, perhaps, but basically an accurate assessment of the politics involved. We are essentially a regulatory agency, and theoretically, we don't have an enforcement branch. Officially, we must defer to the local laws and, thereby, the local law enforcement agencies. But local law enforcement agencies, even one such as the Bureau of Thaumaturgy, cannot in practice cope with situations which are international in scope. Which brings us to the crux of this matter.''

"The fact that you're here," said Slater. "It means we're talking about something very serious. Such as magic used to commit murder. In other words, necromancy.''

"Exactly.''

"You admit it!''

"Absolutely. Only you have it rather backwards. More precisely, necromancy is murder used to commit magic. Ritual murder, accomplished in a manner which allows the necromancer to absorb the life energies of his victims, or to use them in casting a powerful spell. Sometimes the necromancer actually performs the ritual murder. At other times, it may be accomplished by another person in the power of the necromancer, an acolyte, or an entity. A sort of demon.''

"With claws?" said Slater, thinking back to the wounds he'd seen on Sarah Tracy's corpse.

"Not necessarily, but yes, it could indeed have claws. Such as the creature that murdered Sarah Tracy.''

"The creature?''

"Oh yes. I have seen the body and sensed the trace emanations within it. They were very faint, but they were unquestionably there. Sarah Tracy's life energy—or her soul, if you choose to think in those terms—was savagely ripped away from her in a manner calculated to excite maximum terror.''

"Why maximum terror?''

"Because the life force is at its most vibrant at times of sexual excitation and mortal dread. At such times, the aura—to one sensitive to such things—throbs visibly.''

"And you can see that? An aura, I mean," Slater said.

"I can. It is a rare talent. One does not have to be a sorcerer to have it. It must be something you are born with.''

"Can you see mine?''

"Yes.''

"Really? What does it look like?''

"It is a bright, cerulean blue," said Thanatos, "very intense and closely outlining your form.''

"What does that mean?"

"It means, among other things, that I can trust you."

"Well . . . thanks."

"Don't thank me, I simply read them as I see them."

Slater grinned. "What is this, some sort of magic-user's version of good cop/bad cop? First Gorman rails at me and threatens to lock me up and throw away the key, then you cozy up to me and tell me I have a nice aura? Come on, you'll have to do better than that."

Thanatos smiled. "And so I shall. Tell me, Ben, have you ever heard the legend of the Dark Ones?"

CHAPTER
Three

The Beverly Hills Hotel had seen much better days, but then so had most of the city of Los Angeles. Located at the intersection of Sunset Boulevard and Beverly Drive, the hotel boasted a tradition dating back to the early twentieth century, even though nothing was left of the original pink palace that had once been the gathering place of the rich and famous. At various times since the last days of the twentieth century, it had been a hotel, a private residence, a psychiatric hospital, an exclusive luxury apartment complex, and a gambling casino and resort. It had been extensively remodeled several times and most of it had burned down in the riots during the Collapse, but a consortium of private investors had rebuilt it to capitalize on the "new nostalgia." Now, it was once again the place to be seen for the power brokers and the deal makers of the resurgent entertainment industry.

"We're going to be staying *here*?" said Kira as they got out of the limousine.

"This is where Modred got rooms for us," said Wyrdrune,

looking equally bewildered as they went through the lobby doors, with the broom struggling along behind them with their bags.

"What in the bleedin' 'ell is *that*?" said Billy, gazing at the giant golden statue standing in the lobby. It was an abstract figure of a man standing on a round obsidian pedestal. Twin jets of water shot out from his ears into the pool below.

"I think that must be Oscar," Wyrdrune said.

"Oscar who?" said Billy.

"I don't know Oscar who. He was someone famous in the old pre-Collapse days. They sell little foot-high statues of him in all the nostalgia shops. I understand they used to give them out as awards."

"What for?"

"Oh, best film, best actor, best restaurant, that sort of thing. He's the official symbol of Los Angeles."

"What, a skinny bloke with no clothes on?"

Wyrdrune shrugged.

"What's 'e got in 'is 'ands then, a glass o' whiskey?"

"I think it's a sword."

"G'wan! It don't look like no sword."

"It's sort of abstract, see . . . he's holding it pointing downward with the hilt up against his chest and—"

"Will you come on, already?" said the broom. "I'm standing here holding a ton of luggage and you two are *shmoozing* over a statue making with a do-it-yourself *bris*."

The desk clerk cast a dubious eye upon them when they came up to check in, but his attitude changed markedly when everything turned out to be in order.

"Oh yes, of course, Mr. Cornwall's party! We've been expecting you."

He immediately summoned a bellman to conduct them to Bungalow 1. The bellman seemed at a loss when he confronted the broom, holding all the suitcases. He hesitated, glancing from Wyrdrune to the broom and back to Wyrdrune again.

"What, you never saw a suitcase before?" said the broom, dropping the luggage on the floor. "Here. And watch the brown one, it'll give you a rupture if you're not careful."

They were conducted through the lobby and out onto the

garden path leading to their private bungalow. A purple paracat sat in one of the little palm trees, swinging its bushy tail back and forth and singing "My Way" in a squawk-voiced imitation of Frank Sinatra. It was clashing rather badly with a green kittyhawk doing "New York State of Mind" in imitation of Ray Charles. There were more thaumagenetically engineered hybirds singing in other trees around the garden, the cacophony rendering the lyrics indistinguishable.

"Does this sort of thing go on all the time?" said Wyrdrune.

"Fortunately, they tend to quiet down at night," the bellman said, as if he'd answered the same question a thousand times before. "The idea was to teach them a dozen or so nostalgic songs from old pre-Collapse recordings and have them all singing in chorus, but it seems they each have their own favorite song which they insist on singing over and over again." He shrugged. "It gets a bit noisy sometimes. There doesn't seem to be anything that we can do about it."

"Have you tried a BB gun?" said the broom.

Wyrdrune gave it a warning glance and it kept silent till they reached the cabin. Bungalow 1 turned out to be an extremely well-appointed cottage, with luxurious furnishings and a lot more room than their old East Fourth Street railroad flat.

"'Gor'blimey!" said Billy as they entered. "This is really nice, in'it?" He glanced uncertainly at Wyrdrune. "Can we afford it?"

The bellman gave him a strange glance but said nothing. Wyrdrune tipped him, generously, he thought, but the bellman stared at the tip with distaste and left without a word.

"No, we can't afford it, but Modred certainly can," said Kira.

"That still doesn't make me feel any better about staying in a fancy place like this," said Wyrdrune, taking off his hat and cassock and going to the closet. "I don't care how many billions he's got stashed away, I just don't feel comfortable living off his money."

"Let me get this straight," said Kira. "You don't mind stealing, but it bothers you when someone else picks up the tab for a hotel room?"

"It just makes me feel like I'm being given an allowance," Wyrdrune said. He opened the closet door and stepped back in surprise. It was full of clothes. "Hey, I think they gave us the wrong cottage," he said. "Someone's got their clothes in here."

"No, those clothes are yours," said Modred, from behind them.

Wyrdrune turned to face him and Kira gasped.

"Your stone . . ." she said.

The emerald runestone in his forehead was glowing faintly. Kira quickly tore off her glove. The sapphire runestone set into her palm was glowing softly, as well. She glanced at Modred.

"Yes, mine, too," said Modred, coming into the room. He unbuttoned his shirt. The ruby runestone in his chest was glowing, a bit more brightly than theirs.

"They're here!" said Kira.

He nodded. "Yes, I know. I felt it as soon as I arrived. I didn't tell you because I wanted to see if you would feel it, too."

"I didn't feel anything," said Kira, shaking her head. "Not like the last time." She glanced at Wyrdrune. "Did you?"

He shook his head. "No, but his descent from the Old Ones is much more direct than ours. He's more in tune with the spirits of the runestones."

Modred nodded. "It was as if something drew me here," he said. "A powerful feeling, a compulsion. . . ."

"Exactly how we felt when we stole the runestones," Kira said. "Irresistibly compelled."

"At least one of them is definitely here," said Modred.

"But he must not be very close," said Wyrdrune. "Otherwise, the reaction of the runestones would be much stronger."

"That's the puzzling part," said Modred, frowning. "The runestones' response would seem to indicate that the Dark One isn't in close proximity to us, and yet I sense a dark power very close, indeed."

"What does it mean?" said Kira.

Modred shook his head. "I don't know."

"It could mean that the Dark One has one or more acolytes nearby," said Merlin, speaking through Billy.

The difference was remarkable. Billy still looked the same, but his voice became much deeper and lost its cockney accent. His entire demeanor changed—his posture, the way he held his head, the way he moved. His tone of voice, gestures, and mannerisms were instantly recognizable to someone who had known Merlin when he lived. Though it was no longer new to them, it was still a bit unsettling to see the sudden shift in personalities, to interact on a daily basis with someone who was possessed.

"An acolyte?" said Kira. "You mean like Al'Hassan was?"

"Yes, or like those poor creatures in Whitechapel," Merlin said. "The necromancer often uses acolytes and catspaws against his adversaries, working through them, investing them with his power. In this manner, they become not only his tools, but his shield, as well. Through Al'Hassan, they came perilously close to defeating us the first time. We will have to search out and destroy these servants of the necromancer before we can find the Dark One himself."

"Or before 'e finds us," Billy added.

"That's why I've booked us all into this hotel," said Modred. "It's a focal point for much of the business of the entertainment industry, and that's where the power structure in this city lies."

"But how do we know the Dark One is involved with the entertainment industry?" said Kira.

"We don't, of course," said Modred. "However, we know the Dark Ones are enthralled by power and power, whether economic, social, or political, provides a certain measure of protection. And in this town, that kind of power centers around the entertainment industry. Becoming part of it will ensure that all doors will be open to us."

"How do we become a part of it?" said Wyrdrune.

"Very simple," Modred said. "We're going to make a movie."

"What?"

"How the hell do we do that?" asked Kira.

"With the greatest of ease," said Modred. "In the old days, a strong right arm, a keen sword, and a thick head could win you a kingdom, as my father amply demonstrated. However, these days, one no longer wins a kingdom; one simply buys it."

"I get it," Wyrdrune said. "You're going to become a film producer, which will get you in just about anywhere in this town."

"Slight correction," Modred said. "I'm not the only one. You're going to be a film producer, as well."

"Me?"

"And Kira and Billy shall be our executive staff," added Modred.

"But we don't know anything about making movies!"

"You don't have to," Modred said. He indicated the closet. "All you really need to do is dress the part and act suitably eccentric. That shouldn't be very difficult for you. There's a film producer here named Ron Rydell who's going to help us."

"Ron Rydell?" said Wyrdrune. "You mean the one who produced and directed *Curse of the Necromancer*? *That* Ron Rydell?"

"Yes, he owes me a favor for a service I performed for him a few years back. He's consented to act as coproducer in our mutual venture."

"Wow, he's one of the biggest names in the business!" Wyrdrune said. "He made *Curse of the Necromancer, Return of the Necromancer, Revenge of the Necromancer, Bride of the Necromancer, Son of the Necromancer. . . .*"

"*Abbott and Costello Meet the Necromancer*," Modred said wryly.

"Who? I don't remember that one," Wyrdrune said, looking puzzled.

"Never mind, it was a joke," Modred said. "Before your time. The point is, we are merely going through the motions. Rydell will be doing all the work. In fact, he's actually excited about it. He tells me there's a project he's been wanting to do for years, only his backers have always pressured him to do more *Necromancer* films." He glanced at Billy with a smile. "It seems that what he really wants to do is the story of Merlin the Magician."

"You must be joking," Merlin said.

"I'm quite serious," said Modred. "I told Rydell that he could do any sort of film he wanted and what he wants to do is a film about Merlin." He turned to Wyrdrune. "I told him you were something of an expert on the subject, that you'd actually studied with him. Rydell was positively thrilled."

"No," said Merlin. "Absolutely not! I won't allow it!"

"Come now, Ambrosius," said Modred mockingly, "don't you want to leave behind a record for posterity?"

"I've already been through that. I have no intention of seeing my life reduced to another shallow, popular amusement," Merlin said.

"Bit late for that, isn't it?" said Modred.

Billy drew himself up stiffly and gave Modred a haughty look, which on Merlin would have looked imposing, but on a teenager punked to the core, it simply looked snotty.

"It's bad enough I've had to suffer Malory and White and that wretch, Disney, who actually had the temerity to turn me into a fish, to say nothing of all the others, but I shudder to think of what your friend Rydell will bring forth. I've *seen Curse of the Necromancer*. They once showed it at a film festival the students ran in Cambridge. A more ludicrous spectacle I've never witnessed in all my life!"

"Well, look at it this way," Modred said, "this will be your chance to set the record straight."

"Y'know, it sounds like fun to me," said Billy.

"Who asked you?" Merlin said.

"Well, who bloody well asked *you*?"

"Now you listen here, you young guttersnipe—"

"Ey, sod off!"

"*What?*"

"You 'eard me, I said, sod off!"

"How *dare* you speak to me that way?"

"Yeah, an' what're you gonna *do* about it, ya bleedin' old wanker?"

"A man at war with himself," said Modred, chuckling.

"I should have drowned you when you were still a child," said Merlin, scowling at Modred.

"Behave yourself, Ambrosius," said Modred, "or I may call a priest and have you exorcised."

"Hah!"

"In any case, we will be having dinner with Rydell this evening, so I will ask you to be civil, because we need his help."

"How much does he know?" asked Wyrdrune.

"Very little," Modred said. "He suspects my motives, but twenty-five million dollars make for strong persuasion. Still, he wanted to know what I was really after. I told him that I was here to trap a necromancer. Needless to say, he thought I was joking. However, he is not a stupid man, so for his own safety, it might be best if he knew as little about our plans as possible."

"You gave Rydell twenty-five million dollars?" Kira said with astonishment.

"I thought it might not be enough, but it seems he's made films for much less," said Modred.

"That I can believe," said Merlin sourly.

"At first, I thought that merely going through the motions would be enough," said Modred, "but I think that actually making a film would provide a much more solid cover for us. Who knows, I might even make a profit. And, as Billy said, it might be fun. But let's not lose sight of our objective. It will be dangerous, as well. Especially if the necromancer is alerted to our presence before we're ready to make our move. If that happens, it could well prove fatal."

The Lost Souls Mission was located on Sunset Boulevard, just west of Fairfax Avenue in the area known as "the Strip." It was an apt location for a mission with that name. During its heydey in the twentieth century, the Sunset Strip was two miles of swank nightclubs and restaurants, production company offices and talent agencies, souvenir shops and cafés, recording studios and boutiques, and giant, garish billboards overlooking everything. It had gradually degenerated into a combat zone of sleazy bars and sex parlors and during the Collapse, it was quite literally a free-fire zone. Back then, some part of it was always burning. The street gangs took it over in the early post-Collapse days and it had taken years to drive them out so that the area could be redeveloped, but bit by bit, they drifted back to their old stomping grounds.

The result was that the Strip now possessed a bizarre split personality. During the daylight hours, it was a busy commuter business district surrounded by modular clusters of low-rent residential apartments that looked like geometric cliff dwellings or ominous hives for giant killer bees. As night fell, the offices on the Strip were closed and locked securely, the sidewalk cafés hastily retracted all their chairs and tables, and the restaurants that catered to the daytime crowd shut down tight behind steel shutters. Establishments that had remained closed throughout most of the day opened their battered metal, graffiti-covered doors as the nocturnal creatures from the slums up on the hills began to stir. The Strip slowly sloughed off its Dr. Jekyll facade and, as darkness fell, stood revealed as Mr. Hyde, drooling like a hydrocephalic and searching for some sleaze.

The garish, multicolored lights came on as the strip erupted into neon and the billboard war began. The advertising companies who owned the giant billboards had reached a novel compromise with the youth gangs in an effort to keep their signs from being defaced. During the daylight hours, the billboards proclaimed whatever message the renting advertisers desired, whether it was the promotion of a new film, a product, or a personality. At night, the billboard owners made arrangements with the gangs to proclaim whatever message *they* wished free of charge, in return for which each gang became fiercely protective of "their" billboards. A simple transmutation spell placed on the billboards activated the change, so that a huge sign advertising "Natural Magicola, for an instant energy lift!" became a beautiful, young, reclining nude, moaning and writhing slowly while letters of dripping blood formed upon her body, proclaiming "Morlocks Rule!"

The streetboarders clogged the thoroughfare, staging high-speed, violent "freestyle" competitions and raw, driving music would throb from renaissance punk bars and nouveau medieval clubs like Bullwinkle's, Dulang-Dulang, and Spago-Pogo. Hookers of both sexes, often runaways recruited by remorseless pimps, plied their trade without restraint and dealers hawked black market magic potions for power, sex appeal, temporary transmutations, or simply getting high. At such times, the police withdrew discreetly, knowing that discretion was the better part of valor. They had learned their lessons during the Collapse, when most of the city burned. Street violence in combat zones merely served to control the population of the screamers. If the violence erupted into full-blown riots, as it sometimes did, it was far easier and safer to simply gas the crowd into submission than to risk controlling it with riot squads.

It was in this maelstrom of the wild and the aimless that Brother Khasim had established his nonsectarian Lost Souls Mission and it was here he came each night, to minister to the demented and the wayward. The money that he made working for the film production companies as a special effects adept all went to support the mission, which provided food and temporary shelter to anyone who needed it. He referred to his flock as "the children of the streets" and he was tireless in his efforts to solicit contributions to support his work on their behalf. He was well known on the Strip and the street people considered him a saint.

They could not have been more wrong.

The Lost Souls Mission had an unprepossessing exterior. It was a simple, four-story converted office building with a dark brown stone facade. A brass plate mounted on the wall beside the arched entrance to the lobby was the sole identifying sign. Upon entering, one encountered a receptionist who was part of the small permanent staff of the mission, all of whom had once been on the street themselves. All the other help were volunteers, drawn from the streets. The cost of a bed in the shelter was assisting in the kitchen or the laundry, or helping with some small repairs.

Occasionally, there were donations, deposited anonymously in the cash box in the lobby or through the metal slot at the entrance. There were always gratefully accepted and if the money came from ill-gotten goods that had been fenced, well, the donations were anonymous and there was no way of questioning the source. Between such "irregular donations," occasional charitable contributions from wealthy individuals and corporations and Brother Khasim's salary, the mission managed to get by. In fact, it made a considerable profit, but this was carefully concealed and no one would suspect the selfless Brother Khasim of being anything but totally aboveboard.

Every hooker who worked the Strip always made a point of setting "a little something" aside for Brother Khasim and his mission. And Brother Khasim was always so warmly grateful, the one man they could talk to who would not use or abuse them, the one man who did not judge them, the one man they could call their friend. Every pimp and every dealer made it a practice to donate something to the mission, too, if not out of respect for the good brother's work, then out of fear of those above them in the criminal hierarchy of the Strip, who always asked if they had donated something to the cause and always knew somehow if they did not. Every businessman and woman who worked the Strip was squeezed a little, if not through Brother Khasim's charm in asking them directly to "please give anything you can," then through the gangs, who threatened to trash the place if "the brother wasn't taken care of." And the gangs themselves threw in a cut of whatever they took in, which was often a considerable amount, all of which, together with the legitimate contributions, added up to a very tidy sum. It could easily be said that the Lost Souls Mission was the most profitable operation on the Strip.

It was already dark when Khasim came through the door into the lobby. The pretty young receptionist looked up and smiled warmly when she saw him.

"Good evening, Brother Khasim," she said, her eyes practically glowing with adoration.

"Good evening, Kathy," he said.

"How did the filming go today?"

"About the same as usual," Khasim said. "We finally wrapped the film. Quite honestly, I find it tiring and demeaning, but it does help us carry on our work. That makes it all worthwhile."

Her face was shining. "You're always thinking of others," she said, "never of yourself."

"One must always think of others, Kathy," said Khasim. "Especially of those who are less fortunate." He came up close to her and gently touched her cheek. "Always remember, it is by serving others that you best serve yourself."

She trembled.

He briefly visited the free clinic and the crisis center, exchanged a few words with the volunteers there, then went up to the fourth floor, bypassing the shelter dormitories on the third and second. He walked down the corridor to his administrative offices and private residence. He smiled a greeting at the staff as he came through, saying, "I must do my meditations. Please see that I am not disturbed." Then he gestured to open the spell-warded door to his private quarters.

On occasion, such as when the media wanted to do a profile on "the Sorcerer Saint of Sunset Strip," these rooms were opened to outsiders, so that everyone could see how simply and how frugally Brother Khasim lived. The spell-warding was explained by the fact that all the mission funds were kept there, as well as all the records, many of which concerned the intimate details of the broken lives that Brother Khasim tried to patch together. And as Brother Khasim patiently explained, the neighborhood that they were in was, unfortunately, known for its high crime rate and they did not ask questions of those whom they took in.

Indeed, there seemed no other possible reason for spell-warding the premises, which were spartan in the extreme. There was Brother Khasim's private office, which was little more than a small room containing battered, secondhand office furniture and some tattered books. Then there was the consultation room, in which Brother Khasim conducted private meetings with those who sought his help and guidance. Here again, the room was small and dark, with all the space taken up by a used couch, an old wooden desk and chair, a secondhand armchair, a lamp, and a small, stained wooden coffee table. Behind these two small rooms was Brother Khasim's tiny apartment—which invariably humbled those who saw it.

It was like a monk's cell, tiny, cramped by the small, secondhand bed, nightstand, and lamp, with bare walls and no windows. The bathroom was a simple shower cabinet, a toilet, and a sink, the fixtures obviously scavenged from some junkyard. And there was nothing else, except for a battered chest of drawers and a small closet that contained what little clothing Brother Khasim owned. Not even a kitchen. He took his meals, he said, with the other inhabitants of the shelter, any one of whom could testify that he ate as sparingly as a cloistered Buddhist. To all appearances, Brother Khasim was, indeed, a saint. But appearances could be deceiving, especially in a sorcerer's case.

He gestured to close the door behind him. The spell-warding ensured that the only way anyone could gain entrance would be to break the door down, but forcible entry activated another, very different spell, one that only Khasim knew about, since he had cast it. If such an attempt was made, the person making it would never survive to tell about it.

Khasim went directly to the tiny closet in his bathroom and opened the door. He shoved aside the coat and the two spare suits that hung there, both identical and plain, both black, the same as the suit that he now wore. He stepped into the closet, ducking his head beneath the hanger rod, and closed the door, He touched a hidden button and the floor of the tiny closet started to descend without a sound. This special private elevator did not appear on any plans or blueprints and the workers who had installed it had all been placed under a spell to ensure that they would not remember it.

As the elevator descended silently, it went past the third and second floors, past the first floor and the basement to a deeper chamber that had been excavated underneath the mission. As Brother Khasim stepped out of the elevator, he entered a spacious underground apartment suite that would have shocked the mission staff if they had known of it.

The floors were lushly carpeted with imported Persian rugs. The walls were hung with richly embroidered tapestries and paintings depicting graphic, lurid scenes that would have scandalized those who knew Brother Khasim as a deeply moral, saintly practitioner of self-denial. The furnishings were expensive, plush, and sybaritic. There were several Romanesque couches and armchairs more worthy of being called thrones. Large silk cushions were scattered about. A marble bathroom contained a sauna and a tub the size of a

small swimming pool. The bedroom was dominated by a huge
circular bed with mirrors mounted on the walls around it, as
well as on the ceiling. And there were other "furnishings"
kept there as well—paraphernalia of exotic sexual diversions.

And then there were the young women.

There were, at present, eight of them in residence. They
were all very young, shapely, and attractive, several of them
barely in their teens. They were dressed provocatively in silk
and filmy gauze and glove-soft leather, thin golden chains
draped around bare hips and studded collars fastened around
their necks. They were a smorgasbord of sexual temptation,
living beneath the mission exclusively to serve Khasim. Their
eyes were vacant, mirroring the emptiness inside. They had
been kidnapped and enchanted so they had no will of their
own. At a word from him, they would do anything. Anything
at all.

He snapped his fingers and they came to him, helping him
undress and slip into his maroon silk sorcerer's robes and
embroidered velvet slippers. They brought him wine and as
he sat down in his favorite chair, one of them stretched out
on the floor so that he could rest his feet upon her. Another
stood behind the chair, rubbing his temples gently, and two
others knelt beside him, so they could kiss and rub his wrists.
The rest quietly sat at his feet, watching him with blank
expressions, obedient to his slightest whim. He leaned back
against the chair and sipped his wine, shutting his eyes and
enjoying the sensation of his temples being massaged, but
though he looked thoroughly relaxed, his mind was racing.

He picked up the morning paper and stared at it. So Sarah
had a boyfriend who was being held as a suspect in her
murder. He wondered how much the boyfriend knew. It could
cause complications. Sarah had been a whore when she first
came to the mission, a young runaway who sold herself on
the street to keep herself supplied with a nasty little magic
potion called "Bliss." Sold by street dealers in tiny little
stoppered vials, Bliss was not in and of itself addictive, but
the tranquil, blissful state that it induced was so irresistibly
compelling that the user kept coming back for more. Unfortunately, each time it took more and more Bliss to maintain

that ecstatic state. While in the trance, the user would become transported and forget the real world, forget to eat and sleep and drink. Eventually, the user would simply waste away, delirious with inner peace.

Khasim had cured Sarah of her insatiable desire for Bliss, which had not been difficult to do, for it was he who brewed it in the first place. The result was that the girl had become utterly devoted to him. And Khasim had exploited that devotion for all that it was worth.

He had made a mistake with Sarah. She had been young and very beautiful and from the moment she first came to the mission, he had wanted her intensely, but he had hesitated out of caution. The mission was a front that had to be carefully protected and maintained. It was far safer to take women who had no connection with the mission, though on occasion, he did "appropriate" some fresh, young runaway for his private use. However, he was always very careful to make sure that no one would be able to trace her to the mission. If a young girl disappeared and someone came inquiring, knowing that she'd been at the mission, he could always shrug and say that she had left, as many did, because the mission had no power to hold anyone nor did they desire to. They were only there to provide what help they could. Still, a pattern of missing young women who had last been seen at the mission could eventually arouse the curiosity of the police, so Khasim was always careful. With Sarah, he had slipped.

It was easy to enslave a woman with a spell, to utterly take away her will, but with Sarah, that had not been necessary. She became his slave purely of her own free will and Khasim found that exciting. So exciting that it had affected his judgment. He had brought her down to his secret hideaway underneath the mission, but he had hesitated to cast a spell upon her to make her forget what she had seen, fearing that it would dilute the spice of their relationship. Instead, it had ended it. He had overestimated Sarah's blind devotion. What she saw had frightened her and the next day, she was gone. He looked for her everywhere, but she had simply disappeared. Months passed and he had almost forgotten all about her. And then he saw her on the set of *Blood of the Necromancer*.

She was playing a bit part and she recognized him at once. However, the intervening months had done much to erase her fear of him and she began to blackmail him, threatening to expose the ''Saint of Sunset Strip'' as a sadist who kidnapped women off the streets and kept them in enchanted, mindless bondage in a secret harem underneath his humble mission. She actually believed that she could get away with it. She was always careful never to be alone with him and never to allow him to get close enough to touch her, but she was not careful enough. One day, while she was on the set, Khasim went through her purse and found a hairbrush, from which he extracted several loose hairs. And that was all that had been necessary. Once he had those, there would be no escape, no matter where she went.

Only now, it seemed there was a man, a man who might have known about her past connection with him. A man she might have shared his secret with. Khasim reread the account of her death. A ''senseless murder,'' the paper called it, an adjective that implied that there were murders that made perfectly good sense. Well, in this particular case, it had made good sense to Khasim. The newspaper went on to give the address where the murder had taken place and said that the suspect was being held in custody. It even gave his name and said he had been transferred from the hospital to the police station. Khasim smiled. How very considerate of them.

He waved away the women and steepled his hands before his face, fingertips touching his lips. He took several slow, deep breaths, then shut his eyes and began to concentrate. His breathing quickened. Beads of sweat appeared on his forehead. The veins in his temples stood out in sharp relief. The air in front of him seemed to quiver as if with dancing heat waves and bright crimson sparks suddenly appeared, swirling in a whirlpool of brilliant light, like a miniature nebula taking shape before him. It swirled faster and faster and the room grew darker and darker, as if the swirling whirlpool was leeching away the light and then, with a loud concussion of displaced air as molecules whirling through the ether coalesced within the room, an apparition glowing with ionic fire appeared before him. It was but the sparkling outline of a form, no features were discernible, and within it . . . darkness. Deep and utter darkness. It spoke.

"What do you want from me?"

The low and throaty voice reverberated in the room. A woman's voice. A woman Khasim had never seen except in this frightening, dark and featureless, ghostlike incarnation.

"I . . . I have a life for you," he said, struggling to keep his voice steady.

"So. Give it to me."

Khasim nervously moistened his lips. "It . . . it is not here. But I can tell you his name and where he can be found. There is a photograph of him right here in the newspaper. . . . It is important that he be . . . that it be done as soon as possible."

"Another mistake, Khasim?"

"A precaution," said Khasim, swallowing hard. "Someone who might be able to tie Sarah Tracy in with the mission."

"I see. That was careless of you, Khasim."

"I plead your indulgence, Dark Mistress. It shall not happen again."

"That is what you said the last time. Very well. But I need a life first."

The apparition raised an arm and pointed at one of Khasim's women.

"As you wish," Khasim said, and he beckoned the ensorcelled woman forward. "Take her."

"No. You give her to me."

"I?"

"Yes, you, Khasim. You who play games with pain and give away lives so freely should know what it means to take one."

A gleaming, razor-sharp, curved knife with a jeweled hilt suddenly appeared in his lap.

He stared at it with dread.

"Now, Khasim."

His mouth was dry. He licked his lips and picked up the knife. He glanced at the docile young woman who stood before him. He took a deep breath and moved toward her.

CHAPTER
Four

Ben Slater sat in a booth at Flannagan's Bar, cutting into a thick steak and listening to the most incredible story he'd ever heard. Thanatos, the I.T.C. agent, was not eating. He had ordered only a glass of white wine and it stood before him, practically untouched. At his invitation, Slater had decided to continue their discussion over dinner. The paper's lawyer, being naturally suspicious, had at first wanted to come along, but Thanatos had assured him that there were no charges against Slater and that the whole thing had been an unfortunate mistake, whereupon the lawyer had started making noises about suits for false arrest. However, Slater had thanked him and then dismissed him politely. He smelled a story and he wanted to hear what the I.T.C. man had to say.

What he said seemed unbelievable.

"Now let me just make sure I'm understanding you correctly," Slater said. "You're admitting that Sarah Tracy was killed by necromancy, but you're telling me you think the necromancer *wasn't human*?"

"Correct. However, there is one other possibility and that is that Sarah Tracy was killed—indirectly—by an outlaw adept who is in the thrall of an inhuman power. A Dark One."

"One of these immortal beings who lived in ancient times, before the dawn of history," said Slater, repeating what he had just heard. He shook his head. "All right, if they lived before the dawn of history, then how do we know about them?''

"We don't,'' said Thanatos. "At least, not officially. *I* know about them. And so do at least seven other people that I know of. Beyond that, the world is completely ignorant of their existence. However, to explain that fully, I'll have to backtrack somewhat. Some time ago, one of our agents disappeared without a trace while investigating a case here in the States. It involved the theft of three enchanted runestones of unknown properties, part of a consignment up for auction at the Christie Gallery in New York City.''

"Wait a minute,'' Slater said. "Seems to me I heard something about that. Yeah, the heist was pulled in broad daylight, and in a roomful of wizards and sorcerers, to boot. Talk about *chutzpa*!''

"Indeed,'' said Thanatos. "The New York police tried to insist that it was merely a simple 'snatch-and-grab,' as they called it, that there was no evidence that magic was involved in the robbery. This was because they wanted to hold on to the case. However, by the time the trail led to Boston, it became obvious that it was a major crime involving magic use, which made it our jurisdiction. So one of our agents was sent to Boston to coordinate with the police officials there, as well as with the detectives from New York. We never heard from our agent again. We must assume she's dead. Nor was she the only one to die. In the course of their investigation, the Boston police questioned Professor Merlin Ambrosius himself and subsequently, his home was blown up and his body never found.''

"I remember,'' Slater said. "It was the biggest news story of the year.''

His own paper had run it with the banner headline, "MERLIN MURDERED!'' The house on Beacon Hill had been reduced to rubble and it had taken several fire brigades assisted by adepts to douse the flames.

"It had all the marks of a gangland-style killing,'' Slater said. "You had to wonder what possible involvement Merlin could have had with organized crime. That's a story I would have liked to investigate.''

"We did investigate it,'' said Thanatos. "And by the time

we managed to weave all the threads together, we had a very complicated tapestry, indeed. The New York detectives who had the case from the beginning came up with the first lead. They questioned a well-known fence named Rozetti and in return for certain considerations, he admitted that the thieves had come to him with the runestones, but he claimed they cheated him, magically stealing the runestones back again after he had bought them. Another fence known as Fats Greenberg was questioned, and although he denied any knowledge of the runestones or the thieves, the police felt certain he was lying. It seemed that the two thieves had not only stolen the stones, but were running a con with them, selling them over and over and then magically stealing them back again. As a result, the police felt certain that at least Rozetti, and probably Fats as well, had taken out contracts on the thieves. Yet, within a short while, both Fats and Rozetti were dead. Fats was killed in an explosion that consumed his pawnshop and Rozetti was killed in his restaurant by a cobra.''

"By a *cobra*?''

"Yes. No one seemed to know how the snake had gotten there, but when Rozetti's body was found, the telephone on his desk was off the hook and it was established that he had been calling the embassy of the United Semitic Republics, the nation which cosponsored the dig where the runestones had been discovered and which was to share in the profits of the auction. The embassy confirmed that a Mr. Rozetti had, indeed, called them and spoken briefly with a Mr. Mustafa Sharif, ostensibly inquiring about the reward for the recovery of the runestones. Incidentally, it's possible that a skilled adept could have cast a spell that transmuted the snake and sent it through the telephone wires. Mr. Sharif was a highly skilled adept. A sorcerer who studied under Sheik Rashid Al'Hassan himself. We were unable to reach him for comment, as we were informed that he had been sent home. We were, however, able to verify that he kept a cobra for a pet.''

"Jesus," Slater said, shuddering as he imagined a cobra coming through a phone receiver held against his ear.

"An investigation confirmed that the explosion of Fats's pawnshop was brought about by magic," said Thanatos.

"Faint trace emanations of the spell were detected. Around the same time, a similar explosive fire occurred at a penthouse on Fifth Avenue, owned by a Mr. John Roderick. A fortune in art and books was destroyed, to say nothing of the loss of the penthouse and its expensive furnishings, yet Mr. Roderick never even filed a claim. It turned out that Mr. Roderick was not even insured. In fact, Mr. Roderick did not even exist. John Roderick was an alias of a man whom we've been after for a very long time, indeed. A man known as Morpheus."

"*Morpheus!*" Slater gave a low whistle. "I've heard of him. Number one ice man in the business. Nobody's ever even seen him. Some of the cops I know claim he doesn't even exist."

"Oh, he exists, all right," said Thanatos. "And our missing agent, Fay Morgan, had been on his trail for years."

"But how can you be certain that this Roderick guy was Morpheus? I mean, all you had was just a name he'd used as an alias, right? It could have been a coincidence."

"It was no coincidence," said Thanatos. "Discovered in the wreckage of Roderick's penthouse were the remains of a hyperdimensional matrix computer that were positively identified as having been part of Apollonius, a thaumaturgically animated data bank that was hijacked while en route to Langley. It was unquestionably the work of Morpheus. Whoever had destroyed that penthouse had struck out at Morpheus thaumaturgically through Apollonius. I believe that Morpheus had undertaken a contract to find those two thieves and he got too close to Sharif, who was also on their trail. At this point, their trail ran out in New York City, but it was picked up once again in Boston. Before Rozetti died, he gave the police an excellent description of the two thieves. A young male and a young female. The female was known to him as a hustler, a con artist, and cat burglar named Kira. The male he had never seen before, but he said that Kira called him "warlock." The police artist made sketches based on Rozetti's descriptions and they were widely circulated. The Boston police came up with the next lead.

"Several officers had responded to a call of shots fired at the Copley Plaza Hotel," Thanatos continued. "When they arrived there, they found a dead body on the floor of one of the hotel rooms and a suspect standing there with a gun in his hand. A 10mm. semiautomatic, which happens to be the signature weapon of Morpheus. Only this wasn't Morpheus. The suspect denied firing the gun, but there was no one else in the room. He was placed under arrest, but before the police were able to get him out of the hotel room, they fell under a spell in which several minutes passed that they could not account for. When they recovered, the suspect had disappeared. As had the body and the murder weapon. There weren't even any bloodstains remaining on the carpet."

"Sorcery," said Slater.

"Obviously. The room had been registered to a 'Mr. and Mrs. Karpinsky.' The escaped suspect matched the description of Mr. Karpinsky. He also matched the description that Rozetti had given to the New York police. 'Mrs. Karpinsky' matched the description of the girl named Kira. And the description the police on the scene gave of the missing corpse matched that of the U.S.R. attaché, Mustafa Sharif, who had supposedly been sent back home. At this point, the Boston police coordinated with the New York police and with our agent. They discovered that a Melvin Karpinsky, also known by the magename of Wyrdrune, had studied thaumaturgy under none other than Merlin Ambrosius himself, who was residing in Boston."

"You're not suggesting that Merlin was involved in this himself?" said Slater with disbelief.

"One way or another, he must have been," said Thanatos, "and he was evidently killed for it. There's little question that Sharif was working for Sheikh Al'Hassan, and you'll recall what happened to him."

Slater nodded grimly. After Merlin, Al'Hassan had been the world's most powerful mage and he had been done in by a monstrous spell that had apparently gone out of control. No one knew for certain what he had intended, but the story of the result had eclipsed even Merlin's death. The day it happened, it was as if Armageddon had arrived.

People had died horribly as all of New York City was mysteriously blacked out. In Washington, D.C., a huge, demonic entity had appeared during a baseball game in R.F.K. Stadium and slaughtered thousands of people. In China, Peking Station had collapsed, killing two hundred thousand people when the roof of the ten-story-high concourse fell. On the island of Hawaii, Mauna Loa and Kilauea both erupted simultaneously, each volcano belching forth a mushroom cloud of fire-charged smoke that slowly moved off toward the mainland, and within each cloud of fire and ash, something monstrous screeched and there was heard the beating of impossibly large wings. In South America, several huge waterspouts rose up out of the waves and rushed across the Baia de Gaunabara, smashing into the port of Rio de Janeiro and causing untold destruction and loss of life. In Moscow, it rained fire on Kalinin Avenue, the flames consuming the October Concert Hall and spreading to Komsomol Square. Panic-stricken people in the street had turned into blazing torches, many of them dropping down upon their knees to pray even as they burned. And in the U.S.R., at the thaumaturgic epicenter of the devastating spell, Al'Hassan's palace was utterly destroyed as steaming fissures opened in the ground, radiating outward from the palace like spokes on a gigantic wheel.

It was a horrible tragedy of unprecedented proportions and it had brought home to the world the dark side of the power that ended the Collapse. For the first time, people realized what could be done if that power were misused. The word necromancy took on new and frighteningly real meaning. That one man could have caused such devastation staggered the imagination. But how? And why? It seemed that those questions would remain forever unanswered, for Al'Hassan had perished in the conflagration of thaumaturgic energy that he had unleashed and upon his death, his spell had dissipated. The only other person who might have provided an explanation was Merlin, but Merlin was dead. The world, it seemed, had suddenly become a far more terrifying place.

"So you're saying that Al'Hassan was behind all this?" said Slater.

"Al'Hassan was unquestionably involved," said Thanatos. "I believe that it was Al'Hassan, through Mustafa Sharif, who was responsible for the deaths of those two fences in New York and probably for the destruction of Morpheus's penthouse, as well. It all seemed to center on the runestones.

Yet strangely enough, after the storm over what Al'Hassan had done died down, the case was suddenly dropped.''

"Dropped?'' said Slater. "What do you mean dropped?''

"The Annendale Corporation and the U.S.R., who shared joint interest in the artifacts and, consequently, in the proceeds of the auction, simply dropped all charges without any explanation. And Boston Mutual, the insurer of the runestones, also declined to prosecute the case. Obviously, some sort of settlement was reached. It must have been quite substantial. And surprisingly, there was also pressure from within certain government circles. In any event, the investigation was officially dropped.''

"But what about the murder?'' Slater said. "The killing of Sharif in the hotel?''

"What murder?'' said Thanatos with a shrug. "There was no body. No murder weapon. No evidence of any kind that could be produced to prove that a crime had been committed. The runestones were never recovered, our agent never returned, and the matter seemed to end right there. Until what happened in London last year. There was a series of savage murders, unbelievably brutal, that at first seemed to be a routine matter for the police to solve—inasmuch as such heinous crimes can be called routine. What I meant was that there was no evidence of magic use being involved, so it was not officially a matter for the I.T.C. However, we were brought in by the Commissioner of Scotland Yard shortly after what occurred at Carfax Castle.

"Lord Nigel Carfax was a wealthy socialite with enormous political influence. During a weekend festival at his replica medieval castle, some curious events took place that the police were at a loss to account for. Some of the most powerful men in government were in attendance, as well as captains of industry, peers of the realm, the guest list was a veritable Who's Who. And they were apparently being entertained by a considerably less distinguished coterie of young women. The victims concerned were all male, only exactly what they were victims of is difficult to say. Many of them bore wounds such as those that might be inflicted by wild animals, animals with claws and fangs, but none of them could remember a thing and no such animals were ever found on the premises.

Carfax himself was dead, in addition to a number of others. Beneath the castle, we discovered an authentic medieval dungeon and a secret chamber, a temple for conducting a black mass.''

"Carfax was indulging in a little boys'-night-out action with his well-heeled cronies and things got out of hand," Slater said.

"That was what the police believed," said Thanatos, "but I tell you that when I stepped into that underground temple, it was positively throbbing with thaumaturgic trace emanations. Something extraordinary had occurred there. Incredible power had been released. And I saw something else, as well. Something unlike anything I'd ever experienced before.''

He leaned forward slightly and stared at Slater intently.

"You must understand that when I went into that temple, in order to try to sense what might have happened there, I insisted upon being alone. There was not another soul inside there with me. *And yet I saw three auras*. I saw them clearly. Only auras, not people, but each aura clearly outlined a human form. One was a brilliant, emerald green. Another was bright, ruby red. And the third was a deep, sapphire blue. And together, they seemed to form a sort of triangle. A 'living triangle.' I had no idea why that thought occurred to me, but it came in an incredibly powerful intuition. And I knew just as surely that here was the key to finding the answer to the riddle of the missing runestones—one of which was an emerald, one a ruby, and one a sapphire.

Slater had forgotten all about his meal. The rest of the steak lay cold and untouched on his plate and his beer was getting warm. He was completely captivated by the story Thanatos was telling.

"Fortunately, I had better luck in my inquiries of the police this time," Thanatos said. "In Boston, the police were helpful, but ultimately they could tell me nothing. Still, they did discover the identities of the two thieves. In New York, the police were even less helpful, though through no fault of their own. One of the detectives, Dominic Riguzzo, had clearly seen something, but he could not remember what it was. A block of time was missing from his life. He had been enchanted. Whatever it was he had discovered, it had been completely erased from the mind. Interestingly, he was also the last person who saw our missing agent, Fay Morgan. However, I had rather better luck with Scotland Yard.

"The man in charge of the case there was Chief Inspector Michael Blood and he, too, claimed to have suffered some sort of amnesia from the injuries he had sustained, but I was convinced that he was holding something back from me. I could see it in his aura. I pressed him, and when I asked him if the words 'living triangle' meant anything to him, he became visibly distressed. I pressed him further and asked him if he knew anything about three enchanted runestones or anyone named Wyrdrune or Kira and then it all came spilling out.

"He had all the answers I'd been seeking," Thanatos continued, "only he hadn't told anyone for fear that no one would believe him. The missing runestones were keys to an ancient and powerful spell that had held the Dark Ones prisoner in a hidden chamber deep beneath the earth. During the Annendale dig, Al'Hassan had found the hidden chamber and he had removed the runestones, in effect taking the keys out of the lock. What remained was to open the door, but Al'Hassan lacked the power to do that and he had lost possession of the runestones. They wound up among the artifacts to be sold at auction. Al'Hassan had planned to buy them back, through Mustafa Sharif, but before he could do that, the stones were stolen."

"By Wyrdrune and Kira," Slater said.

"Precisely. According to Blood, who had spoken with them, they claimed they were *compelled* to steal the stones, compelled by the runestones themselves, which are in some magical sense alive, the repository of the life forces of the Old Ones who had imprisoned the Dark Ones ages ago. And the runestones had chosen them because of their descent from one of the Old Ones, from whom Merlin was descended, as well. Somehow, the runestones had . . . linked up with them, joined their life energies with theirs to resist the Dark Ones, who had finally been released by Al'Hassan. That was the reason for that cataclysmic spell of his, to utilize all the energy of those thousands of lost lives to enable the Dark Ones to break free of their confinement. They are loose upon the world now, and I believe that at least one of them is here in Los Angeles. And that means that the three runestones must be here, as well, or soon will be.''

"You said there were three people that the runestones had linked up with," Slater said. "This young wizard, Wyrdrune, the cat burglar, Kira . . . but who's the third?"

"Morpheus," said Thanatos.

"*Morpheus*? Why Morpheus?" said Slater.

"Because he is descended from the Old Ones, too," said Thanatos. "Morpheus is none other than Modred, son of King Arthur Pendragon and the sorceress, Morgan Le Fay, whom I had known as agent Fay Morgan. Al'Hassan had killed her and Morpheus killed Al'Hassan, but he was too late. The Dark Ones had already been released."

Slater simply stared at him

"You don't believe me," Thanatos said.

Slater exhaled heavily. "Well, you have to admit it's a pretty incredible story. I mean, if Morpheus was really who you say he is, then he'd have to be about two thousand years old!"

"How old was Merlin?" Thanatos countered.

"Well, all right, but that wasn't exactly the same thing," Slater said. "Merlin was placed under a spell. He was sort of in suspended animation all those years."

"Yet he was nevertheless alive," said Thanatos. "Look, Ben, prior to the Collapse, no one believed in magic, and yet it was around them all the time. They simply didn't know how to utilize the natural thaumaturgic forces. Or at least most of them didn't. There were some who did it unconsciously. Some people were able to develop extrasensory perception. Others had fatal diseases that suddenly, inexplicably went into remission. There were individuals who seemed to be able to do things that others couldn't, such as inducing spontaneous combustion or moving objects with the power of their minds. All these things are documented, Ben. Why is it that some people live so much longer than others and never seem to get sick? And why is it that today, even with the same thaumaturgic training available to everyone, most people who try simply can't accomplish very much and some can't do it at all, while others simply seem to have a natural affinity for magic?''

"I don't know, why do some people have artistic talent and others don't?" countered Slater. "Why are some people better athletes or better mathematicians? It's a matter of genetics."

"Exactly, Ben! Don't you see, centuries ago, the Old Ones must have interbred with us! Eventually, all that was left of them were the legends. Examine the folklore of the ancients and you will inevitably find recurring, common threads, stories of an older, godlike race of beings. The Celts called them the Old Ones. The Egyptians and the Greeks worshiped them as gods. The Arabic tribes knew them as the Djinn and the American Indians called them Kachina. Look at all the myths that have been handed down to us, stories of witches, warlocks, shapechangers, and vampires. What was *really* behind the Spanish Inquisition and the Salem witch trials? Were those people merely the victims of primitive superstition or did they know something we've forgotten?"

"Why are you telling me all this?" asked Slater. "If it's really true, then I should think the *last* thing you'd want to do would be to tell the press."

Thanatos smiled. "That's exactly how Gorman feels, but you see, Gorman hasn't really thought it through. To be sure, if this story were to come out, there'd be mass hysteria, especially after what Al'Hassan did. On the other hand, I don't think you'll print it."

"Why not?" said Slater. "It would be the biggest damn news story in the world. I'd be crazy not to print it."

"But where's your proof?" said Thanatos. "I would simply deny that this conversation ever took place. I'd say you fabricated the whole thing."

"What if I had you on tape?"

"You don't," said Thanatos. "And if you were carrying a recorder, do you seriously think I'd have told you all this without taking precautions? Even if someone were eavesdropping on us at this very moment with directional microphones, all they'd hear would the meaningless gibberish. And if I chose to, I could easily cast a spell of forgetfulness upon you so that you would not even remember meeting me."

"Like they did to that New York cop who saw something," Slater mused. "Only they didn't do it to your English detective, what's the name, Blood? Why not him?"

"I'm not sure," said Thanatos. "I can only guess. Perhaps they belatedly realized that if Blood told all he knew, it would sound so incredible that odds were no one would believe him. Perhaps they thought they could use his help again."

"You said there were at least seven people who shared this secret," Slater said.

Thanatos nodded. "The two thieves, Wyrdrune and Kira, Morpheus or Modred, Chief Inspector Blood, a Frenchwoman named Jaqueline Monet, a somewhat eccentric professor named Sebastian Makepeace, who claims to be a fairy—"

"A what?"

"A fairy," said Thanatos. He cleared his throat. "Not the kind you think. According to my information, he actually believes himself to be a sprite."

"You mean like in Peter Pan?" said Slater.

"Uh, yes, only somewhat larger. Professor Makepeace weighs about three hundred pounds."

"A three-hundred-pound fairy?" Slater said. "Are you putting me on?"

"I'm not, but perhaps Professor Makepeace is," said Thanatos. "He cuts a very flamboyant figure at New York University and in the café society of the Village. One would never suspect such a man of having connections in deep-cover government intelligence."

"Which he does?" said Slater.

"He does, indeed."

"All right, but that's still only six," said Slater.

"The seventh is a cockney boy named Billy Slade," said Thanatos. "A street urchin of thirteen who's already been in more than his share of trouble. And according to Chief Inspector Blood, young Billy Slade is the most fascinating of the bunch."

"Why's that?"

"He's possessed."

"Possessed," repeated Slater, not sure he'd heard correctly. "You mean like in speaking in tongues, puking green slime, and throwing furniture around?"

"Well, perhaps not quite that dramatic," Thanatos said, "but if it's true, it's dramatic enough. Blood claims he's possessed by the spirit of Merlin Ambrosius."

"Oh, come on!" exclaimed Slater. "What the hell are you feeding me here? You actually expect me to *believe* all this?"

Thanatos regarded Slater with a steady stare. "You see what I mean, Ben? I told you that you were never going to print this. You don't even believe it yourself. How would you expect your editors, much less your readers, to believe it?"

"They wouldn't, of course," said Slater. "Not without proof, anyway."

"Which is why I'm telling you all this," said Thanatos. "I also need proof. Chief Inspector Blood refused to testify, not that I can blame him. He knows very well that without proof, he'd be laughed off the police force. I believe him, but I need to find proof to convince my superiors. And to do that, Ben, I need your help."

"Why me?"

"Because you know this city. As the old saying goes, you know where all the bodies are buried. I'm a stranger here, whereas you have contacts. You could save me a great deal of time and time is of the essence."

Slater sighed and shook his head. "Well, I've heard some pretty wild stories in my time, but nothing to match this. Assuming it's all true—and mind you, I'm not assuming anything at this point—then this is the biggest story to come along since Merlin was released from his enchantment. What makes you think you can trust me to keep quiet about this? I am a reporter, after all."

"And one with a great deal of credibility, from what I hear," said Thanatos. "Which is precisely why I *don't* want you to keep quiet about it. I *want* the story to be told, but first we need incontrovertible proof. One of the greatest assets that the Dark Ones have is that no one knows about them. Gorman is a bureaucrat and, unfortunately, he thinks like one. He doesn't know the full extent of what I've told you just now. He thinks we're faced with a renegade sorcerer practicing necromancy and his first instinct is to keep it covered up, both to keep from warning the perpetrator that we're on to him and to keep the public from being panicked. Can you imagine how he'd react if I told him what I've just told you?''

"He'd either think you've lost it or he'd go over your head and bring the entire B.O.T. and your superiors at the I.T.C. down on your neck," said Slater with a grimace. "Typical bureaucrat mentality. C.Y.A.''

Thanatos frowned. "C.Y.A.?''

"First rule of bureaucracy," said Slater. "Cover Your Ass. They're all the same. Or at least most of them are. You seem to be an exception. Why is that?''

"Because first and foremost, I am a sorcerer, not a bureaucrat,'' said Thanatos. "If I was interested in money, I would have remained in corporate sorcery, but that held little fascination for me. In fact, it bored me to tears and I found that I was constitutionally incapable of playing corporate politics. I joined the I.T.C. not because I was interested in power or position, but because I wanted to do something constructive. I've seen far too many abuses of thaumaturgy in my time. And I wanted to do something about it. I suppose that makes me sort of a policeman.''

Slater nodded. "What it makes you is a street cop. And that's something I can understand, even if your beat is in the Twilight Zone.'' He grinned. "Okay, I guess I'm in. Where do we start?''

A waiter approached their table. "Excuse me, sir,'' he said, "is you name Thanatos?''

"Yes?''

"There is a call for you from a gentleman named Gorman. He says it's very urgent.''

"Thank you.'' Thanatos glanced at Slater. "Excuse me, I'll be right back.''

A moment later, he returned, a grim expression on his face.

"Let's go,'' he said. "Our friend has struck again.''

Slater got up quickly. "What happened?''

"The suspect in the death of Sarah Tracy,'' Thanatos said. "Her boyfriend, Victor Cameron. He was just discovered torn to pieces in his cell.''

CHAPTER
Five

The red and blue paragriffin in the palm tree behind their table was stuck on the first chorus of "Memories," singing it over and over again in a plaintive, squawking voice. The broom reached for the bowl of fruit in the center of the table and pitched a nectarine at it with unerring accuracy. The paragriffin gave a loud yelp and fell to the ground like stone, its silvery scales clinking on the patio tile. The broom shuffled over to the unconscious creature and swept it underneath a bush.

"I don't know about this," said Rydell, gazing dubiously at the broom.

"Listen, if I want *schmaltzy* singing at the table, I'll go to Little Italy," the broom said. It picked up a menu and perused it quickly. "What kinda menu is this, I ask you? What is this duck pizza? Who needs a greasy bird mucking up the mozzarella? Don't people in Los Angeles eat any normal food?"

"You don't even eat, so what do you care?" Wyrdrune said.

"*Nu?* So I don't eat. Someone's got to watch out for your digestion, *boychik.* I promised your mother I'd take care of you, may she rest in peace. Here, this is what you need, the club special, a nice chicken salad sandwich—wait a minute. *With raisins? Gevalt!* Who puts raisins in chicken salad?"

"Come on, Broom, relax, will you please?" said Wyrdrune, taking the menu away from it. "I'm just going to have a hamburger and some fries."

"What do they put in the hamburger, glazed fruit bits?"

"Broom. . . ."

"You ask for ketchup, they probably give you some kinda sauce made from peach brandy—"

"Will you put a lid on it, please?"

"Fine. Eat this *chaloshes*, get an ulcer, see what I care."

"That thing sounds just like my mother," said Rydell. "Its spooky."

"I know, but it sorta grows on you," said Wyrdrune.

"Yeah, like a fungus," Kira said wryly.

"You should get a festering boil on your *tuchis*," said the broom.

"Listen here, stick—"

"Will you stop?" said Wyrdrune. "Broom, why don't you go clean up our rooms, make yourself useful."

"So, all of a sudden, I'm a maid," the Broom said, leaving with a sniff, which was somewhat incongruous, since it didn't have a nose. "Fine. That's all I'm good for. You work your bristles down to the nubs and this is the thanks you get. . . ."

Rydell shook his head with amazement. "I've never seen anything like it," he said. You know, maybe we could use it in the film."

"Bite your tongue," said Wyrdrune. "It's hard enough to live with as it is."

Rydell glanced at his watch, "Well, they ought to be here by now," he said, "but knowing Jessica, she'll show up just a little late. Not enough to piss you off, but enough to make you notice. She's refined it to an art. And of course, Landau can't possibly arrive before Jessica, even though he's probably been waiting in the parking lot for the past half hour, so they'll be coming in together whenever she arrives."

He glanced around at them. "Okay, now here's how it's going to go. Jerry's going to talk a lot. He always does. He's going to come on like he's the biggest name in the business and act as if you're not going to get him cheap, but you're going to get him cheap because I made him and he needs the work. He's just wrapped my latest picture yesterday and since I always control postproduction and the final cut, he's got nothing to do, besides which, he's probably broke already. I don't know what the hell he does with all his money, but he never seems to have any. Jessica is going to play a slightly different game. She's going to come on as if she's got about a dozen offers because she's this year's reigning sex symbol and she may actually have a few. However, she'll be dying to do this film because I've had word leak out that it's going to be a quality picture and she wants to show the world that she can do more than just wet her lips and breathe hard. She's also going to try to figure out which one of you she can manipulate and whoever she decides that is, she'll start coming on to you, hard. She can really put it out, but take my word for it, it's a control thing and nothing more than that." He grimaced. "Half the guys in the country fantasize about Jessie Blaine. If they only knew that all they'd have to do is ask. . . . If you want my advice, if she gives you the come-hither, you'll shine her on, because she's trouble. However, she is box office, so we'll use her."

"What part did you have in mind for her?" asked Wyrdrune.

"She'll want Morgan Le Fay, but she's going to get Queen Guinevere," Rydell said.

Modred glanced at him and raised his eyebrows, but said nothing.

"Typecasting," Merlin mumbled.

"You keep quiet!" Billy said.

"What?" Rydell said. "Ah, never mind, here they come. Fashionably late, as usual."

Johnny Landau and Jessica Blaine took their time strolling across the lounge, making sure that everybody had a good opportunity to notice them. And just in case anyone forgot to look, Landau made a big show of scanning the tables, spotting Rydell and calling out, "Yo, Ron!" and waving.

"When they come to the table, don't get up," Rydell said, so that only they could hear.

"Why not?" said Wyrdrune, looking puzzled.

"It's a power thing. If you get up for them, you give up some power. Look, you've got the money, right? That makes you king. Kings don't get up for anybody."

They all remained seated as Landau and Jessica came up to the table.

"Ron, darling! I hope we're not too late," gushed Jessica, quickly positioning herself so that Landau could pull out a chair for her and she could go through the introductions sitting down. She immediately reached her hand across to Wyrdrune and flashed a dazzling smile. "Hi, I'm Jessie Blaine."

Landau was now left hanging and had to stand awkwardly as Rydell performed the introductions.

"Jessica Blaine, Johnny Landau, this is Mel Karpinsky, Michael Cornwall, and their associates, Kira . . . uh. . . ."

"Just Kira."

"Right. And . . . uh. . . ."

Billy just sat there, kicked back with his boots up on the table.

"Billy Slade," said Wyrdrune, indicating Billy.

Landau shook hands all around, but when he got to Billy, Billy just stared at his outstretched hand. After an awkward moment, Landau let his hand drop.

Jessica stared at Billy for a moment, not quite knowing what to make of him or what to say. She finally settled on, "Cute hair."

Billy growled at her.

Wrydrune reached over and shoved his feet off the table. "You'll have to excuse Billy," he said. "He's not quite housebroken."

"Look, Ron," said Landau, "before we go any further, I have to tell you that I absolutely *love* your concept. As you know, we just wrapped *Blood of the Necromancer* and I've already got about eight new projects on my desk, but I can tell that what you've got here is something really special. It's exciting. It's focused. It's sexy. It sounds like the sort of thing I could really get my teeth into. That, plus working with you again, well, what can I say? I haven't actually committed to anything yet, although we've reached the serious discussion stage of this one deal, but hell, you and I have got some history, right? That's gotta count for something. Still I've practically given my word. . . ."

"Well, that's all right, Johnny, I understand," Rydell said. "If your plate is full, your plate is full. I wouldn't want you to back out of any deals for my sake."

A look of alarm came into Landau's eyes.

"Well, now I haven't actually made any *firm* commitments, yet. True, there are one or two projects I find pretty interesting, but if the deal's right, I think we might be able to work something out.''

"Well, I suppose we can talk about it,'' Rydell said, abruptly switching gears and turning to Jessica. "What did you think of the script, Jessie?''

"I thought it was wonderful,'' she said. "Morgan Le Fay is a fascinating part. I see her as sort of—''

"Actually, I was thinking of you for Guinevere,'' Rydell said.

"Guinevere?'' said Jessica, her smile slipping.

"Oh yes. She was the central figure in the Arthurian saga, you know.''

"But this film is about Merlin. In this script, Guinevere is a much smaller part than Morgan Le Fay.''

"Well,'' Rydell said with a shrug, "it's still not the final draft, you know.''

"Who were you thinking of for Morgan Le Fay?''

"I was thinking of maybe using an unknown,'' Rydell said.

"An *unknown*? In the starring role?''

"Well, Merlin is the starring role,'' Rydell said.

"Who have you got in mind for Merlin?'' Landau said quickly, anxious to get back into the conversation.

"Burton Clive.''

"Burton Clive? Really?''

"He really likes the script,'' Rydell said. "He wants to do it. Anyway, the casting isn't entirely up to me, you know. Our backers have a say in this. After all, it's their money, right, Michael?''

"That's right, Ron,'' said Modred, picking up his cue and moving his leg out of reach of Jessica's foot beneath the table. "We all agreed from the beginning that casting is something that has to be very carefully considered. And the choice of director is important, too. In fact, it's vital. If Mr. Landau's already made other commitments, then perhaps that other fellow you were suggesting, what was his name?''

"You mean Bob Tomasini?''

"Yes, that's the one.''

"*Tomasini*?" Landau said, a look of panic in his eyes. "On a project of this scope? Hell, Ron, he's just a kid! You can't be serious."

"Well, I don't know what to tell you, Johnny," said Rydell. "You're telling me that you've got all these other projects and you're taking meetings left and right and it sounds like you've got a deal that's going to go through at any minute—"

"Well, yes, but I haven't actually made any *firm* commitments, you understand. . . ."

By the time the meeting was over, Rydell had practically reduced Landau to begging that he be allowed to direct the film and he had convinced Jessica that while Morgan Le Fay was the larger female role, the part of Guinevere was in fact the meatier one and would get her the most favorable attention from the critics.

"See, the secret of taking a good meeting is to gang up on 'em," Rydell explained after they left, "and if you can't gang up on 'em, keep 'em off balance. Never do a one-on-one if you can help it. And whatever you do, never deal directly with an agent. Always end run 'em, play the agent off against the talent and vice versa. The talent's always going to be easier because they want the job and the agent simply wants to cut the best deal. So in a situation like that, you play the talent off against the agent, as if you really want the talent, but the agent is the one that's going to queer the deal. The exception is when you're dealing with a big-name talent who won't budge unless you offer the right numbers. There, you play the agent off against the talent, because the agent wants that bottom line commission and you make as if the talent's got an attitude that's going to price 'em right out of the deal. You'd really like to use 'em, but hey, your backers won't allow you to sign a contract that's a budget buster, so your hands are tied."

"So basically, it's just a hustle," Kira said.

"Yeah, it's all a game," Rydell said with shrug.

"And you have to go through this kind of thing every time you make a picture?" Wyrdrune said.

"Every time. Some are worse than others. This one's going to be a snap."

"You've really got Burton Clive for Merlin?" Wyrdrune said.

Rydell grinned. "Impressed? Don't be. Clive's a major talent and one of the biggest names in the business, but the problem with being a major talent and one of the biggest names in the business is that when you get there, you don't get a lot of work. Your whole career becomes much more precarious. The minute you get there, everybody and their mother-in-law starts sending you scripts, but you've got to be very careful about what you choose to do. It's got to be the sort of part that will reinforce your major talent/big-name image and help you build on it if you can. A part that would have allowed you to shine the year before you made it, the kind of part that had critics saying you were going to be a big star simply won't make it anymore because if you play a part like that *as* a big star, they'll be ten times as tough on you and say it wasn't a part worthy of your stature or that you're taking 'lesser roles.' They'll say you were miscast or, worse yet, 'underutilized.'

"The other thing is the money," Rydell continued, after taking a sip of mineral water. "The minute you start getting the big-name money, you can't ever take one penny less or the whole thing goes out the window. That, plus the thing with the right roles, automatically cuts down on the amount of work you get. And even if you do start getting offered one wonderful script after another, you've still got to be very careful because if you start doing too many pictures, you're going to get overexposed and the next thing you know, you're not getting the good scripts anymore and you're talking about doing a TV series. Burton Clive is in that Neverneverland between a rock and a hard place. He's a big-name star, a major talent, expensive as hell, and difficult to work with. He hasn't done a picture in five years, but he's recently started showing up in all the right places, just being visible to let people know he's still around. That means he's hungry. And I knew if he was hungry, I could cut a deal with him."

"Hungry?" Wyrdrune said. "With all the money he gets, he's hungry? He must be a multimillionaire."

"He probably would be, if he was smart," Rydell replied,

"but you don't run into too many actors who are smart. If they were smart, they wouldn't be actors."

"Even so," said Kira, "with the kind of money Burton Clive must make, if all you did was put it in a bank, you could retire and live off the interest."

"Not in this town," Rydell said. "This town is like a Venus flytrap. It eats you alive, especially if you're well known and successful. You bite and claw and scratch your way to the top and then you have to bite and claw and scratch ten times as hard to stay there. What happens is you become extremely visible and everybody judges you by every little thing you do. You've got to buy a ten-million-dollar mansion in Bel Air because that's how someone in your position is supposed to live and if you *don't* live that way, then everybody starts to wonder if maybe you can't afford it and that's death in this town. If they think you can't afford to go first cabin all the way, then it means you're second-rate. So you've got to drive something that makes a statement about you and you have to wear clothes that reflect your standing in the business, which means you've got to get them from the same overpriced designers as everybody else who's worried about the same thing. You've got to be seen in all the right places, and the right places are all ludicrously expensive. You've got to give a party for all the right people every now and then and make sure that it's catered by the right caterer and protected by the right security agency and the floral arrangements done by the right florist, the bar stocked with whatever the current most unobtainable wine is and so on and so on and so on. It never ends. It's like being a junkie. No matter how much you score, it's never enough."

"If it's such a drag," said Billy, "then why do you do it?"

"Because it beats working, kid," Rydell said with a grin. "And it's kinda fun, playing with all the glitterati and putting them through their paces, but in order to appreciate it, you've got to have the right kind of attitude. See, I was broke for so many years that I learned to get by on very little. I've been blade dancing all my life. There's an old nostalgia song that's got a line that goes, 'Freedom's just another word for nothing left to lose.' Bottom line? If my career fell apart tomorrow, I've still got enough set aside so I can retire to a small cabin in the Colorado Rockies and write books. I won't have a mansion or a chauffeured limo or fancy clothes or tables at all the best restaurants in town, but I could easily do without all that. I regard it all as just the cost of doing business. See, the trap snaps shut on you when you think you can't do without all that stuff, when your material possessions become the measure of your self-esteem. When that happens, you've lost yourself. You've been El Laid and you might as well hit the Strip and be an honest whore. End of sermon. So, you guys ready for a party?''

"Ey, I'm always ready to party,'' Billy said.

"You'll like the bash, kid,'' said Rydell. "You'll fit right in. It's at Spago-Pogo. Everybody who's anybody is going to be there.''

"Who's the host?'' said Modred.

"You are,'' said Rydell.

"Me?"

"You and your partner, Mel. Its a private party to kick off Warlock Productions and launch pre-publicity for *Ambrosius*, your new feature presentation.''

"*Pre*-publicity?'' said Wryrdrune. "What the hell is pre-publicity?''

"That's publicizing the fact that you're going to publicize something,'' explained Rydell. "The fact that it's a private party ensured that everybody important in this town had to bend over backwards to wrangle an invite.''

"When did you have time to send out invitations?'' Modred asked.

"What invitations? I booked the club, hired a band, and told the management it was a strictly private deal for Warlock Productions; absolutely no one gets in unless they're on the guest list. The phones in my office started ringing off the hook within twenty minutes, people saying they'd lost their invitations and wanting to make sure their names were on the list. Of course, they hadn't been invited, but they figured if *they* hadn't been invited, then whoever was running Warlock must really be worth meeting. So, by noon, we had a guest list and all the phones in town were melting down from people tying to get the scam on Cornwall, Karpinksy, and associates. You wanted to meet the heavyweights in this town?" He snapped his fingers. "Easy. All you had to do was snub them. So tonight, they're all coming to meet you."

There was nothing left of Victor Cameron. He had been quite literally torn to pieces and those pieces had been flung all about the jail. Bloody gobbets of flesh and viscera were everywhere, sticking to the walls and hanging from the ceiling. Even his bones had been scattered. It was as if he had exploded. The smell was indescribable. Gorman and Rebecca Farrell were both waiting for them when they got there.

"What the hell is *he* doing here?" said Gorman when he saw Ben Slater.

"He's with me," said Thanatos. "What happened?"

"With all due respect," said Gorman, "are you sure you know what you're doing? Bringing the press in on this is—"

"I know exactly what I'm doing," said Thanatos. "And I'm not in the habit of explaining myself. The matter is closed. Now what happened here?"

Gorman flushed and gave Slater an unfriendly glance but chose not to risk pursuing the matter any further.

"Nobody saw anything," Rebecca said. "The other prisoners report hearing a sound that some of them described as a loud pop, others described it as 'a sort of whump,' and then they heard Cameron screaming. He screamed once— they said they'd never heard anyone scream like that before—and then the scream was cut off in a gurgle or a 'wet sound.' The guards responded immediately, but it was all over by the time they got here. There were pieces of him all over the place and no sign of whatever did it to him."

"A manifestation," Thanatos said.

Gorman glanced uneasily at Slater. "Either that or he exploded," he said.

"No, a manifestation," Thanatos repeated, staring intently into Cameron's cell. "I can see it."

"What?" said Gorman. "You mean it's still *in* there?" Involuntarily, he backed away.

"No, it's gone, but I can see the trace emanations of its aura," Thanatos said. "It's fading even as we stand here."

"What does it look like?" Slater said, looking from the interior of the bloody cell to Thanatos. He couldn't see anything in there except the grisly remains of Victor Cameron.

"I can't quite make it out," said Thanatos, staring intently into the cell. "It's like a shadow . . . a dark shadow with a faintly glowing border all around it . . . a figure. . . . I can't tell. . . ." He sighed. "It's gone now. Let's get out of here."

"Well, so much for your suspect," Slater said with a glance at Rebecca as they left the jail.

She said nothing.

"Slater, what you saw and heard in there was strictly off the record," Gorman said.

"No," said Thanatos. "No, I want him to report *exactly* what he saw and heard in there."

"I'm not sure that would be wise—" Gorman began, but at a warning glance from Thanatos, he broke off abruptly.

"I don't suppose you want me to mention the aura that you saw in there?" asked Slater.

Thanatos shook his head. "No, I want you to be certain to mention it. But I would avoid drawing any conclusions. I suggest you simply give my name and report that I 'claimed' to have seen an aura in the cell. That way, you wouldn't be reporting hearsay as fact."

"True," said Rebecca. "And he'd also be setting you up."

"I hope so, Captain Farrell," Thanatos said. "I sincerely hope so. Because at the moment, we have hardly anything to go on. Have you come up with anything more on Sarah Tracy?"

"As a matter of fact, we have," Rebecca said. "She had just finished working on a film for Ron Rydell. Ask me what the title was."

"What was the title?"

"Blood of the Necromancer."

Thanatos raised his eyebrows.

"Thought you'd like that," said Rebecca.

"Has anyone spoken with Mr. Rydell yet?" Thanatos said.

"Not yet."

"Well, perhaps we should make his acquaintance. In the meantime, Gorman, I'd like you to find out as much as possible about Mr. Rydell and his films. Especially any adepts who might have been involved in his productions. I'd like all the B.O.T. files on any such individuals."

"I'll get on it right away," said Gorman.

"I'll call the paper and see what the entertainment editor's got on him," said Slater.

"Good idea. It may not get us anywhere," said Thanatos, "but on the other hand, who knows?"

"So long as it doesn't get us to wind up like Victor Cameron," Slater said with a shudder.

"There are worse things than what happened to Victor Cameron, Ben," said Thanatos grimly. "Much worse."

Spago-Pogo was the current "in" club among the chic set of L.A., although one couldn't tell by looking at it. Located on the Strip, it was a blocky and unattractive building, looking like a big, black, windowless cube with a flashing blue sign out front that seemed to jump up and down in a pogo stick effect. Over the years, the building had gone through any number of incarnations, from warehouse to massage parlor to S & M bar and almost all the possible permutations in between. Now it had become an upscale nightclub featuring live entertainment, nostalgic pre-Collapse cuisine, and a colorful celebrity clientele that enjoyed a decadent evening on the Strip. The cover charge varied depending on the featured attraction and on some nights, such as this one, it was impossible to get in at all unless by special invitation.

The place was already jammed by the time they arrived in Rydell's chauffeured limousine. The club's full complement of head-breakers was out in force, controlling the crowd massed around the entrance and keeping out the riffraff. The broom had remained behind in their rented cottage to play solitaire and watch TV, not caring to sample L.A.'s nightlife. Besides, its favorite TV show, "Hobbittmashers," was on. Wyrdrune was relieved. The broom had a nasty habit of always saying the wrong thing at the wrong time. It simply wasn't to be trusted.

They ran the gauntlet of fans and photographers and then they were inside, where a band was playing, but not so loud that people couldn't talk. Leggy waitresses were threading their way among the tables and there were a few couples on the dance floor, but mostly everyone was busy table-hopping and being seen.

"What are we supposed to do?" asked Wyrdrune as they were being led to their table.

"It's a party," Rydell said. "What do you usually do at parties?"

"Get drunk and bust up the place," said Billy.

"Hey, just look around," Rydell said. "I'm sure you'll find someone to accommodate you. I'll get up and introduce you and from there on, you guys are on your own."

As they were seated, he made his way over to the stage. He spoke briefly to one of the musicians in the band. The musician nodded and gave a signal to the band. They played a couple of flourishes and then he stepped up to the mike and said, "Ladies and gentlemen, can I have your attention please?" A moment later, after the crowd had quieted down, he added, "Your host for this evening, Mr. Ron Rydell."

The drummer did a roll and a few rim shots as Rydell stepped up to the mike amid the applause. He blew into it several times.

"Hello, this thing working? Can you all hear me out there? Yeah? All right. First of all, on behalf of myself and my new associates, Warlock Productions, I'd like to welcome all of you to the festivities. I see a lot of old familiar faces out there. Hell, I see some people that I've slept with *twice*!"

Laughter.

"All right, seriously now, as you all know, we're about to start production on a new, big-budget feature which a lot of you have already heard about, I'm sure, and this party is to officially launch our production, so I'd just like to take a moment or two to introduce my new associates at Warlock Productions . . . Michael Cornwall, where are you, Mike? Stand up and take a bow."

Modred stood up to a flourish from the band and applause from the crowd.

"And Mel Karpinsky, ladies and gentlemen, stand up, Mel, don't be shy."

Wyrdrune stood up and waved awkwardly at the crowd as they applauded.

"It's all right, guys, relax, I'm not going to make you give any speeches," said Rydell, and for some reason, the crowd seemed to think that it was funny. Wyrdrune realized that anything Rydell said would be laughed at or applauded, as the occasion seemed to call for, simply because Rydell was footing the bill.

"And speaking of speeches," Rydell went on, "here's a man who's always got one ready, our director, Johnny Landau. Johnny, where are ya, babe? Come on up here and say a few words!"

Landau sprang to his feet and made his way over to the mike amid the applause. He then proceeded to make some fatuous remarks about the "greatness" of Ron Rydell and the "vision" of Warlock Productions in teaming up to make "the greatest story ever told" about "the greatest mage who ever lived." He went on at some length about how "honored and humbled" he was to have been selected from among all the directors who "had fought for the privilege" of making *Ambrosius!* and how "pleased and delighted" he was at having been "singled out" to work with Ron Rydell once more and that he "had immediately dropped everything" when Rydell phoned him with the concept and so on and so on. He then introduced "the radiant" Jessica Blaine, taking care to refer to her as "our leading lady," despite the fact that hers was not the leading role. Jessica stood up and radiated and then Landau introduced "our star, the one and only, the celebrated Burton Clive!"

Clive stood up and was duly celebrated. He was a robust man with a florid face, an aquiline profile, and shaggy, curly dark hair shot through with gray. He bowed with an expansive gesture and it was clear that he had already been doing some celebrating himself, as he was a bit unsteady on his feet. However, he managed to make it back down to his chair more or less intact.

Billy suddenly straightened in his seat. "Good God," said Merlin, "*that's* the man who's going to play me?"

"He's what Rydell refers to as 'bankable talent,' " Modred said.

"He's what *I* refer to as a drunk!" said Merlin, pulling out his pipe and packing it with his special sorcerous blend of tobacco, which smelled different with every puff. "Besides, he doesn't look anything like me at all."

"Well, I'll admit that he isn't exactly a wiry five foot four thirteen-year-old with an overly elaborate hairstyle," Modred said, "but I suppose a bit of makeup would fix that."

"Very funny," Billy said, and immediately switched back to Merlin. "You know perfectly well what I meant."

He snapped his fingers and a small jet of flame came out of his thumb. He puffed his pipe alight and clouds of lavender-scented smoke subtly changing to the heady smell of melting chocolate drifted across the table. By the time he got it going, the aroma had changed yet again and now the pipe smelled like a buffalo steak cooking on a grill.

"What difference does it make what he looks like?" Modred said. "For God's sake, Ambrosius, we're not here to make the story of your life. That's only a cover. In case you've forgotten, we're after—"

He suddenly winced with pain and clapped his hand to his chest.

At the same time, Kira gasped and clutched her gloved right hand.

And Wyrdrune felt a sharp, hot, stabbing pain in his forehead.

Khasim had just entered the club.

CHAPTER
Six

Khasim did not sense that anything was wrong, but from the moment he walked into the club, he felt a vague unease he couldn't quite explain. He glanced around and his gaze fell on the three special effects technicians, Bert Smith, Mort

Levine, and Joe Gallico. They were standing together at the bar and staring at him. He could guess why. They all felt threatened by him. They were concerned about their jobs and their dislike of him was obvious. However, he couldn't afford to be bothered by their petty jealousies and insecurities. He had something much more important to be concerned about.

And her name was Jessica Blaine.

He wasn't sure when the idea had first taken form, but he knew the exact moment when it had become an overwhelming obsession. It was the moment when they had filmed the climatic special effects scene in *Blood of the Necromancer*. In the film, the character that Jessica was playing had been captured by the necromancer and was about to be sacrificed to "the Evil One" when the hero arrived in the nick of time. As the conjured demon leapt at her where she lay helpless on the altar, the hero released the potent charm given to him by the necromancer's jealous mistress and the demon was banished back into the netherworld. Khasim's job in that scene had been to stand in for the actor who played the necromancer and conjure up the demon illusion, then make it disappear as if defeated by the hero's charm. The other scenes had all been filmed already, with the actors playing the necromancer and the hero performing in the scenes occurring immediately before and after the special effects sequence. All that had remained was for Khasim to conjure up the special effect and for Jessica to film her reaction shots. Something had happened to Khasim during the filming of that sequence.

He wondered what the others would have thought if they knew the demon had been real. On a subliminal level, Jessica had sensed it, which was why her terror had been as real as the demonic entity itself, but Khasim had never doubted that he could control it. Since he had started serving his Dark Mistress, his powers had increased a hundredfold. Without her, he was at best an adequate wizard who had barely squeaked through his certification exams. However, from the moment that she first appeared to him in her darkly glowing, featureless state, he had felt his powers increasing exponentially. He had stood for certification as a sorcerer and passed easily. And he was getting stronger still. All it took was the occasional "gift" of a life to the Dark Mistress.

Lately, she required more and more frequent "gifts," but Khasim always obliged her. He always told himself that they were, after all, the sort of lives no one would miss. Street people. Women who held themselves so cheaply that they sold their bodies to any man who happened by.

Khasim did not love women. He did not know what love was. Perhaps he understood love as a concept, intellectually, but he had certainly never felt it. And strangely enough, Khasim did not hate women, either. Both love and hate were emotional extremes that were completely foreign to him. What Khasim lived for was manipulating people, especially women. Using them for his own self-gratification. It was far less a matter of lust than of control. What motivated him was the obsessive desire to exercise power over others. A psychiatrist would have diagnosed him as a sociopath, utterly without a conscience, totally self-centered, and capable of feeling no pain other than his own.

To Khasim, the women that he used were little more than pawns in a bizarre and complicated chess game. In a very real sense, he defined their existence only in terms of the moves that he could put them through. Their feelings, their desires, their rights, even their very humanity were not an issue to him. Some part of him was dead inside . . . or perhaps more accurately, it had never even lived. The ability to control the lives of others gave him a feeling of self-worth, a sense of satisfaction and identity that he could achieve no other way.

The Dark Mistress understood this and she had made it easier for him, feeding a hunger that she knew to be insatiable. And in supporting his psychosis, she was doing to him exactly what he did to others. Khasim understood that all too well, yet he had no choice but to accept their strange and frightening symbiosis. And it was something that was easy to accept, since it fed his appetites so well. Only those appetites kept on increasing. The cravings were becoming more and more intense.

When they had filmed that scene and he had stood up on that promontory, looking down at Jessica chained to the altar, a thrill of anticipation had gone through him. He had actually started to tremble. And when he had conjured up the demon, Jessica's terrified reaction had positively galvanized him. The sight of the demonic entity had touched off an instinctive, primal fear in her and watching it had excited Khasim unlike anything he'd ever experienced before. *He* had done that to her! *He* was the demon who had terrified her so! Watching her scream and thrash in terror on the altar, it was all Khasim could do to make the demon disappear. Part of him had wanted to see her torn apart.

Ever since that moment, he had not been able to stop thinking about her. Jessica Blaine was different. Very different. She was not some naive runaway or potion addict who struggled for a living on the Strip, someone who would become just another statistic if she disappeared. She was an internationally famous actress, a sex symbol desired by men all over the world, a woman whose standing in the business gave her power and position. And in one magic, blissful moment, he had reduced her to a mewling, frightened little animal. Ever since that moment, the way she looked at him was different. It was there, planted deep down in her psyche, the certain knowledge that *he* was the one who did that to her and the recognition that he could do it to her again, anytime he chose. The thought intoxicated him and he was sure that it excited her.

And now a new craving had started gnawing at him. He had lost track of all the lives he had presented as "gifts" to the Dark Mistress, but in the past, she had always taken them herself. When he had asked her to claim the life of Victor Cameron, she had demanded one of his captive women as a gift and insisted that he take the life himself. The idea had frightened him at first. And then, as his fingers had closed around the jeweled hilt of the knife that she had given him, that same thrill of anticipation had run through him, much stronger than before. As he held the knife, he realized that here was the ultimate manipulation, the final control. Power over life and death, resting in his hand. He had slit the woman's throat and watched in fascination as the bright red blood welled up in the deep cut and then washed down her throat like water overflowing in a sink. His mouth had gone dry and his breath had caught. He had started to tremble as he shook with the paroxysm of—

The voice of Bert Smith snapped him out of his reverie. "You gonna be workin' on this picture, too, Khasim?"

It took him a moment to focus on the man. "Yes," he replied, after taking a deep breath. "Mr. Landau called the mission earlier and left word that my services would be required."

"Is that so?" said Joe Gallico sourly. "I wonder if there'll be any work left over for us."

"I understand there are going to be quite a few effects sequences in this film," Khasim said, not particularly wanting to pursue the conversation, but the special effects men had hemmed him in.

"Yeah, and you can do all of 'em all by yourself, isn't that right?" said Mort Levine. He was drunk.

"If necessary, yes, I could, but you know as well as I do that it would be far more expensive that way."

"Unless maybe you decided to start cutting your prices so you could pick up *all* the work," said Mort. "Then where would that leave us?"

"I have no intention of cutting my prices," Khasim said, trying to remain outwardly composed. 'Brother Khasim,' after all, had a certain reputation to maintain. "Why should I do that? I need the funds to support my work at the mission."

"Yeah, only if you dropped your prices for the smaller, less complex effects, you could still charge the full going rate for the big ones you do now and still pick up more funds for your damn mission from the stuff we'd lose out on."

"It almost sounds as if you're trying to talk me into it, Mr. Levine," Khasim said.

Bert gave his colleague a sharp look, then turned back to Khasim. "Nobody's trying to talk anybody into anything," he said. "We're only trying to find out your intentions because our jobs could be at stake."

"That is hardly something I can control, Mr. Smith," Khasim said. "Frankly, I have no intention of pricing you out of your jobs, but a lower grade adept, a wizard, or even a warlock for that matter, could easily undercut your prices and there would be nothing you could do about it. My mission is full of people who mistakenly believed that the world owed them a living. I do what I can to help them, but most of the damage was caused by their own attitudes, you see. In life, there are no guarantees, no promises. Conditions in life are ever changing and a man must know how to adapt to them if he is going to exercise any control over his destiny. If you are concerned about adepts making inroads into your business, then unless you can compete with them, I might suggest that you look into training for some other line of work. And now if you gentlemen will excuse me. . . ."

He had spotted Jessica Blaine.

"What is it?" Merlin said, and Billy's face showed his concern.

"He's here!" said Wyrdrune.

"You're certain?"

"There can be no doubt of it," said Modred, anxiously scanning the faces all around them.

"Which one is he?"

"I don't know," said Modred. He glanced at Wyrdrune. "Can you tell?"

"No. But his presence is undeniable." He slipped his headband back briefly to show Modred that his runestone was glowing brightly.

"Kira?"

She shook her head. Unconsciously, she had balled her right hand into a fist.

"We have to find him," Modred said.

At that moment, Ron Rydell came back to rejoin them, bringing several people along with him.

"I brought some folks who'd like to meet you guys," he said, and started performing the introductions. "Mike, allow me to present Sheila Smythe of *Celebrity* magazine"—he went on to cue him smoothly—"you know that great piece she did on Jessica last month . . . Sheila, Michael Cornwall of Warlock Productions, and this is his partner, Mel Karpinsky. . . ."

"Very pleased to meet you," Modred said in a courtly tone, taking her hand. "We were discussing your piece earlier. I found it very insightful, wouldn't you agree, Ron?"

Rydell smoothly picked up the ball and started dropping a few specifics from the article, so that Sheila Smythe would think they had both read it, when in fact Modred had not only not read it, but also he had never even seen a copy of *Celebrity* magazine. He had already found out all he needed to know about Sheila Smythe when he touched her hand. She was not the one. As Wyrdrune was being introduced to Sheila, Modred glanced at him and their eyes met. They were both thinking the same thing. There had to be at least several hundred people in the club. How could they possibly sort through them all? And then he noticed that Kira and Billy had both slipped away into the crowd.

"Warlock Productions?" Thanatos said.

"That's right," said Slater. He had just gotten off the phone with the paper's entertainment editor. "They're having a big to-do tonight over at Spago-Pogo on the Strip. Private party to kick off a new coproduction venture between Warlock Productions and Rydell, a film about your old professor, Merlin Ambrosius."

"Indeed? How very interesting. And what do we know about Warlock Productions?"

"Nothing," Slater said. "They seem to be a brand-new outfit, came out of nowhere, but word is they've got a lot of money. That party tonight is supposed to be a very hot ticket. Invitation only."

"Perhaps we should attend," said Thanatos.

"They probably won't let us in," said Slater.

Rebecca flashed her shield. "They'll let us in," she said. "Let's go."

"Miss Blaine."

"Brother Khasim!"

Jessica Blaine was, as usual, surrounded by a throng of men, none of whom looked very pleased by the addition of yet another rival for her attentions, but they relaxed somewhat when they heard her call him by name and introduce him, for the benefit of those who hadn't heard of him, as the man who ran that wonderful mission down the Strip, doing all that wonderful work with the street people.

"Miss Blaine, I merely wanted to say hello and once again apologize for what happened during the filming of that—"

"Oh, I've forgotten all about it," she said breezily, though her eyes clearly revealed that she hadn't forgotten it at all, that she would never forget it for as long as she lived. "And you really must stop calling me Miss Blaine. I'm Jessie to my friends."

He smiled. "Very well, Jessie. And I am simply Khasim to mine. Being called 'Brother' somehow always makes me feel as if I should be tending a garden in a monastic retreat."

"And you're not a monk, is that what you're telling me?" she said with a mocking smile, but there was challenge in her eyes.

"Well, not exactly," he replied. "Monks are generally cloistered in contemplative isolation, are they not? I don't think they make movies."

"Who knows what they do in there?" she said, grinning. "Anyway, I take it Johnny's got you back to do the effects for *Ambrosius!*"

"Yes, I haven't actually spoken with him yet, but he called and left a message, asking me to come tonight. He said there would be quite a few effects sequences in this film."

"That's what I hear," she said. "After all, it *is* about the greatest mago who ever lived. I don't think anyone's actually seen the script yet. Ron's being very secretive about it."

"Which part are you playing?"

"Queen Guinevere."

"Of course. I should have guessed," he said. "A woman of surpassing beauty and overwhelming passion. I would say it's perfect casting. Who is the lucky man who's playing Lancelot?"

"I don't know yet. The part hasn't been cast." She smiled. "Why don't you ask Ron if you could read for it?"

"*Me?* You're joking, surely."

"Oh, I don't know, why not?" she said. Jessica turned away and, taking his arm, started to drift away from the others, much to everyone's disappointment. "You're about the right age for the part and you're certainly attractive enough to pull it off. Unless you're worried about the love scene."

"The love scene?"

"Mmm-hmm. I understand there's going to be a very torrid love scene between Guinevere and Lancelot." She glanced up at him with a sly smile. "You know, I've always wondered what it would be like to make love with a sorcerer." She moistened her lips with the tip of her tongue. "Think of the possibilities."

"Jessica! There you are!" Johnny Landau came plowing through the crowd like an icebreaker. "Hey, Khasim, glad you could make it! You're going to handle the effects for us, of course? We're going to need some really spectacular sequences on this one."

"Yes, well—"

"Good, good, it's all settled then. Have you met Burton Clive yet?"

"No, I—"

"He's right over there by the bar. Why don't you go up and introduce yourself? You'll be doing a lot of standing in for him. Jessica, there's somebody I want you to meet. . . ."

As he pulled her away, she turned and gave Khasim a smoldering look over her shoulder. Khasim thought that before too long, something decidedly unpleasant might happen to Johnny Landau.

Kira and Billy worked their way through the crowd, scanning all the faces. Kira had taken off her glove and she held her right hand close to her side, cupping it to cover the glow of the sapphire runestone. It would tell her when they were close. And they were slowly closing in. She could feel it.

"Hey, whoa, darlin'! Don't run by so fast! Stop and say hello!"

A young man grabbed her by the elbow as she went past and spun her around. He was well built and tall and blond and slickly groomed, wearing a silk, laced dueling shirt that was open to his waist. There were several amulets around his neck. His teeth were perfect and he was darkly tanned.

"My name's Lance," he said. "Lance Stevens, Megasound Recordings. So, tell me, you watch TV or do you have a job?"

"Excuse me—"Kira began, but he interrupted her.

"Excuse you? Oh, now come on, we haven't even had a chance to get to know each other! Loosen up a little."

"I said, *excuse* me," Kira said, twisting away from him and moving on.

"Whoa, whoa, wait a minute, sweetheart—" He started after her, but Billy stood in his way.

"Look, piss off, mate, she's with me," said Billy.

Stevens glanced down at Billy with surprise. "What's this? You don't even look old enough to be in here, little man."

"Ey, she ain't interested, right? Get the message? In other words, sod off!"

"What the hell does that mean? You mouthin' off at me, you little shit? Get out of my way before I give you a spanking."

He reached out to shove Billy aside, but as he did so, Billy's hand darted into the pocket of his leather jacket and brought out a butterfly knife. As Lance grabbed him by the coat, Billy snicked the blade out with a quick flick of his wrist and pressed the point into his groin. Lance froze with a surprised expression on his face.

"Don't push it, mate, unless you want to sing soprano. Got me?"

"Why, you little son of a—"

"Ah-ah!" Billy pressed the point home slightly and Lance gasped.

"All right! All right, you little bastard!"

He let him go. Billy backed up, flicked his wrist to close the blade, and put the knife away, but the moment he turned to follow Kira, Stevens lunged at him.

Billy spun around suddenly, only it was no longer Billy. His eyes blazed with blue fire and twin beams of bright blue thaumaturgic energy shot out from them, striking Stevens in the chest. It happened much too quickly for anyone to fully register what had occurred. There was a very brief, incandescent flash and for a fraction of a second, Stevens was wreathed in a bright blue glow, and then he simply stood there, stunned—and stark naked.

Somebody cut loose with a high-pitched scream. Stevens shook his head to clear it and then, with a shock, realized that all his clothes had suddenly disappeared. He yelped and hunched over, covering his privates, but not before everyone around him had seen his shortcomings revealed. He bolted through the laughing crowd, scuttling bent over toward the exit.

Khasim heard the commotion and turned to see what had happened. His gaze fell on Kira, who was coming toward him through the crowd, scanning all the faces around her intently. She hadn't seen him yet.

Khasim's gaze was drawn down to her right hand. There seemed to be some sort of blue glow coming from inside it. He stiffened and his eyes glazed over. He pulled the hood of his cloak up over his head, turned, and started heading quickly and purposefully for the door.

Kira felt the stone start throbbing. She looked quickly to her right and then her left and spotted a hooded figure moving away from her, through the crowd. Suddenly, the runestone in her palm was burning.

"It's him," she said. *"Billy, it's him!"*

She started pushing her way through the crowd.

On any given night, one was apt to see just about anything on Sunset Strip, but neither Thanatos nor Ben Slater nor Rebecca Farrell were quite prepared for the first thing they saw when they pulled up in front of the entrance to the club.

It was the sight of a naked man struggling with a woman dressed in an expensive designer cloak. The cloak seemed to be the object of their altercation. The naked man was desperately trying to get it away from her and had succeeded in yanking it partway off her shoulder, but the woman had paid a small fortune for the cloak and she was hanging on like grim death.

Her companion, another young woman, had joined the fray and as they pulled up, she was in the process of belaboring the naked man about the head and shoulders with her purse. He was attempting to fend her off with one hand while he continued trying to wrest the cloak away from her friend with the other, but he was rapidly losing the contest. In fact, as Slater, Thanatos, and Farrell got out of the police car, the outcome was suddenly decided by a punishing haymaker to the naked man's essentials. He made a sound like a squeaky disc brake and slowly sank down to the sidewalk like a balloon deflating. Lance Stevens was not having a good night.

"All right, nobody move!" Rebecca said. "Police!"

"Don't worry," said the woman with the cloak, "he's not going anywhere."

A crowd was gathering around them. With all the focus of attention upon the writhing naked man and the two angry women standing over him, no one noticed the hooded figure leave the club and duck quickly into the alleyway beside it. Nor did anyone notice when, a moment later, Kira came running out and stopped on the sidewalk in front of the entrance, looking both ways up and down the street. She hesitated, started toward the knot of people on the sidewalk, then abruptly changed her mind and ran to the alley. For a moment, she stood at the mouth of the alleyway, staring into it intently, then she went in.

Billy came shoving through the crowd, ignoring the outraged protests of the people he pushed aside as he made his way to Wyrdrune's side.

"Come on," he said, grabbing Wyrdrune's arm and pulling him away from a studio executive. "Kira's spotted him! Where's Modred?"

"I don't know, he was here just a second ago. I'll use the mind link—"

"No time! Come on!"

They hurried for the door.

Kira walked slowly down the dark alleyway, listening for the slightest sound. She'd been just behind him and there was no sign of him when she came out the door. He had to have come this way. Whatever was going on out in front of the club could be just a diversion or it could have nothing to do with him at all. Either way, she couldn't let him get away. And the runestone throbbing in her palm told her that she was on the right track.

She stopped and listened.

She couldn't hear anything except for the muffled sounds of music coming through the wall of the club. Her right hand was trembling; the runestone seemed to be vibrating in her palm. He was here, close by, waiting for her. She was sure

of it. She glanced over her shoulder nervously. Where the
hell was Billy? He'd been right behind her when she left the
club, or so she thought. She reached inside her leather jacket
and felt the bone handle of the commando knife in its sheath,
sewn securely into the inside of her jacket. She started to
summon up the mind link—

And at that moment, something hit her.

Wyrdrune and Billy came running out of the club and the
first thing they saw was a small crowd gathered on the sidewalk. There were two police vehicles at the curb, a patrol
unit, and an unmarked car. For a moment, Wyrdrune had the
terrible image of Kira stretched out on the sidewalk, dead,
but then he saw a man with a blanket draped over him being
handed into the patrol car and he breathed a sigh of relief.

"Do you see her?" asked Billy.

"No," said Wyrdrune as they both looked up and down
the street for any sign of her.

"Kira!" Billy shouted.

Thanatos heard the name and spun around.

And suddenly they heard her scream. "Billy!"

It came from the alleyway. Wyrdrune and Billy took off
at a dead run. Thanatos grabbed Slater by the arm.

"Come on, Ben!"

They pushed their way through the crowd of curious onlookers.

The jarring impact on her back had knocked Kira to the
ground, but a lifetime of survival on the streets of New York
City had given her incredibly quick reflexes in addition to
the strength and acrobatic skills she had developed as a cat
burglar. She instinctively dropped down to her knees, using
her attacker's downward momentum to fling him off her back.
As he leapt at her again, she came up quickly with the knife
and slashed at her assailant. There was an unearthly howl of
pain and Kira froze.

What she was facing wasn't human. The figure in the
hooded cloak had two arms and it stood on two legs and it
was dressed in human clothing, but there the similarity ended.
She couldn't see too clearly in the darkness of the alley, but
she could see enough to make out that the creature's face
was covered with fur and its mouth was less a mouth than a

muzzle, with saliva dripping from its fangs. The eyes were yellow, lambent like a wolf's, and it growled as it crouched before her, clutching itself where she had wounded it.

"Jesus Christ . . ." she said, and then she heard Wyrdrune call her name.

"*Warlock!*" she shouted, and as she called to him, the creature came at her again.

It caught her knife hand and slammed her up against the wall. She could feel the warmth of its fetid breath as it snarled, its muzzle inches away from her face, and then the stone in the palm of her right hand flashed brightly, illuminating the alley with its sapphire glow, and a beam of pure thaumaturgic force lanced out from it and struck the creature in the face.

The monster screamed.

"*Kira!*"

Wyrdrune and Billy came running into the alley. Billy flung out his arm and blue fire crackled around his outstretched fingers as Merlin sent a bolt of thaumaturgic energy flashing toward the creature. It missed and struck a dumpster, causing the metal to soften and run like molten plastic. Wyrdrune tore off his headband and the emerald set into his forehead flashed with green fire, sending a bright green beam of force directly at the creature, but before it could strike home, the creature disappeared. It had thrown up its cloak and simply vanished.

Wyrdrune and Billy came running up to Kira.

"Are you all right?" said Merlin, with concern.

She nodded.

"*Okay, hold it right there! Police!*"

Rebecca Farrell stood at the mouth of the alley with her gun drawn. There were two other officers beside her, as well as Thanatos and Slater.

"Shit," said Wyrdrune. He grabbed Kira and Billy, quickly mumbled a teleportation spell under his breath, and all three of them disappeared.

The police officers opened fire.

"*Hold it! Hold it!*" Rebecca shouted. "*Cease fire!* What the hell are you shooting at?

The two officers looked at her sheepishly and put their guns away.

"What the hell was all that about?" asked Slater.

"Get over to the club," Rebecca said to the two officers. "Cover the backdoor and get some backup over here. I don't want anyone to leave until we've had a chance to ask some questions."

Thanatos simply stood there, staring at the spot where they had stood. There was no longer anybody there, but he could distinctly see two auras . . . one bright blue, and one bright green.

CHAPTER
Seven

Khasim had never felt such agonizing pain before in his entire life. It burned like fire, no, worse than fire, it felt as if his face had been torn off and then the raw, bloody, throbbing flesh beneath slathered with sulfuric acid. He materialized in his hidden sanctuary underneath the mission and collapsed to his knees, crying out and hammering his head against the floor, his hands covering his ruined face.

"Help me . . . help me. . . ." he moaned.

He struggled to his feet, but crashed into a coffee table and fell to the floor again, whimpering and moaning like a wounded animal.

"Help me, Mistress. . . . Help me, please. . . ."

His captive, spellbound women came in answer and he grabbed the first one that came near him, pulling her down to the floor. His hood fell back and she saw his face. She screamed.

He raised his hand, a furry paw with long, razor-sharp claws, and brought it down hard, again and again and again, until she screamed no more. And then he lunged at the next one and brought her down as well, tearing at her throat with his teeth.

Behind him, a darkly glowing figure stood like a three-dimensional shadow outlined in a thin border of bright light, a light that seemed to grow brighter as each unfortunate woman died. Finally, having slaughtered them all, the pain-racked beast that was Khasim huddled on the floor, pawing at the rug with bloody claws and whimpering. The shadowy, dark form stretched an arm out toward him and gradually, the pain began to ebb. Khasim spasmed on the floor as he slowly reverted to his human form. His face was horribly disfigured, but as he lay there, twitching and shaking, gasping for breath, his wounds magically healed. Moments later, there was no trace of the disfigurement caused by the thaumaturgic beam or of the knife wound that Kira had inflicted on him.

Slowly, Khasim got up to his hands and knees, facing the specter in the corner. "Thank you," he said, his voice a ragged croak. "Thank you, Mistress, thank you. . . ."

"*You failed me, Khasim,*" she said, her sepulchral voice echoing throughout the room.

"Forgive me, Mistress. I did not think. . . . That is, I meant to. . . ." He shook his head, bewildered. "I don't know what happened. I don't know how. . . . Who was that girl?"

"*She is my enemy, Khasim. And you let her live.*"

"I tried, Mistress, but—"

"*But you failed.*"

Khasim hung his head and nodded miserably. "Yes, Mistress. But there were those others—"

"*Have I ever failed you, Khasim?*"

"No, Mistress. Never."

"*Have I not given you everything you ever asked for?*"

"Yes, Mistress," he said in a small voice, afraid to look up at her dark, featureless form.

"*And yet still you fail me.*"

"I'm sorry, Mistress," he said, his voice barely above a whisper. "I won't fail you again."

"*If you do, Khasim, I will have your life,*" she said.

He trembled. "I will find her, Mistress, I swear it. I will

find her and make you a present of her life. But who is she? And that blazing jewel, what was it?''

"There are three of them, Khasim, and you can be thankful that you only encountered two of them tonight. When they are all together, the runestones are invincible."

"The runestones?"

"A sapphire, an emerald, and a ruby. Three enchanted gems imbued with untold power. Each is bonded to a different individual, melded with their life force. Without the runestones, they are nothing, but when the three stones are in concert, their power is almost limitless. Yet separately, they can be defeated."

"Then I shall do it, Mistress. I will track them down and I will bring you these enchanted stones.''

"No! They must be destroyed!"

"Destroyed? But if they have such power, then surely—''

"Do you question me, Khasim?"

"No, Mistress.'' For a brief instant, he glanced up at her, then quickly looked away.

"When the time comes, I will tell you how the stones must be destroyed,'' she said. *"But for now, we must prepare. I must make you stronger so that you may deal with them and for that, we need more lives, Khasim. Many more lives."*

"Look, I don't know what's going on," said Ron Rydell, "but is anybody filing charges here? I mean, has there been some kind of crime committed? What's this all about?''

"We would merely like to ask you a few questions, Mr. Rydell, that's all,'' Rebecca said. "You wouldn't mind just answering a few questions, would you?''

"Look, Captain, I've got nothing against cooperating with the police, you understand, but I don't really think I'm out of line if I demand to know what the hell is going on. Don't get me wrong, I'm not looking for any trouble, but you come in here without any warrants, you interrupt a private party, and you inconvenience a lot of very important people. I sure as hell hope you have a damned good reason for all this! I mean, has somebody been killed, or what?''

"First of all, Mr. Rydell,'' Rebecca said, "we do not require a warrant to enter public premises—''

"It was a *private* party—"

"That makes no difference. I'm sorry if your guests are being inconvenienced, we'll try to wrap this up as soon as possible. In fact, if we could proceed, we could finish that much sooner and—"

"Wait a minute," Rydell said, looking at Slater. "I know you. Ben Slater, right? The columnist?"

"Have we met?" said Ben.

"No, I recognized you from your picture. I read your column all the time."

"Thank you."

"You're a hell of a writer."

"Thanks again."

"Could we please get on with this?" Rebecca said, slightly exasperated.

"You usually let newspaper people tag along on your investigations, Captain Farrell?" countered Rydell.

"Mr. Slater is not officially part of this investigation," said Rebecca patiently. "However, he is assisting in an unofficial capacity and . . . why the hell am I explaining this to you?"

"This is where you're supposed to say, '*I'll* ask the questions, Rydell,' " Rydell said with a grin.

Slater tried unsuccessfully to suppress a smile.

"Perhaps *I* should ask the questions," Thanatos said.

"And who are you?" Rydell said.

Thanatos reached into his coat pocket and took out his I.D. Rydell glanced at it briefly and raised his eyebrows.

"I.T.C., huh? Okay, so I'm impressed." He glanced from Rebecca, to Ben and back to Thanatos. "Precinct captain, big-time investigative columnist, and now a field agent for the I.T.C. Something sure as hell is up. But you guys aren't going to tell me what it is, right?"

"Right," said Thanatos.

Rydell nodded. "Okay. Fine. Then you can take your questions and shove 'em, because I haven't done anything wrong and I'm not saying anything until I know what the hell this is all about. What do you think about that?"

"I think that would be rather ill advised, Mr. Rydell," said Thanatos calmly. "Because, you see, if you refused to cooperate, I could ask Captain Farrell to place you under arrest.''

"On what charge?''

"Oh, I'm quite certain she could think of something,'' Thanatos said nonchalantly. "Of course, it probably wouldn't stick, but by the time your attorney managed to get you released, there would have been plenty of time for me to place you under a spell of compulsion, forcing you to answer any questions I might choose to put to you. Such as, have you anything at all to hide, Mr. Rydell?''

Rydell licked his lips nervously. "You couldn't do that.''

"Certainly I could.''

"That's illegal.''

"Well, in point of fact, the law is somewhat nebulous on that point, since in a case such as this, it becomes a rather complicated question of jurisdiction. However, I could easily avoid potential difficulties by questioning you and then making you forget you'd ever been questioned. In any case, I don't see where it would make a great deal of difference to you either way . . . unless, of course, you *had* something to hide. But then again, most people do, don't they?''

Rydell turned pale. He swallowed hard and took a deep breath, letting it out slowly. "All right, you've made your point. What do you want to know?''

"What was the purpose of this occasion tonight?'' asked Thanatos.

"To publicize my next film, *Ambrosius!*''

"Which you are coproducing with another company, is that correct?'' said Thanatos.

Rydell stared at him. "I see you've already asked some questions,'' he said. "Yeah, that's right. My backers for this film are Warlock Productions.''

"And are they here tonight, as well?''

"Well, yeah, it's their party,'' Rydell said. He looked around. There were a lot of people at the bar, the others were all milling around, watching and talking among themselves, trying to figure out why the police had crashed the party. "I don't see them anywhere,'' Rydell said, "but they're probably around here someplace.''

"Probably?''

"Well, yeah, I guess. I mean, I didn't see 'em leave."

"What are their names?"

"What?"

"The principals of Warlock Productions," Thanatos said. "Your new partners. What are their names?"

"Mike Cornwall and Mel Karpinsky."

"I see. There are only those two?"

"Well, there's their . . . uh, executive assistants. . . ."

"And what are their names?"

Rydell hesitated, unsure of where this was leading. Knowing exactly who and what his partner was made him even more uneasy. He wondered how much the I.T.C. man knew.

"Billy Slade and Kira . . ." He shrugged and shook his head. "I don't know her last name. She never uses it."

"Would she happen to be a striking brunette, about five foot six, slim, with a penchant for wearing black leather jackets and a glove on one hand?"

"Yeah, how did you know?"

"And would Billy Slade be a teenaged boy with an outlandish hairstyle and a cockney accent?"

"Yeah, but—"

"And Mel Karpinsky, he'd be in his mid-twenties, with long, curly blond hair, usually wearing either a hat or a headband?"

"That's right. Listen, how did you—"

"And Michael Cornwall would be blond, bearded, and muscular, with gold-rimmed eyeglasses, an elegant wardrobe, and a British accent?"

Rydell glanced nervously from Thanatos to Rebecca. "What *is* this? What's going on?"

Thanatos looked up at Rebecca. "I think we're finished here, Captain Farrell," he said, standing up from the table.

Rebecca seemed surprised. "You don't want to take him in for questioning?"

"No, I don't think that will be necessary. I think Mr. Rydell has told us all he knows. Let's leave him to enjoy his party." He turned back to Rydell. "I'm sorry if we've inconvenienced you and your guests, Mr. Rydell. We're quite finished now, so we'll be leaving. Thank you for your cooperation."

Rydell simply stared at him, not knowing what to say.

Thanatos started to leave, but then he hesitated and turned back. "By the way, I would appreciate it if the next time you see him, you could give your partner, Mr. . . . uh . . . *Cornwall*"—he stressed the name ironically—"a message for me. Tell him that an old friend of his mother's said hello."

Once they were outside, he turned to Rebecca and said, "I think Mr. Rydell should be watched closely. I suggest you assign your most experienced detectives to the task, people who are expert at not being spotted. Rydell probably wouldn't spot them in any case, but our Mr. Cornwall, he's a horse of an altogether different color."

"You know a lot more about this case than you've told me, Thanatos," Rebecca said. "I think it's about time you filled me in on all the details. I don't like working in the dark, especially when I know you're telling Slater more than you've told me."

Thanatos paused and seemed to consider for a moment. "You're quite right, Captain Farrell. Please make no mistake, I fully appreciate your position. However, if I've told Ben Slater more than I've told you, it's because he does not have to account to a police administration that may not quite see eye to eye with me when it comes to my methods of handling this case."

"Are you saying you don't trust me?" she said.

"It's not a question of trust," he replied as they headed back toward the car. "You misunderstood me. You may recall that a number of times, I've commented on the jurisdictional problems inherent in this case. Officially, what we have here is a homicide that has occurred within your jurisdiction. Unofficially, we've all acknowledged that necromancy is behind it, which makes it the jurisdiction of the Bureau. However, this case is also directly connected with a series of grisly murders that took place in London last year, as well as a number of other deaths, and that would make it my jurisdiction. Unfortunately, I can't prove that, at least not yet, so officially, I can't take charge of the case. Gorman can at least prove necromancy, but he doesn't want to go public with it, so he won't officially take charge, either. And that, Captain Farrell, leaves *you* officially in charge, so that you can officially take all the heat while Gorman and I unofficially pursue the case. You see where I'm heading, don't you?"

"You're saying that what I don't know, I can't be held responsible for," she said.

"Precisely. I knew you'd understand."

"I understand just fine, but I still think it stinks. I don't work that way, Thanatos. If you and Gorman want to cover your asses officially, that's your business, but I take full responsibility for what happens in my precinct and I want to know what's going on."

Thanatos studied her thoughtfully for a moment, then nodded. "All right. Only not here. Where can we go to talk?"

"My place isn't too far from here," said Ben.

"Fine, we can go there. But first, we'd better have someone detailed to keep an eye on Rydell. It's liable to be a very long night and you can be certain that before it's over, people are going to die."

Wyrdrune materialized back in their cottage at the The Beverly Hills Hotel with a pop of displaced air.

"Boy, that was close," he said. "We almost got ourselves shot by . . ."

His voice trailed off as he suddenly realized he was alone.

"Oh no," he said, shutting his eyes and bringing his hand up to his forehead. "Don't tell me. . . . Kira? Billy?"

He ran over to the closet and opened it.

"Kira?"

There was no one inside.

"Billy?"

He ran to the door and opened it. There was no sign of them outside, either.

"Oh, hell," he said, thinking of all the places he might have accidentally teleported them to. "Now what've I done?"

There was a sudden pop of displaced air and Kira and Billy materialized before him.

Wyrdrune breathed a sigh of relief. "There you are! Where *were* you?"

"Where *were* we?" Kira said irately. "Where you tele-ported us, you bonehead! Up on the roof! If it wasn't for Merlin, we'd still be there!"

Billy shook his head and spoke with Merlin's voice. "I just can't understand it. Why you can't master a simple spell like teleportation. . . ."

"He masters it all right when it comes to himself," said Kira sourly. "*He* arrived where he was supposed to, didn't he? But me he drops into fountains, dumpsters, pops me into closets, up on the roof. . . . One of these days I'm liable to wind up inside a wall and *then* what do I do?"

"Look, I'm sorry, but I was in a hurry. In case you didn't notice, they were about to start shooting at us!"

"We would have been perfectly safe if you'd left it up to me," said Merlin. "You were always so impetuous, Kar-pinsky, so impatient! All things considered, it's a miracle that you've survived this long."

"Hey," said Wyrdrune, "*I'm* not the one who died, re-member?"

"Very funny."

"Haven't you two forgotten something?" Kira said. "What about Modred?"

"Modred can take care of himself," said Merlin. "The important thing is, are *you* all right?"

Kira nodded. "Yeah, I'm okay." She held up her right hand, palm open. "Thanks to this."

"Did you get a good look at him?" asked Wyrdrune.

She shook her head. "No, not before he changed. I took a piece out of him, though."

"That probably won't help us, either," Merlin said. "Un-less he's been fatally injured, the Dark One can heal him. It would require a strong infusion of life energy, but the Dark Ones and their acolytes have never hesitated when it came to murder."

Wyrdrune watched as Billy clasped his hands behind his back and slowly started pacing back and forth across the room, the way Merlin always used to do in class.

"What puzzles me is the rather serendipitous arrival of the police," he continued. "Even if someone had reported a disturbance almost immediately, there could not have been enough time for the police to respond so quickly.''

"Maybe they just happened to be driving by," said Wyrdrune. "There *was* some sort of a disturbance outside the club.''

"Yes," said Merlin, "only along with the uniformed officers, there were also several in plain clothes. Detectives. Why would detectives respond to a public disturbance?''

The phone rang. Since he was right next to it, Merlin picked it up.

"'Allo?" said Billy. He listened a moment. "Michael? No, 'e's not. I dunno where 'e is." He paused. "Yeah, 'e's 'ere. 'Old on.''

He held the phone out to Wyrdrune. "It's Rydell. 'E sounds a bit frantic.''

Wyrdrune took the phone. "Hello, Ron?''

"Where the hell did you guys disappear to?" Rydell said. "The police were just here!''

"The police?" said Wyrdrune, glancing up at the others. He put down the receiver and turned on the speakerphone so they all could hear. "Why? What happened?''

"Suppose you tell me," Rydell said. "The precinct captain herself was here. And Ben Slater, the columnist, was with 'em, too. He's the top investigative reporter in the city, in case you didn't know. And they knew all about you. The guy asking the questions was an agent of the I.T.C., no less.''

"Wait a minute," said Wyrdrune. "The I.T.C. was asking questions about us? What did you tell them?''

"I told them we were working on a film together, what was I supposed to tell them? That's all I know! And, believe me, I don't *want* to know anymore! The I.T.C. guy threatened to take me down to headquarters and put me under a spell of compulsion to answer questions, questions like do I have anything to hide? You tell our friend 'Michael' about that, okay? I don't know how much he's told you, but you tell him it wouldn't look too good for either of us if I was made to answer questions like that!''

"Take it easy," Wyrdrune said. "The man was bluffing.

He couldn't question you like that. It's against the law. It's a violation of your rights."

"Yeah, that's what I told him," said Rydell. "And you know what he came back with? He said it didn't matter, because he could put me under a spell to forget it ever happened. Said it calm as you please, right in front of a precinct captain and a newspaperman, no less! And they didn't even bat an eye!"

"What else did they ask you?" Wyrdrune said.

"Nothing. The guy just asked me who the principals of Warlock Productions were and then he described you to me and asked if the descriptions matched."

"Hold it," Wyrdrune said. "*He* described us to *you*? You mean you described us to him, don't you?"

"No, man, I mean he described you to me, right down to a 'T.' And he said something else, too. I don't know what the hell it means. He said, 'Tell Mr. Cornwall'—and he said it like he knew it wasn't his real name—'that an old friend of his mother's said hello.'"

Wyrdrune looked at Kira and Billy with a worried expression. "What else did he say?"

"Nothing. After that, they left. Look, I don't know what you guys are into and like I said, I don't want to know, okay? But whatever it is, do me a favor, just tell me this—does it have anything to do with me and with the film?"

"No," said Wyrdrune. "It has nothing to do with you or with the film."

"You're sure?"

"Ron—"

"Well, look, whatever it is, please, just keep me and the movie out of it. And when you see him, you tell our mutual friend that we've got to talk. No, wait, maybe that's not such a hot idea. I don't want to see anything interfere with the production. We're building sets, we're scouting locations, we're getting ready to do wardrobe, I've got a thousand things to worry about without having the police around, so maybe you guys just shouldn't come around, huh? I don't want to worry about anything happening to shut me down—Jesus, you don't think they'd do that, do you? They wouldn't shut me down?"

"I don't see why, Ron," Wyrdrune said. "You're not doing anything wrong. You're just making a movie."

"Right. Right. So let's keep it that way, okay?"

"Fine, Ron. Don't worry. Everything will be all right."

"Ask him who the agent was," said Merlin.

"Oh, Ron? By the way, who was the agent that you spoke to?"

"Foreign guy. He used a magename. Thanatos. Why?"

"Nothing, just curious."

"Yeah, I'm sure," Rydell said. "Look, you're not going to get me mixed up in anything, are you? You're not going to pull out and leave me high and dry?"

"What are you worried about, Ron?" said Wyrdrune. "You've already got the money, right?"

"Yeah, right, but—"

"But nothing. Just make your film, Ron. Stop worrying so much. Good-bye."

Wyrdrune hung up the phone and shook his head. "For all he knows, we're wanted for mass murder or something and all he's worried about is his movie."

"That's Hollywood," said Kira.

"He's nobody's fool, that's for certain," said Merlin thoughtfully.

"Who, *Rydell*?" said Wyrdrune.

"No, no, I was talking about Thanatos," said Merlin.

"The I.T.C. agent?" Kira said. "You know him?"

"I taught him," Merlin said. "His truename is Bryant Winslow. I named him Thanatos because I often joked that he would be the death of me. He was one of my most gifted students, but he was far from zealous in his application." He glanced pointedly at Wyrdrune. "Not unlike some others I could mention."

Wyrdrune grimaced.

"What did he mean with that line about being an old friend of Modred's mother?" Kira asked. "He couldn't possibly know about Modred, could he?"

"Morgana was also an agent of the I.T.C.," said Merlin. "And her death was the one loose end that we could not tie off. If Thanatos was assigned to investigate it, it's just possible that somehow he's managed to piece it all together."

"But how?" said Kira.

"There's only one explanation I can think of," Merlin said, fishing his pipe out of his pocket and filling it. "He must have spoken with Chief Inspector Blood."

"I don't believe it," Wyrdrune said. "Blood helped us. He understood what we were up against. Hell, he was *there*, he saw it! He wouldn't set the I.T.C. on us!"

"No, I don't believe he would," said Merlin, puffing his pipe alight. The pungent aroma of melting rubber wafted across the room. "Unless he believed that he was helping us."

"How does talking to the I.T.C. help us?" Wyrdrune said wryly. "Al'Hassan was an official of the I.T.C., remember?"

"Yes, I remember all too well," said Merlin, his pipe now giving off an odor of fresh-baked, apple-cinnamon pie. "Still, perhaps the I.T.C. *could* help us."

"A bunch of sorcerers turned bureaucrats?" said Wyrdrune derisively. "Even if we could get them to believe us, they'd only wind up starting a panic, getting in the way and getting themselves killed. They wouldn't stand a chance against the Dark Ones. You tried to stand against them by yourself and look what happened."

"Please, don't remind me," Merlin said, blowing out a stream of violet-scented smoke. "You think I enjoy being trapped in the body of this prepubescent leather fetishist?"

"Ey, 'ow d'ya think *I* feel?" Billy said. "You think I like 'avin' an old geezer like you stuck in me 'ead, all the time moanin' and gripin' and makin' me smoke this bloody bog moss?" He took the pipe out of his mouth, made a face, and spat on the rug. "Gor'blimey, what 'orrid stuff!"

"If you don't mind, I happen to enjoy it!" Merlin said, making Billy put the pipe back into his mouth.

"Yeah, but I'm the one what's gotta smoke the bleedin' mess!" He took the pipe out of his mouth again and brought his hand back to fling it across the room.

"Don't you dare!" shouted Merlin, stopping the arm in mid-swing. "That's a four-hundred-year-old, hand-carved Algerian briar!"

Billy struggled, having a tug-of-war with his own arm

muscles as he tried to throw the pipe while Merlin restrained him.

"Leggo me arm!"

"Stop that, you little holligan! Stop it, I say!"

"Do you people know what *time* it is?" the broom said, swaying sleepily into the room. It had a red nightcap stuck on the end of its handle.

"Go back to sleep, Broom," Wyrdrune said wearily.

"Who can sleep with all this *tummel*? It's almost two o'clock in the morning! It took me hours to get to sleep after listening to those *fercocktuh* birds all day long and now I have to listen to young Mr. Split Personality *kvetching* at himself? Who needs this, I ask you? Is it too much trouble to go to bed like normal people?"

"Listen 'ere, you scraggly old loo swabber," said Billy, "you shut yer cakehole! Wherever the 'ell yer bleedin' cakehole is!"

"Did he just call me a toilet brush?" the broom said in an outraged tone. "Was that what you called me, *a toilet brush? Gevalt!* I don't have to take that kind of talk from someone who wears his hair like a Shetland pony and dresses like a stolen car."

"Right," said Billy, snaking his hand out and grabbing the broom around the handle. "I'm gonna tear out all yer bleedin' bristles!"

"No, you're not," said Merlin.

"I am, too!"

"You are *not*!"

"Let me go, both of you!" the broom cried.

"Billy. . . . Professor. . . . " Wyrdrune said.

"You stay out of this!" said Merlin. "I've had about enough disobedience from this young whelp!"

"Whelp, eh?" said Billy. "I'll whelp you right upside the 'ead, I will!"

"That would be a neat trick," Kira said. She stepped up to Billy, grabbed a handful of his crested hair, and held her knife against it.

"Ey!"

"Let the damn stick go and settle down, or else I'll scalp you, you little twerp."

"Awright, awright!" said Billy, letting the broom go. It quickly retreated to the closet. "But I *still* ain't smokin' this dreck!"

And he tossed the pipe across the room.

"*Ahhhh!*" cried Merlin, and Billy suddenly started smacking himself in the head.

"Ey! Stop it! Cut it out!"

"You rotten little pismire! You've had this coming to you!"

"Stop it, you crazy old git!"

Wyrdrune rolled his eyes at Kira. "It's going to be a long, long haul," he said, shaking his head with resignation.

"Cheer up," she said. "It could be a lot worse."

"Yeah? How?"

"It might not have been Billy that Merlin decided to possess. He could've chosen one of us, instead."

Wyrdrune turned pale. "Don't," he said. "Don't even *think* it!"

The door opened and Modred came in. One look at the expression on his face and they all instantly became silent.

"I'm afraid we have a rather serious problem," he said, looking around at them. "There's more than one of them."

CHAPTER
Eight

"What do you mean there's more than one of them?" said Wyrdrune.

"There's more than one necromancer," Modred said. He glanced at Kira. "Are you all right?"

"Never mind me, I'm fine," she said. "What do you mean there's more than one necromancer? Are you saying there are *two* Dark Ones?"

"There are at least two, and perhaps more," said Modred.

"How do you know?" said Wyrdrune.

"It's obvious how he knows," said Merlin. "His runestone sensed their presence."

"More than that," Modred said. "I saw them."

"You *saw* them?" Wyrdrune said, his eyes wide. *"Where? When?"*

"In the alleyway, when Kira was attacked. It was a close call," he added. "I had a rather narrow escape myself."

He took off his jacket and they saw that his sleeve was red with blood.

"You've been shot!" said Kira.

Modred glanced at her and smiled slightly. "Yes, I know. I'm afraid I caught a bullet when the police officers started shooting. Careless of me. I'd say they overreacted somewhat, wouldn't you?"

"Let me have a look at that," said Merlin.

"No need," said Modred. "The wound is already almost healed."

He took off his shirt and they saw that he was right. Not only had the wound stopped bleeding, but it had already closed and new skin was quickly forming.

Modred examined the wound thoughtfully. "I've always healed more quickly than ordinary humans, but never quite as fast as this."

"The runestone?" Kira said.

Modred nodded. "Unquestionably. It's healing me even as we speak."

It was true. The bullet wound was healing right before their eyes. Merlin looked for an exit wound, but there wasn't one.

"What about the bullet?" he said with some concern. "It's not still in there, is it?"

"No, it was expelled," said Modred, going to the closet to get a fresh shirt. "I've never experienced anything like it. The bullet was literally forced out of my body through the entry wound, as if by some sort of telekinesis." He glanced at Wyrdrune. "As I recall, you also healed very rapidly after our first battle with the Dark Ones. Our symbiosis with the runestones seems to be responsible. They're using their energy to accelerate our normal healing functions. You know,

I'm beginning to think that short of a mortal wound, we can survive almost anything."

"Perhaps," said Merlin, "but that's no reason for becoming careless. Surviving a physical attack is one thing. A magical attack is something else, again. Which brings us back to the essential point of this discussion. How can you be certain that what you saw were Dark Ones? Tell me what happened."

"At the moment Kira was attacked," he said, tucking in his shirttails, "I suddenly felt. . . ." He hesitated and then shook his head. "No, it wasn't a feeling, exactly. It was more like an extremely powerful intuition. I simply *knew* somehow that Kira was in trouble."

"I know what you mean," Wyrdrune said. "I felt it too, right after Billy came to get me in the club. The minute we got outside, I knew Kira was in danger."

Modred nodded. "Yes, we already know we can call upon the runestones to forge a psychic link between us. Only it also seems to be an involuntary function, something that happens by itself only when the runestones feel it's absolutely necessary."

"That would make sense," said Merlin. "Such a link, established thaumaturgically, requires considerable lifeforce energy which the runestones would understandably want to conserve. Go on."

"Anyway," Modred continued, "the moment I sensed that Kira was in trouble, I bolted outside through the rear door of the club. I'm not sure how I knew to head for the alleyway, but I simply did. I ran down the back steps and the moment I turned the corner into the alley, I saw that creature teleport to escape from your attack. When the police arrived, I would have made myself scarce just as you did, only in that instant, I also saw something else.

"They were behind the dumpster," he continued, "not twenty feet away from me. It was dark, but they were outlined with thin borders of bright light, an effect rather like a solar eclipse. Two shadowy, indistinct, ghostly figures. I had the momentary impression that they were *hovering*, floating just above the ground. They turned toward me for an instant and then suddenly they were both gone. They simply disappeared.

Before I could react, the police had started shooting and I was hit. I don't think they even saw me at the back of the alley. The police, that is. They must have instinctively started shooting when you teleported. It was probably a shock reaction, their fingers involuntarily tightening on the triggers. I was hit by a stray bullet. It knocked me down, which was rather fortunate, or I might have been more seriously wounded. I figured that you'd probably come back here and so I followed.''

"And you're certain about what you saw?" asked Merlin.

Modred nodded. "There can be no doubt. The runestone reacted very strongly. I had a sudden, sharp, searing pain in my chest, as if the stone had suddenly become white-hot. I think the Dark Ones must have sensed it, too, which must be why they left so quickly. I have to admit that puzzles me. I was alone and there were two of them. Why didn't they try to kill me?"

"Perhaps it was because they couldn't," Merlin said. "They were not physically there. What you saw were only their manifestations, projections of their astral selves. Which is not to say they had no power, but they wouldn't be at full strength unless they were actually physically present." He picked up his pipe and started tamping the tobacco back down with his thumb.

"'Gor', you're not gonna fire that bloody thing up again, are you?" Billy protested.

"Quiet, Billy," Merlin said, scowling as he snapped his fingers and lit his pipe with a jet of flame that shot out of his thumb. "I have no time to argue. We must plan carefully. We've obviously lost the element of surprise. But then, in a sense, so have the Dark Ones. True, we don't know where they are, but we now know that there are at least two of them. The question is, are there anymore?"

"I'd say the question is will they stay and fight?" said Modred. "Or will they disappear now that they know we're on to them and turn up somewhere else?"

"It's possible," said Merlin. "When they broke free of the spell that confined them, they scattered far and wide, each thinking only to escape from the power of the runestones. Separately, they could never be as strong as the three of you together. But they have had some time now, time in which to gather acolytes and murder to increase their strength. Time to learn not to repeat the mistakes they made with Al'Hassan. There will be no more wholesale butchery such as they accomplished through him, because any spell strong enough to kill people in such vast numbers would also be strong enough to enable you to trace it to its source. And that would be the last thing that they would want.''

Merlin paced back and forth across the room, puffing out huge clouds of aromatic smoke. The smell of nuts roasting mingled with the heady odor of fresh-baked raspberry tarts, then changed once again to the unpleasant scent of mothballs.

''No, I think they've learned from their mistakes,'' he said, continuing his pacing. ''They will try to increase their powers gradually, so as not to give away their exact location. We know of at least one acolyte and you can be sure that there are others. They will use those acolytes to kill for them, just as in the ancient days, when they appointed priests to conduct their sacrificial rituals. They have had to establish a sanctuary for themselves and find people they could use to serve their purposes. They will not be anxious to abandon what they have accomplished here and start all over somewhere else. At least, not unless they have no other options left. The fact that there are two of them suggests there may be more and that, in turn, suggests that they have a leader among them. And that's very disturbing news, indeed. Still, I doubt they will risk a direct confrontation. At least not yet. Not unless they're forced to. They will use their acolytes against us first. And as we've already seen, those can be quite dangerous enough.''

''Well, we know that at least one of them is someone who was invited to the party tonight,'' said Modred. ''I'll get a complete guest list from Rydell. I'm not sure how much help it will be, but we'll have to start someplace.''

''I think you'll find that your friend Rydell isn't very anxious to see you at the moment,'' Wyrdrune said. ''He called a little while ago. The police were questioning everybody in the club and he said there was an I.T.C. man with them who seemed to know all about us. Does the name Thanatos mean anything to you?''

Modred frowned and shook his head. "No. It's a mage-name?"

"His real name is Bryant Winslow," Merlin said. "He was once one of my students. Now it seems he's a field agent with the I.T.C."

Modred shook his head again. "The name means nothing to me."

"He said he was an old friend of your mother's," Kira said.

"Did he?" Modred said, raising his eyebrows. "How very interesting."

"You think it's true?" said Wyrdrune.

Modred shook his head. "I can't believe she'd have told anyone at the I.T.C. who she really was, much less told them about me, especially since I'm on their 'most wanted' list. And Rydell doesn't know who I really am. So unless this Thanatos is running some kind of a bluff, there are only three other sources where he could have learned that agent Fay Morgan was really Morgan Le Fay and that I was her son. Jacqueline Monet, Sebastian Makepeace, and Michael Blood. Jacqueline would never talk and Makepeace . . . no, he may be as crazy as a bedbug, but he's utterly reliable. Besides, I've known both Sebastian and Jacqueline for years and they've always been completely trustworthy. Which leaves our friend, Chief Inspector Michael Blood of Scotland Yard."

"That's what Merlin figured," Kira said.

Modred grimaced. "I never did trust policemen. I should never have made an exception in his case."

"I can't believe that Blood would sell us out," said Wyrdrune. "He helped us, remember?"

"Yes, and now it appears he's being just as helpful to the I.T.C.," said Modred wryly.

"Wyrdrune's right," said Billy. "Mick wouldn't give us up. 'E's on our side. It's like ole Merlin said, if Mick told this Thanatos bloke about us, it's because 'e thought Thanatos could 'elp us."

His expression suddenly changed as Merlin spoke through him.

"There's a simple enough way to find out for certain," Merlin said. "Why not call Blood and ask him?"

"You think he'd tell the truth?" said Modred.

"You always did have a suspicious nature," Merlin said. "That can be useful on occasion, but unfortunately, in this case, it's preventing you from seeing the obvious. We've already deduced that Blood's the only one who could have told Thanatos about us. If he tells us that he's never heard of Thanatos, then we'll know that he betrayed us. If he admits it, then we can simply ask him why."

Modred nodded. "All right. Call him."

Merlin picked up the phone and called the desk. "Overseas operator, please."

A few moments later, Scotland Yard had answered and Merlin asked to speak with Chief Inspector Michael Blood.

"I see, sir. And who shall I say is calling, please?"

"Tell 'im Billy Slade."

There was a slight pause, then Blood was on the phone. Billy put him on the speakerphone so that all of them could hear.

"Billy? Is that really you?"

"It's me, Mick. 'Ow've ya been, old sod?"

"Thank God! Where the devil *are* you? I've been trying to get in touch with you, but your New York number's been disconnected!"

"We're in Los Angeles," said Billy.

"Los Angeles? Why didn't you tell me you . . . wait, you said 'we.' Are the others with you?"

"We're here, Michael," Wyrdrune said.

"Wyrdrune? Is Kira there, as well?"

"Right here, Mike."

"Sebastian?"

"No, he's still in New York."

"What about . . ." He hesitated, obviously not wanting to say Modred's name out loud. ". . . our other friend?"

"I'm here as well, Michael," Modred said. "Can you talk?"

"Well, I'm in my office, but it can't hurt to be cautious, you understand? I'd just as soon not use your name on these premises."

"Yes, I quite understand," said Modred. "You said you'd been trying to reach us?"

"Yes, I needed to tell you about a chap called Thanatos, an agent with the I.T.C."

Wyrdrune glanced at Modred and smiled.

"Go on," said Modred.

"He came to me recently, asking a lot of questions. Officially, he was investigating the disappearance of one of their agents. Fay Morgan. But he was asking a lot of questions about what happened here, as well. At first, I played it cool, telling him I didn't see the connection between the case their agent was investigating in Boston with what happened here in London, but then he started telling me about the runestones, about Wyrdrune and Kira and Sharif and Al'Hassan and those two fences in New York and the fire in the penthouse of John Roderick. . . . He had it all just about completely put together. And he'd tied it in with what happened here, as well."

"And so what did you tell him?"

"Well, at first I stuck with my amnesia story, but he saw right through that. I didn't know how he knew, but he looked me straight in the eye and as politely as you please, told me I was lying through my teeth. Now I'll tell you, I've spoken to all sorts in my time, from petty thieves to homicidal maniacs to my father's stuffy friends in Parliament and I've always thought I could take just about anyone without flinching, but let me tell you, this chap gave me a dead level stare that went right through to my bones. I tried to put the best possible face on it and I acted all put out. I told the bastard to get out. He didn't move. He simply sat there staring at me with that implacable gaze of his and then he asked me to tell him about the living triangle."

Modred, Wyrdrune, and Kira exchanged astonished glances. Billy simply sat there, stroking his nonexistent beard thoughtfully, as Merlin always had a tendency to do.

"Well, as you can imagine," Blood continued, "that knocked the pins right out from under me. I simply sat there, staring at him, unable to respond. Thanatos just watched me for a moment, and then he proceeded to tell me an amazing story. He said he'd been out to the Carfax place. I hadn't known that. He'd apparently gone over my head with that one, straight to the Commissioner. I hadn't a clue he'd seen it. He'd been in the dungeons, down in that underground temple where it all happened. He told me that he'd sensed indescribably powerful thaumaturgic trace emanations down there, as if an incredible amount of thaumaturgic energy had been released.

"He'd ordered everybody out so that he could get the feel of the place alone. And then told me something that set me right back on my heels. He said he'd seen three *auras*. A red one, a blue one, and a green one, standing apart in a sort of triangular formation, interconnected by patterns of thaumaturgic force. Apparently no one else could see them, but he could, because he could detect auras. Actually see them. He said he could mine, which was how he knew that I was lying to him earlier. Something about some sort of color shift, I didn't completely understand it all, but apparently it had nothing to do with his thaumaturgic training. He said he'd been a sensitive from birth and that his training as a sorcerer had only increased it."

Modred glanced at Billy. "Is that true?" he said.

"'Ow the 'ell should I know?" Billy said.

"He's asking me, you dolt," said Merlin. He shook his head. "I don't know. It's possible, but it's extremely rare. I never knew that Thanatos was a sensitive."

"Why would he have concealed it from you?" said Modred.

"Difficult to say," said Merlin. "Thanatos never was the most forthcoming of individuals. He always had a sort of curious inscrutability about him. On the other hand, come to think of it, he always seemed to know whenever I was asking a trick question or planning a pop quiz. Go on, Michael. What did he say then?"

"He said he knew that what happened in the States with the theft of the runestones was connected with what happened to Al'Hassan, as well as with the murders here in London and the incident at Carfax Castle. He said that the I.T.C. knew that Al'Hassan was killed while casting an immensely powerful necromantic spell, but they did not know for what purpose. And then he said he had a theory of his own, one he hadn't shared with his superiors at the I.T.C. because he had no proof. He said he was convinced that Al'Hassan had discovered something in that dig in the Euphrates Valley, something apart from the artifacts they found. He'd been down there. And he said there was a wall of solid rock in the deepest part of the excavation, and that he'd sensed something *behind* that wall, as if a tremendous amount of thaumaturgic energy had been released.''

"Did he try to break through it?" Wyrdrune said softly.

"No. He said he was afraid. He didn't know why, but he felt a fear that chilled his bones right to the marrow. And then he looked at me and in a very quiet sort of voice, he said, 'Al'Hassan released something down there, didn't he? Something very old, and very powerful and terrifying.' He said that if he wanted to, he could put me under a spell of compulsion to tell him what I knew, but he'd rather I told him of my own free will, because he knew I was protecting someone and he had a feeling that the people I was covering for would need all the help that they could get.''

"And so you told him," Modred said.

Blood sighed. "Of course I told him. I told him everything. What else could I do?"

Modred nodded. "I suppose you had no choice. And what was his reaction?"

"He turned pale and remained silent for a while, then he thanked me and asked me to keep what I'd told him to myself. And then he asked me to get in touch with you and let you know that he was coming. He said to tell you that he would help in any way he could. He said he had a deep personal stake in this, as well."

"In what way?" said Modred.

"Fay Morgan," Blood said. "Your mother." He hesitated. "Apparently, the two of them were lovers."

"What?"

"He showed me a ring he wore," said Blood. "A large fire opal in a silver setting. It was engraved with some peculiar symbols. He said you'd know what it meant."

For a moment, Modred didn't say anything.

"You know what he's talking about?" said Kira.

Modred nodded slowly. "It was my mother's. It was given

to her by my grandmother, Igraine. Gorlois gave it to her as a token when they wed." He took a deep breath and let it out slowly. "It means they were much more than lovers. It means they were man and wife."

"Morgana?" Merlin said, astonished. *"Married to a mortal?"*

Kira stared at Modred. "Then that means Thanatos is—"

"My stepfather," Modred said. "It seems I have a stepfather who is younger than me by some two thousand years."

"I . . . I hope I did the right thing," said Blood.

"It seems you had very little choice," said Modred.

"If you need me," Blood said, "I can hop the next plane—"

"No," said Modred. "No, you stay where you are. But there is something you can do."

"Name it."

"Get in touch with Jacqueline. And then call Sebastian in New York. Tell them we're staying at the Beverly Hills Hotel and ask them to get out here right away."

"You've got one of *them* out there, haven't you?" said Blood.

"No," said Modred. "We have two of them. And perhaps more. Thanatos was right. We're going to need all the help that we can get."

"I'll call them right away," said Blood.

"Good-bye, Michael."

"Good-bye, my friends," said Blood. "And good luck."

It was getting late when Gorman arrived at Spago-Pogo, but the party was still in full swing. He showed his identification to the man at the door, who merely rolled his eyes and said, "Hell, go right ahead. We've had half the police force here tonight already."

Once inside, Gorman stood near the entrance for a while, allowing his eyes time to grow accustomed to the dim light. The music was loud and the dance floor was packed with writhing bodies. The bar was packed, as well. Gorman recognized the celebrated actor, Burton Clive, laughing and leaning back against the bar with his arms around two stunning young women. His thick, graying hair was in a state of disarray, his lace jabot looked wilted, and his expensive suit was thoroughly rumpled. The celebrated Burton Clive looked as if he had already done more than his share of celebrating. Gorman made his way over to the bar.

"Mr. Clive?"

"Yes, dear boy, what can I do for you? You want an autograph? Happy to oblige."

His eyes were bleary and his balance was uncertain—in fact, it appeared as if the two young women were literally holding him up—but remarkably, that magnificent, stentorian voice literally dripping with Old Vic was as clear as a church bell. Clive was infamous for his epic drinking bouts and it was said that on numerous occasions, he had played demanding leading roles on stage while so drunk that he could barely see. It had sounded improbable at the time, but seeing him now, Gorman believed it.

"No, sir, thank you, but I don't want your autograph." He held up his I.D. "Agent Gorman, Bureau of Thaumaturgy."

Clive squinted at the I.D., but he was clearly incapable of reading it. He turned to the woman on his left and said, "What's it say, darling?"

"What he said, Bertie," the woman replied.

"Ah! Excellent! Excellent, indeed! An honest-to-goodness sorcerer, eh? I'm about to play a sorcerer, did you know that, Agent . . . sorry, what did you say your name was?"

"Gorman. Phillip Gorman."

"Phillip! Excellent name! My father was named Phillip. Which reminds me . . . bartender! Be a good lad and 'phillip' this glass!"

"Have you see Mr. Rydell?" said Gorman.

"Ronald?" Clive said, swaying back around to face him, leaning against the ample busoms of his support posts. "Oh, he's gone. Left some time ago, after the police departed. You with that lot? Understand there was some shooting or something. Did somebody get killed?"

"I wouldn't know about that, sir. I was looking for Mr. Rydell."

"Oh, well, he's gone. Come and have a drink."

"Thank you, sir, but not while I'm on duty. Perhaps you

could help me. You're familiar with his productions, aren't you? You're currently working on one, isn't that right?''

"About to start filming the role of a lifetime!" Clive declaimed with a wild sweep of his arm that almost pitched him headlong to the floor. "Merlin Ambrosius! Spawn of an incubus! Court wizard to King Arthur Pendragon! Father of Modern Thaumaturgy! Greatest mage of all—"

"Yes, yes, I understand," said Gorman hastily, anxious to forestall an impromptu soliloquy. "Are you familiar with the man who conjured the special effects on his last feature? A man named Brother Khasim?"

"Certainly, dear boy. The Sorcerer Saint of Sunset Strip, they call him. Keeper of Lost Souls! Master of illusion and—"

"Yes, yes, is he here tonight?" said Gorman.

"He left about the same time the Warlock people did. I suppose it wouldn't be seemly for a saint to be seen getting sloshed in nightclubs, what?"

"Damn it," said Gorman.

"The other special effects chaps are still around, though."

"Are they? Where?"

"Right over there," said Clive, leaning forward and overbalancing, catching himself at the last moment by putting his palm flat against Gorman's chest. He pointed at the far end of the bar. "Those three chaps over there," he said. "Bert, Mort, and . . . somebody or other. Always together. The three witches, I call 'em. That's from Shakespeare, y'know. *Macbeth!* The Thane of Cawdor! The—"

"Right, thank you, Mr. Clive," said Gorman, departing quickly. He hastened toward the far end of the bar and approached the three special effects men. "Gentlemen, may I have a word with you, please?"

"Who're you?" said Joe Gallico, slurring his words slightly.

Gorman flashed his I.D. again. "Agent Gorman, Bureau of Thaumaturgy. I'd like to ask you some questions."

"It's about Khasim, isn't it?" said Mort Levine. "I knew it! I just knew there was something screwy about that guy!"

"What makes you say that, Mr. . . . ?"

"Levine. Mort Levine." He jerked a thumb at his partners and said, "Bert Smith. Joe Gallico."

"Bert, Joe," said Gorman, nodding to each of them. "What makes you think I wanted to know about Brother Khasim?"

"Don't you?"

"Would you answer my question, please?"

"Okay, for the record, I don't like the s.o.b., okay? I never did. All that holier than thou bullshit about saving souls and helping people and he comes muscling in on our business, taking the bread right out of our mouths. . . ."

"So you have some personal animosity?"

"Some what?"

"You don't like him."

"Didn't I just get finished saying that?"

"Yes, but you still haven't told me why you thought I wanted to know about him."

"All right," Levine said, "Look, we did some checking, see? There was always something about that guy that rubbed me the wrong way."

"Me, too," said Joe.

"So we did some checking," Bert Smith said.

"Merely because he rubbed you the wrong way?" said Gorman.

"No, it was much more than that," Levine said. "Like, how come he could pull off illusions nobody else could do? Okay, so he's a sorcerer, which makes him a higher grade adept than anyone else in the business, but even though I'm not an adept, I know a thing or two about magic use. I know that if you pull off a complicated spell, it tends to make you tired 'cause it uses up your energy, isn't that right?"

"Yes, that's right," said Gorman.

"Well, Khasim was *never* tired," said Levine. "And hell, on our last picture, he popped an effect that should've knocked him out."

"What sort of effect?" asked Gorman.

"He manifested a demon," said Bert Smith.

"He did *what*?" said Gorman.

"It was illusion," said Levine. "But, damn, you should've

seen it. Let me tell you something, it takes a hell of an effect
to impress a pro, and that was sure as hell impressive. Never
saw anything like it. Landau was so knocked out by it, he
gave Khasim a bonus.''

''Landau?''

''Johnny Landau, the director. See, the scene called for
the necromancer to summon up a demon that was going to
attack Jessica . . . that's Jessica Blaine, she was the female
lead. She was chained down to this altar and Khasim was
standing in for Jay Solo, who plays the necromancer in the
films. Anyway, Khasim was up on this big rock and he was
supposed to conjure up this demon effect. And what he came
up with didn't look *anything* like what was in the storyboard.''

''It was pretty scary, I gotta admit,'' said Joe Gallico,
nodding over his beer.

''They'd drawn this thing that looked like a werewolf or
something, but Landau told Khasim he wanted something
really special, really dramatic, and Khasim sure as hell de-
livered, let me tell you. It was huge, with sparks and flashes
going off inside it, like an electrical storm, and it screamed
like a runaway express train. Scared Jessica half out of her
mind, it was so real.''

''Even got the hoofprints right,'' Joe said.

''What hoofprints?'' Gorman said.

''He threw in some hoofprints on the ground,'' said Bert.
''We had a camera crane shooting from a high angle, I guess
he thought it would look more real if the thing left hoofprints,
only they never showed up on film. For a while there, he
had us so convinced, we thought he'd conjured up a *real*
demon, because of those hoofprints, but of course, that would
be crazy. Still, it just goes to show you what the hell of an
effect it was.''

''I figure it should've wiped him out,'' Mort Levine said,
''but he looked fresh as a daisy when it was over. Apologized
for scaring Jessica to death, then sauntered off, calm as you
please, as if he pulled off tricks like that every day of the
week. And that got us thinking. I mean, if the guy's that
good an adept, why the hell is he wasting his time in the
motion picture business? He could get ten times as much from
some major corporation.''

"I'll tell you the truth," said Bert, "we never did buy this social worker thing of his. It costs a lot of money to go to school for all those years and then get certified, right?"

"It is rather expensive," Gorman admitted, prodding him on.

"Right, that's what we figured," said Levine. "It's got to put a serious dent in the bank account, right? And most adepts have to get student loans and such. So you gotta recoup, right? Does it figure that somebody like that turns his back on all the money to be made in corporate sorcery and goes in for charity work with a mission?"

"It does seem rather unusual," said Gorman.

"Well, we did some checking," said Levine. "I called in a few favors. And . . . well, listen, can I tell you something off the record?"

"Go ahead."

"We got a printout of his B.O.T. file."

Gorman raised his eyebrows. "Those are strictly confidential. How on earth did you manage that?"

"I'd rather not say, all right? I don't want to get anyone in trouble. Anyway, guess what we found out?"

"He struggled all the way through thaumaturgy school and barely squeaked past his adept certification," Gorman said.

Levine made a face. "Right, of course. Stupid of me. You've already seen his file. Anyway, you said it was off the record. We're not going to get in trouble for this, are we?"

"I'll forget you ever told me," Gorman said, making a mental note to follow up on it and find out how they got their information.

"Anyway, you saw the file," said Levine. "How does someone who barely managed to get certified as a lower grade wizard suddenly breeze through his sorcerer's exam? He never took any additional training. At least it didn't show on his file." Levine shrugged. "I don't know, I thought maybe we'd get something on him, like maybe he'd been convicted of some kind of white collar thaumaturgical crime or something, but there wasn't anything like that on his record."

"Tell him about the mission thing," said Joe.

"Yeah, Brother Khasim's Lost Souls Mission," said Levine. "I don't know what it is with this 'brother' business. Is he hooked up with some religion or what? What is he, a monk? He takes in a lot of money to keep that mission going. Contributions. He's got a reputation now and he's made contacts with a lot of people in the industry who can help him out, but where'd he get the scratch to get the whole thing started up? No one seems to know. And nobody donated that building to him. He paid for it in cash. *In cash*."

"You *have* done some checking, haven't you?" said Gorman. "You seem to be very well informed."

"Well, when you've worked in this town as long as we have, you make lots of connections with all sorts of people," Bert Smith said. "To be honest, we've been worried about our jobs. A guy like Khasim could make us obsolete. We're only being used for incidental effects as it is. On this new picture, Khasim's picking up all the big gags. He's got a lot of people in our business worried, especially some of the lower grade adepts. They've never had to compete with a full-fledged sorcerer before and it he starts cutting his prices and matching what they get, they'll all be out of work."

"Us, too," said Joe, staring deep into his glass.

"You got something on Khasim?" Levine said hopefully. "Has he done something?"

"Just a routine investigation," Gorman said. "But I'd appreciate it if you kept your eyes open and let me know if he does anything that seems at all unusual." He held up his hand and a business card suddenly appeared between his index and middle fingers. "You can reach me at that number. Or ask for Captain Farrell. Anything you say will be kept strictly confidential."

"Sure," Levine said, taking the card. "He *has* done something, hasn't he? I just knew he wasn't on the level."

"Thanks for your help, gentlemen," said Gorman. "I'll be in touch."

He was suddenly extremely anxious to meet Brother Khasim and have a look around the Lost Souls Mission.

CHAPTER
Nine

The first one was easy. He caught her strolling west down Sunset, near the Fairfax intersection. Her short skirt was slashed right up to her waist and her spike-heeled boots clicked sharply on the pavement as she cruised in a leisurely fashion down the boulevard, every step a hip shot. He quickly spoke a teleportation spell and vanished, to reappear in an alleyway just ahead of her. He waited till she drew even with him, then he called to her from inside the alley.

She paused, hesitating as she peered into the darkness, then said, "Come out here where I can see you."

He stepped out of the shadows.

She recognized him instantly. "Oh, it's you, Brother Khasim. For a second there, I thought—"

His eyes started to glow with a hellish green fire.

The words suddenly froze in the hooker's throat. The green lambence of Khasim's stare was reflected in her eyes. She stiffened and slowly started moving toward him, into the darkness of the alley. A short while later, Khasim came out alone.

He found his second victim only two blocks farther on. It was late and all the night flowers were out in full bloom. He could pluck them at his leisure. Only there was nothing leisurely in the way he went about it. A sense of desperate excitement was welling up within him and he practically trembled with anticipation as he approached the young girl standing on the corner. She couldn't have been a day over sixteen. His eyes were already burning with green fire when she turned to face him and there was a brief, sharp intake of breath as her mouth fell open with surprise, then her gaze unfocused and she stiffened. Helplessly, she followed him around the corner and into a darkened doorway.

There was the soft, dull, thumping sound of something striking flesh repeatedly and she sank down to the ground. Khasim bent over her, working swiftly, and moments later, he was on his way once more, searching for the next sacrificial victim. Behind him, where the young hooker lay sprawled in the doorway, a shadow seemed to detach itself from the darkness and glide after Khasim.

Rebecca Farrell sat staring at Thanatos, not knowing what to say. She shifted her gaze to Ben Slater, who sat across from her at the table in the kitchen of his apartment, watching her somberly.

"Is this for real?" she said.

Slater nodded silently.

Rebecca expelled her breath heavily. "Jesus."

"Jesus has nothing to do with it," said Slater wryly.

"So you're telling me these people, these Dark Ones—"

"Not people," Thanatos said, interrupting her. "At least not as you and I would know them. The Dark Ones are not human."

"Well, *whatever* the hell they are, you're saying they've been alive for all these thousands of years, kept prisoner in some hole in the ground, hidden in a secret underground temple in the Euphrates Valley? How'd they manage to stay alive?"

"Well, for one thing, they're immortal," Thanatos explained.

"Great," Rebecca said. "How are we supposed to fight something we can't even kill?"

"Fortunately for us, they can be killed," said Thanatos. "Of that, there is no question. Apparently, they just don't die of natural causes, such as old age, for example, or disease. Keep in mind that most of this is merely theory and supposition. I have no empirical knowledge of the Dark Ones, just what I've been able to piece together through secondhand reports and obscure, veiled references in ancient, forgotten thaumaturgic texts. I suspect that what probably happened after the Dark Ones were imprisoned was that their life functions slowed to an almost imperceptible level.''

"You mean like suspended animation?" Slater said.

"Probably something very similar; perhaps some form of cryptobiosis," Thanatos said. "I don't know if anybody really knows for sure, except perhaps for the three possessors of the runestones." ,

"If they're the ones with all the answers, then why aren't we looking for them?" asked Rebecca. "Let's bring them in and hold them for questioning."

"It's rather difficult to detain someone for questioning who's capable of teleportation," Thanatos replied dryly. "You saw what happened earlier tonight. According to Chief Inspector Blood of Scotland Yard, these people are quite capable of taking care of themselves. Wyrdrune is a gifted, if somewhat erratic, warlock whose natural abilities, when augmented by his runestone, should place him at the level of a high grade wizard, at the very least. Kira is a cunning cat burglar and con artist whose streetwise instincts, coupled with the power of her runestone, should make her a very formidable young woman, indeed. Billy Slade might be a mere boy of thirteen, but if Merlin's spirit has possessed him, then he's become the most resourceful teenager on the planet, and the most dangerous, as well. And as for Modred . . . well, we're talking about a man who's got some two thousand years of knowledge and experience to draw on, a man who isn't even fully human. None of them are, really. At least, not anymore. With people such as these, one doesn't simply walk up to the front door, flash a badge, and expect them to come down to headquarters and answer some routine questions."

"So what are we supposed to do?" Rebecca said. "Sit on the sidelines and just watch?"

"No, most emphatically not," said Thanatos. "By now, we can be reasonably certain that Mr. Rydell has communicated with his new partners and passed on the particulars of our discussion with him. I fully expect that we will be contacted very soon. In the meantime, we need to start compiling information as quickly as possible. Ben from his various sources on the street and you, Rebecca, from the police department. We're looking for certain patterns. Not only murders, but disappearances as well, kidnappings where no demands for ransom were ever received. Somehow, somewhere, a pattern must emerge that will give us a clue where to start looking for the Dark Ones and their servants. It shouldn't be long before Gorman's had a chance to track down the information I requested. Meanwhile, we can monitor what's happening on the Strip. I have a strong intuition that before the night is out, the Dark Ones will make their presence felt.

Gorman pushed open the door to the Lost Souls Mission and stepped inside. It was an unpretentious lobby, with a few potted plants placed here and there and several chairs set back against the walls. It was late and it was very quiet. A somewhat bedraggled-looking young man was bent over his desk in the reception area, reading a lurid horror comic book. Gorman rapped on the desk sharply, startling him.

"Yeah, what is it?" said the young man in a somewhat surly tone. "I mean . . . uh, how can I help you?"

Gorman showed the young man his I.D. "Agent Gorman, Bureau of Thaumaturgy," he said, looking the young man directly in the eyes.

"Yes, sir?"

"Is Brother Khasim in?"

"No, sir. He's out for the evening. Is there something I can help you with?"

"I understand that Brother Khasim lives here at the mission, isn't that right?"

"Yes, sir, he has quarters on the top floor."

"I would like to see them, please."

"Sir?"

"I would like to see Brother Khasim's quarters," Gorman repeated. "I would like you to show them to me." His gaze was still locked with the young man's. He didn't blink. Little lights danced in his pupils.

The young man blinked twice and flinched slightly, but he couldn't tear his gaze away from Gorman's.

"I . . . I'm sorry, sir, but I . . . I don't think I can do that."

"Yes, you can."

"I . . . I . . . I really think. . . . I think you'd need a warrant . . ."

"I don't need a warrant," Gorman said deliberately, willing the young man into submission.

"You . . . you don't need a warrant," the young man repeated dully.

"You are going to show me Brother Khasim's private quarters," Gorman said.

"I'm going to show you Brother Khasim's private quarters," the young man said flatly. His gaze had become unfocused.

"If anyone asks what we are doing, you will say that I am from the studio and Brother Khasim sent me back to get some script notes. Now what will you say?"

"Brother Khasim sent you back to get some script notes."

"Good. After you take me to Brother Khasim's private quarters, you will return here and you will forget that I am up there. In fact, you will forget that I was ever here. You will forget my name. You will forget we ever spoke or saw each other. You will not remember anything about me at all."

"I will not remember anything about you at all."

"Take me up there now."

The young man got up somewhat stiffly and said, "Follow me, please."

By the time the first body was discovered in the alley, Khasim had already accounted for four more. He had killed them all within an area encompassing eight blocks and he wasn't finished yet. The raging bloodlust had risen to a fever pitch within him.

By the time the detectives, the assistant medical examiner, and the lab man had arrived to take over from the beat cops who had initially responded to the call, Khasim had stalked and killed three more women. While the lab man took his pictures and filled out his forms and the detectives together with the assistant medical examiner puzzled over the curious markings carved into the dead woman's chest, Khasim's second victim was discovered, only two blocks away, on the same side of the street. The detectives hurried to the scene and found another dead hooker, slain the same way as the first, stabbed to death, with the same curious runes carved into her chest. The medical examiner asserted that both women had been killed within minutes of each other, and very recently, at that. Within the hour. And as they were examining that body, the patrol officers discovered a third one only half a block away.

With disbelief, the detectives radioed for backup and started following a trail of bodies that led them east on Sunset Boulevard. All were killed in exactly the same way, all mutilated in the same manner, carved with the same indecipherable markings. They realized that they had to be literally within blocks of the killer as he steadily, diabolically slaughtered his way east toward La Brea Avenue. The scream of police sirens cut the night as they tried to cordon off the area and the people on the Strip, like livestock sensing a predator in their midst, started milling about fearfully, darting across the street, running aimlessly in all directions, and huddling in doorways. In short, doing everything except going inside where it was safe, seeking instead the illusion of safety in numbers, following the herd instinct of the streets.

Back at Ben Slater's apartment, they followed the reports over the police frequency on Slater's portable radio.

"This must be it," Rebecca said, quickly getting to her feet and starting for the door. Slater grabbed his hat.

"Wait," said Thanatos, calmly sipping his coffee and making no move to get up from the table.

"What for?" Rebecca said. "This is just what you were telling us would happen! We've got to get down there right away!"

Thanatos glanced at her and raised an eyebrow. "Rebecca, have you forgotten that I can teleport us directly to the scene in an instant?"

She grimaced sheepishly. "Oh. That's right."

"We can follow the progression of events from here," said Thanatos. "We will listen, and wait, and see what develops. When the confrontation comes, we will be there."

Rebecca and Ben exchanged glances and came back to join Thanatos in the kitchen.

"Relax. Have some more coffee," he said, while voices crackled back and forth over the radio.

"How can you be so calm?" said Slater. "Women are being slaughtered down there even as we sit here and you say relax and have some more coffee?"

"I assure you, Ben, that at the moment, I am anything but calm," said Thanatos, staring into his coffee cup. "In fact, I'm trying very hard to steady my nerves, because I'm rather frightened." He looked up at them. "I have to depend upon the element of surprise, you see, and that means I have to pick my moment carefully. The police must provide the necessary distraction. Because if I cannot strike quickly, decisively, and without warning, then I'm not sure I'll have a second chance."

"*This is Unit nineteen, we've got another one! Alley behind the Whip and Chain club. . .*"

"*Roger, Unit nineteen, we copy, all units—*"

"It won't be long now," said Thanatos, as Slater and Rebecca stood behind him, listening intently. "It seems they've got him hemmed in. Unfortunately, that isn't going to help them."

He turned to the radio and gestured at it. "Attention all units," he said, and a second later, they heard his words repeated over the police band. "*Attention all units. Attention all units. The perpetrator is a magic-user. Repeat, the perpetrator is a magic-user. Exercise extreme caution. Locate, but do not attempt to apprehend. Repeat, locate, but do not attempt to apprehend.*"

"What are you doing?" demanded Rebecca.

"If they try to apprehend him, he may escape," said Thanatos. "Or he may turn on them and kill them all."

"*This is Unit twenty-one, suspect in sight, white male, dark clothes, running down alley off Sunset and Alta Vista, repeat suspect in sight—*"

"This is it," said Thanatos, getting up out of his chair. He glanced at Ben and Rebecca. "Perhaps you'd both be safer here."

"Not on your life," said Rebecca. "Get us down there. Now."

Thanatos grimaced tightly. "All right. Give me your hands."

Gorman hesitated at the door to Khasim's private quarters. The young man who had brought him up had gone back downstairs and there was no one else around, yet Gorman still hesitated. Carefully, he put his hand out, placed his palm flat against the door, and closed his eyes in concentration. Like a safecracker feeling the tumblers falling into place, Gorman felt the faint surge of thaumaturgical trace emanations through the door. Yes, it was as he'd suspected. The door was spell-warded. He smiled.

He backed well away from the door and turned, looking around the outer office, where the administrative volunteers did all the work that kept the mission going. His gaze fell on one of the heavy wooden desks. He stretched his arms out, spoke a levitation and impulsion spell, and concentrated. The heavy desk started to rise. When it was about three feet above the floor, he guided it around and toward the back of the room, then with a grunt of effort, impelled it hard toward the door to Khasim's office. The desk hurtled across the room and smashed into the door.

There was a crash as the door splintered and broke inward and at the same time, a bright, searing flash of light filled the room. Gorman threw his arm up to protect his eyes as the desk was incinerated in an instant. When the smoke cleared, the way was open. Just to be on the safe side, Gorman picked up a chair and tossed it through the doorway. It landed with a clatter inside Khasim's office. Well, so much for subtlety, he thought, as he entered the office. But at least he was inside.

A thorough search produced nothing. Gorman grimaced with disappointment. It didn't make any sense. Why spell-ward the entrance if there was nothing in here to protect? Somehow, he had to have missed something. He searched the office once again, with no more result. Yet he did not give up. He knew he was right. He knew there was something here that Brother Khasim had been anxious to conceal, anxious enough to spell-ward the entrance with a spell that would instantly kill an unwary intruder. He looked through Brother Khasim's desk again, he tore his bed apart and carefully examined the mattress, he looked through his clothes in the closet . . . and then he spotted the small switch on the inside wall. Why hook up a switch *inside* the closet, especially if there was no light fixture in there? He threw the switch and there was a soft humming sound. Gorman frowned with puzzlement, and then he noticed that the floor of the closet had started to descend.

"Well, well, well," he said to himself. "How very interesting. Now why would someone want to hide an elevator in a closet?"

He reversed the switch and waited for the floor to come back up, then stepped inside and threw the switch again. The floor started to descend once more. Khasim tried to estimate the distance. Was there a false wall on one of the lower floors? But no, after several moments, he realized that the elevator had gone past the street level and down to the basement level . . . and still lower. What the hell, he thought, there's another basement *below* the basement? And then the elevator stopped and Gorman stepped out into Khasim's secret underground apartments.

He gave a low whistle as he stepped out into Khasim's sprawling living room and took it all in. "Well I'll be damned. . . ." he said.

And then he saw the bodies.

Officer Zeke Paterno spotted him first. The squad car was slowly cruising down the Strip, Paterno's officer adept partner taking care of the driving while Paterno flashed the spotlight into shadowy doorways and dark alleys. Just as they were passing an alley near Sunset and Alta Vista, Paterno suddenly said, "Stop, Al!"

Al Carlson, the driver adept, held the squad car motionless as Paterno adjusted the light. The high intensity beam illuminated a dark figure in the alleyway, crouched down over something . . .

"Jesus, that's a body," said Paterno. "Get on the horn, we've got him!"

And before Carlson could react, Paterno was out of the car and running toward the alley.

"Zeke, wait! Dammit, we're not supposed to—" The squad car dropped about a foot to the ground with a jarring thud as Carlson stopped concentrating on his levitation spell and grabbed the radio mike. "*This is Unit twenty-one, suspect in sight, white male, dark clothes, running down alley off Sunset and Alta Vista, repeat suspect in sight—*"

"Hold it right there! Police!" shouted Paterno, pulling his 9mm from his holster as he ran. The suspect looked up and for a brief moment, Paterno caught a glimpse of a white face, eyes bulging, jaws slack, and then the suspect was off and running down the alley.

"Stop!" Paterno shouted. "Stop or I'll shoot!"

The suspect kept fleeing. Paterno brought his gun up in a two-handed combat stance and fired three shots rapidly. The suspect stumbled but kept on going.

"*Damn,*" Paterno swore. And then he saw the mutilated body lying in the alley. "Oh, Jesus. . . ."

He took off after Khasim. All around him, the night was filled with the sound of police sirens as all units converged on the area. The suspect reached the end of the alley, where it T-boned into another alley running parallel with Sunset. Paterno, who like most of his fellow officers was not a marathon runner, was breathing hard as he gave chase. At the far end of the alley, a squad car pulled up, blocking off the exit. Paterno saw the suspect veer sharply to the left, down another alley between two buildings, heading back toward Sunset.

"Stop, you son of a bitch," Paterno gasped as he pumped his arms and legs, trying to close the distance.

Breathing hard, he turned into the alley, paused, saw the suspect about halfway down, still running, checked to see that there was no one in the line of fire at the other end of the alley, raised his pistol, aimed carefully, and squeezed off another three rounds. The fleeing suspect went down.

"Gotcha, you bastard," Paterno said with satisfaction.

Behind him, he heard the siren as Carlson brought the squad car around. Another police cruiser came up to block off the mouth of the alley. Red and blue flashing lights reflected off the brick walls as Paterno approached the fallen suspect.

Suddenly, the suspect sprang up with a growl and Paterno found himself face-to-face with something inhuman. Its leathery, batlike face leered at him demonically as it bared its dripping fangs and screeched like a demented harpie. For one fraction of a second, Paterno froze, stunned into immobility, and in that one fraction of a second, the creature lashed out with a clawed hand and Paterno felt the gun plucked right out of his grasp. He only had time for a shocked gasp before the creature tossed the gun aside, grabbed his head between two immensely powerful hands, and turned it around one hundred and eighty degrees, snapping his neck and killing him instantly.

The officers at the far end of the alley opened fire. The creature jerked twice as bullets struck it, then threw out an arm and a bright blue bolt of thaumaturgic energy shot out from its outstretched claws and enveloped the police officers and their cruiser. There was a blinding flash of light and an eardrum-shattering concussion as the police officers and their cruiser exploded in a spray of viscera and shrapnel.

Carlson watched it all with stunned disbelief. And then the creature turned toward him. Desperately, he tried to focus on his levitation and impulsion spell, but fear destroyed his concentration. He threw himself across the seat, tumbled out the passenger side door, and ran right into Thanatos, Ben, and Rebecca, bowling them over as they materialized directly in front of him. Behind him, the police cruiser exploded as it was struck by a bolt of thaumaturgic energy and Carlson cried out as several pieces of jagged metal shrapnel struck him in the back.

By the time Thanatos scrambled back up to his feet, the alley was deserted.

Gorman stared down at the bodies of the half-clad women and fought down his revulsion as nausea surged up within him. They had been literally torn apart, savaged as if by some wild beast. Blood was everywhere, soaked into the luxurious, handwoven rugs and splattered on the expensive wall hangings. It looked like a seraglio turned into an abattoir.

In the bedroom, he found implements of perversion that disgusted him almost as much as the grisly sight outside in the living room. He also found the bloody corpse of yet another naked young woman, chained to the wall. So much for the so-called Sorcerer Saint of Sunset Strip, he thought. The benevolent Brother Khasim was a foul, depraved necromancer who kidnapped young girls and kept them prisoner in his underground lair, violating them repeatedly and then sacrificing them in his unholy rites. That such a twisted creature should be a sorcerer and that he should use his training in the thaumaturgic arts for such a bestial, abominable purpose filled Gorman with an outrage so profound that he began to tremble.

His gaze fell on the huge, black-canopied bed, covered with black satin sheets and a black brocade coverlet with the mirror mounted overhead and his lips twisted down in disgust at the thought of what had gone on there. Rage welled up within him, a fury he was unable to control. He swept his arm out in a violent gesture and the bed burst into flames. The fire quickly spread to the canopy and within seconds, the entire bedroom was a conflagration. Gorman retreated back into the other room, turned . . . and then stopped cold.

He was no longer alone.

Huddled, bleeding on the floor, was Brother Khasim. He was on his knees, clutching himself, his breaths coming in sobs. His clothes were dirty and torn, spattered with blood, some of which was his own. He had been shot several times and he was whimpering with pain. He looked up at Gorman and held out a bloody hand.

"Help me. . . ." he said.

"*Help* you?" said Gorman, barely able to restrain his fury. "I ought to kill you, you son of a bitch!"

And then he noticed that Khasim was looking *past* him. He turned and saw something dark and featureless standing close behind him. It was the last thing he ever saw.

CHAPTER
Ten

It was a long night on the Sunset Strip. It began with a murder spree that ended with the deaths of a dozen women and three police officers and to make matters still worse, the perpetrator had managed to escape. Nor was that the end of it. A raging conflagration at the other end of the Strip had destroyed the Lost Souls Mission and it was almost morning by the time the fire was extinguished. When it was over, the routine investigation to determine if arson could have been the cause unearthed the truth about Khasim. They found the concealed elevator, which, along with two hidden ventilation shafts, had acted as a forcing cone for the flames. These, in turn, led them to the discovery of the secret rooms underneath the mission and the charred remains of several more female bodies, as well as the body of one male. The bodies had been burned beyond recognition, but they were able to identify Gorman by his flame-blackened B.O.T badge. The media descended on Rebecca Farrell and the fire marshals. They didn't like being told that there would be no comments until a "full investigation" was completed, but it was what they had to settle for.

Outside on the street, Thanatos leaned back against the rear seat of the police cruiser and wearily massaged the bridge of his nose. The first gray light of dawn was starting to show and he was exhausted.

"I don't understand," he said in a weary voice. "Why didn't he call me? What on earth made him go in alone?"

"Gorman probably thought he could handle it," said Slater, sitting beside him, sipping a container of coffee. "And if he'd called you in, he wouldn't have been able to take full credit for the bust. A B.O.T. man beating out an I.T.C. agent on a necromancy case. It would've looked good on his record. Or maybe he just couldn't wait because he was hot on the scent. It's probably the same reason Paterno tried to bring down Khasim all by himself. The game was afoot. They couldn't resist the chase.''

"Unfortunately, we're left with no proof that the killer was Khasim,'' Thanatos said.

"Who else could it possibly be?" said Rebecca, twisting around in the front seat. "What do you think he was doing down there in that secret chamber of his, conducting meditation sessions? With all those chains and handcuffs they recovered from the fire? Those women were murdered in some kind of twisted, necromantic rites. Gorman discovered his nasty little secret and confronted him, so Khasim killed him, too, then set the fire to cover up his crimes.''

"It certainly looks that way,'' Thanatos said, "but what we have is still only circumstantial evidence. Admittedly, it's very strong circumstantial evidence, but it may not be enough to make a charge of necromancy stick, much less multiple murder charges.''

"Are you kidding?" Slater said. "How the hell do you figure that?''

"Put yourself in a defense attorney's place,'' Thanatos replied. "With those bodies burned the way they are, it will be almost impossible to establish what killed them. The defense would almost certainly argue that they probably died in the fire. A fire that could well have been caused by Gorman, for all anyone knows. And there's no way to tie in those deaths with the murders on the Strip tonight. The only one who got close enough to the killer to make a positive identification was Officer Paterno and, unfortunately, we'll never know what Paterno saw because he became one of the victims.''

"Maybe Paterno can still identify the killer,'' said Rebecca. "According to Carlson, Paterno put at least two bullets in him, maybe more. And we've got Paterno's gun. All we have to do is match up the slugs taken out of Khasim and we've got him. I've got an A.P.B. out and we can alert all the hospitals—''

Thanatos shook his head. "Don't bother. If Khasim is seriously wounded, a hospital will be the last place he would go. Unless he was mortally wounded, he could be healed thaumaturgically and for that he will turn to his Dark Lord."

"What about the fact of the secret rooms themselves?" Slater said. "And all those restraints they found. Chains embedded in the walls, for Christ's sake!"

"Brother Khasim was widely known for his work with addicts," Thanatos said wearily. "The withdrawal symptoms from some of the street potions available today can be quite frightening, often inducing psychopathic behavior. As a defense attorney, I would argue that the purpose of that secret chamber was to treat the most violent cases of potion withdrawal, to allow them to submit to being voluntarily restrained before the most serious onset of the withdrawal symptoms."

"You know, for an I.T.C. agent, you think an awful lot like a crooked lawyer," Rebecca said wryly.

"Virtually all the crimes involving magic use we have to deal with are corporate crimes," said Thanatos. "And multinationals employ entire batteries of crooked lawyers. You have to learn to think like one or else you can't hope to secure convictions. It has a tendency to make one somewhat cynical."

"So where does that leave us?" Slater asked.

"Unfortunately, it leaves us right back where we started," Thanatos replied. "Searching for patterns. Necromancers feed on death. Tonight was an example, only a small example, of what they're capable of. Nor, I suspect, will it be an isolated incident. Brother Khasim was sent out on a rampage tonight, to kill as many times as he could. Sacrifices to increase his Dark Lord's power. Causing a train wreck or an apartment building to collapse would have made that much more life energy available for quick consumption, but so powerful a release of energy might also have alerted the runestones and perhaps enabled them to focus in on the Dark One. One life at a time, one right after another, is a great deal slower, but a lot more surreptitious from the point of energy release and its thaumaturgic absorption, which leaves behind trace emanations that can be detected by sensitives."

"So what does that mean?" said Slater.

"It means the Dark Ones must know the runestones are nearby," said Thanatos, frowning. "They're getting ready, trying to increase their power. The confrontation must be drawing near."

"Then it's time we brought in these people with the runestones," said Rebecca. "If they've really got a way of locating these necromancers, I want to know about it. And I don't care how dangerous the Dark Ones are, I don't want magic-using vigilantes running loose in this city. We have laws for dealing with criminals and—"

"Oh, Becky, for God's sake, stop sounding like a department P.R. flack," said Slater. "You had half the damn police department on the Strip tonight and they couldn't even stop Khasim. And he was only human. Imagine what one of these Dark Ones would be capable of doing."

"So what would you have me do, Ben?" she replied hotly. "Sit back and do nothing while a goddamn mage war takes place on the streets?"

"And just how do you intend to stop it?" Slater asked.

She turned to Thanatos. "You said these Dark Ones could be killed just like a human, right? Guns will stop them?"

"Yes, they can be killed," Thanatos admitted. "However—"

"Then if that's what it takes, the law will do it, not some group of vigilantes. Officially, it's still my case—"

"I'm afraid not," said Thanatos. "After what happened tonight, there's no hope of keeping the lid on it anymore and I have more than enough grounds to officially take charge of the case. In fact, with the death of a B.O.T. agent involved, I have no choice."

"I see," she said curtly.

"Believe it or not, I'm doing you a favor," Thanatos told her. "It's my hide they'll scream for now, not yours."

"Whatever you say," she said flatly. "So what do you want me to do?"

"Coordinate with all police agencies, on the local and on the state level as well, and check for cases involving unsolved murders, serial killings, rituals slayings, disappearances, anything that could indicate necromancy. A pattern is bound to be there. You'll find it. In the meantime, Ben, see what you can learn from your sources on the street. We're looking for any unusual occurrences, especially disappearances of people who might not ordinarily be missed, such as homeless individuals; anything at all that could suggest illegal magic use. The Dark Ones cannot function in a vacuum. They must have their minions, like Khasim. They must have a source of life energy to empower their vile spells. Someone somewhere *must* know something.''

He sighed wearily as the police cruiser pulled up in front of his hotel, the MacDonald Wilshire. It was dawn.

"Do what you want to get things started and then try to get some rest," he said. "For now, all we can do is wait."

He left them and went through the golden arches over the hotel doors, up to his room on the forty-second floor. He hoped he was doing the right thing, but he wasn't sure of anything anymore. Perhaps he should have told Rebecca that the bearers of the runestones were not exactly "magic-using vigilantes," that since the runestones were animated by the collected life force of the Old Ones who had made up the Council of the White, they in fact represented an authority older than any human law. However, he wasn't sure she would have appreciated his point. He wasn't sure that anybody else would, either, particularly his superiors at the I.T.C. In fact, there was very little that the I.T.C. would appreciate about the way he was conducting this case . . . if they knew about it.

Officially, all the I.T.C. knew was that he was investigating the disappearance of one of his fellow field agents, Fay Morgan. He did not tell them that he already knew that she was dead, killed in a battle with the Dark Ones. Nor did the I.T.C. know that he and Fay Morgan had been secretly married, or that Fay Morgan was really a two-thousand-year-old sorceress named Morgan Le Fay or that one of the world's most wanted criminals, a man known to the I.T.C. only by the name "Morpheus," was actually her son, Modred, the last survivor of Camelot. They did not know about the true nature of the runestones and they did not know about the Dark Ones. That was an awful lot for them not to know, yet despite his sense of duty, Thanatos could not bring himself to tell them.

For one thing, he could not be certain it would be the right thing to do. As an agent of the I.T.C., there was no question but that he should have told his superiors about all the information he'd uncovered, but as an adept, he was not convinced that it would be the proper thing to do. He had his oath of office to the I.T.C., but over and above that, he was sworn to the Ambrosian Oath, which every magic-user, from the lowliest warlock to the highest mage had sworn. And in taking that oath, he has sworn not only never to abuse the old knowledge that Merlin brought back to the world, but also to use it only for the greater good. Only what was the greater good in this case?

It was one thing to share his knowledge with people like Rebecca Farrell and Ben Slater, whose auras showed him that they could be trusted, but if he were to report the results of his investigation so far to his superiors at the I.T.C., it would have to go through normal channels and be classified and filed, analyzed and considered, discussed and verified, subjected to all the slowly grinding processes of a large and unwieldy bureaucracy and, as was inevitable in any bureaucracy, there would be leaks. The information would be certain to get out to an unprepared and unsuspecting public and there would be a worldwide panic. Every magic-user would wind up under suspicion in the ensuing climate of fear and distrust.

Yet, at the same time, the Dark Ones' greatest strength was that the world at large did not know of their existence. It left them free to move among the humans who were once their chattel and whom they hoped once more to enslave. It left them free to gather human acolytes and form a perverse and evil priesthood that would serve them; free to recover from the weakening effects of their eons-old confinement and increase their evil power even more.

Thanatos did not know what to do. He felt trapped in the middle, caught up in something bigger and more frightening than anything he'd ever experienced before. And he was too exhausted to think clearly. He turned the key in the lock and entered his hotel room.

And suddenly discovered than he was not alone.

The police cruiser took them both back to the station, where Rebecca assigned detectives to check with their other local and state police agencies, looking for any pattern of crimes that might indicate that necromancy was responsible. In the meantime, Ben took out his little black book and started making calls to sources who had given him information in the past, with instructions to ask around and get back to him through his remote pager the moment they heard anything. The city was just starting to wake up for the next day by the time that they were through.

"You about done?" Rebecca asked him, coming over to the desk that he was sitting at.

Slater hung up the phone. "That was the last call. Now it's like Thanatos said. We wait."

"You look tired," she said.

"So do you, kid."

"I am, but I don't think I can sleep."

"Me neither."

"Breakfast?"

"Sure, why not?" he said. "I've got to put something else in there on top of all that coffee before it eats a hole in my stomach."

They went downstairs and Rebecca checked out an unmarked cruiser powered by a thaumaturgic battery. They'd driven several miles before Slater realized that they were heading back to her place. He glanced at her questioningly as he recognized the route.

"We're going back to your place first?" he said.

"I could use a shower," she said. She sniffed. "And you could do with one, as well."

"That bad?" he said.

She grinned. "No, just kidding. But you're welcome to take one anyway. I can put on some coffee and whip us up some steak and eggs."

"Sounds great," Ben said, thinking about other breakfasts that they used to have together. It seemed like a long time ago. He forced the thought from his mind. "What do you make of this whole thing?"

She sighed and shook her head as she drove. "I don't really know what to make of it, Ben. It all sounds so incredible. A race of immortals that once lived on this planet and dominated primitive man. It seems so hard to believe, yet it would explain so much about our legends and our mythology, about our religions, about history's unanswered questions, about why some people have powers of extrasensory perception and why some people can easily learn to use magic while others can't do anything, no matter how hard they try.''

"Yeah,'' Slater said with a grunt. "And then there was the other graphic evidence of what was done to Sarah Tracy, not to mention her boyfriend.''

Rebecca shuddered. "There've been other murders like that, just as you guessed in the first place,'' she admitted. "Same pattern, mostly hookers and street people. But as bad as they were, I'd never seen anything like what was done to Victor Cameron. It was as if he was just . . . shredded. There wasn't even a body, just . . . entrails and blood. God, all that blood splattered everywhere. . . .''

"I know,'' said Slater. "It makes me wonder how the hell you stop anything like that. What can you do with someone who can actually conjure up demons? And while we're on the subject, remind me to ask Thanatos just what exactly a demon is, anyway.''

"Gorman briefed me on that at the beginning,'' Rebecca said. "Don't ask me to explain exactly how it works, because that part of it I didn't understand at all, but as near as I can make out, it isn't some creature summoned up from hell or anything like that. The conjured demon is essentially an alter ego of the necromancer, a sort of psychic projection of his inner personality, what psychiatrists call the id.''

"No kidding?'' Slater said. "You mean like turning your subconscious self into a monster and sending it out to kill?''

"Something like that,'' Rebecca said. "Gorman said that in its mildest forms, the principle behind it accounts for such parapsychological phenomena as feeling pain when someone very close to you is injured or maybe having a dream in which a close relative comes to you and says goodbye and you find out the next day that they'd died that night.''

"Yeah, I heard of that happening,'' said Slater.

"Well, according to Gorman, people who have experienced things like that have an innate genetic potential for thaumaturgy.'' She grimaced. "Which I guess could be another way of saying what Thanatos claims, that somewhere way back along the line, one of their ancestors was an Old One. Anyway, say your son gets hurt. The theory is that at that precise instant, perhaps not even consciously, he thinks of you, because you were the one he always came to for protection. And he subconsciously does this projection thing and you feel the pain because he's reached you. Or say your mother's dying. Maybe she's thinking of you at the moment of her death, wishing she could say goodbye, and her projection comes to you in a dream.''

"What if your son or your mother hates your guts?" asked Slater.

"You mean can the psychic projection hurt you?" said Rebecca. "No. At least, not according to Gorman. There isn't enough energy involved or something. Even with white magic, a sorcerer would have to expend a great deal of energy, and he couldn't do it without severely depleting himself. But with necromancy, where you use someone else's life force—''

"I get the picture," Slater said.

They pulled up in front of Rebecca's building and she parked the car, flipping down the visor with it's printed "Police Officer on Duty" card clipped to it, so that the car would not get ticketed or towed away. Her apartment hadn't changed much since Slater had last seen it. She was still an utter disaster as a housekeeper. She didn't apologize for it like most people did, saying "Excuse the apartment, it's a mess; I didn't have a chance to clean." Rebecca's apartment was *always* a mess and her cleaning methods were sporadic and haphazard, at best. Like many women, Rebecca had a habit of taking off her shoes the moment she came in and they had a tendency to remain wherever they fell when she took them off. As a result, one could find shoes all over her apartment. The rug was covered with long orange-blond hair from her pet snat, Snuggles, a thaumagenetically engineered creature that was half snail and half cat. It had no legs and its rubbery underside would cling to just about anything. To Slater, it always looked like a giant hairball sticking to the wall.

"Snuggles?" Rebecca called as she kicked off her shoes. "Snuggles, where are you, Snuggles?"

A thirty-pound ball of fur dropped from the ceiling and plastered itself to Slater's head.

"Aaah! *Jesus!* Get this hairy slug off me!"

"Ooh, Snuggles, *there* you are!" she cooed, prying the snat off Slater's head. "Did he scare you, Snuggles, did he? He won't hurt you, nooo. . . ."

"Me hurt him? Hell, I think he gave me whiplash," Slater grumbled, rubbing his neck. He never could understand why perfectly sensible women turned into total mushminds whenever they spoke to their cute, furry little pets.

"Fooood," Snuggles said, sounding like a Munchkin on downers. "Food, foood."

"You want your food, Snuggles?" said Rebecca in a high-pitched, little girl voice.

"I think he wants his food," said Slater wryly.

Rebecca glanced at him and shook her head in reproof.

"What?" said Slater. "Go feed the little hairball. Meanwhile, I'll take you up on your offer and go grab a quick shower."

"You know the way," she said.

Yeah, Slater thought, I know the way. He sighed and headed for the bathroom. He was brought up short the moment he walked in. He had almost forgotten about Rebecca's bathroom. It seemed to be one of nature's more peculiar laws; the more trouble a woman took to care of her appearance, the messier her bathroom was.

Slater's personal toiletries included one bottle of shampoo (no rinse), soap, roll-on deodorant, toothbrush, toothpaste, floss, mouthwash, shaving soap and brush, razor, and witch hazel for aftershave. He could get the whole kit and kaboodle into one small leather traveling case. Rebecca, on the other hand, had what seemed like a dozen different bottles of shampoos and rinses and conditioners and color highlighters and hot oil treatments and PH balancers and styling gels and moisturizing agents—and that was only for her *hair*. Her face required another thirty or forty some odd bottles and tubes and jars, most of which were scattered in profusion on the bathroom countertop. As he stripped for his shower, Slater thought that with all that junk and all the time she spent putting it on, she had still looked best to him first thing in the morning.

He stepped into the shower and put his face directly in the spray, enjoying the invigorating feeling of the water beating down on his skin. He started to soap himself. His once dark chest hair was now mostly gray. Getting old, he thought. Too old for going on crusades and chasing necromancers and thinking wistfully of a certain police captain who was just about young enough to be his daughter. It had been nice while it lasted. Now, he was just a harmless old friend whom it was safe to ask back to her apartment. At least it seemed that they were friends again.

He heard a soft click as the shower door opened and then he felt her hands on his back, her fingernails softly stroking down his shoulders. He turned and she came into his arms.

He knew who they were even before the boy spoke and said, "Good morning, Winslow," calling him by his truename.

He caught his breath and stared at Billy. *"Professor Ambrosius? Is that really you?"*

Billy stepped forward with his swaggering walk, thumbs tucked into his belt. "Nah, it's really me, mate, but ole Merlin's in 'ere, too." He held out his hand. "Billy Slade," he said.

Thanatos shook it and then watched in bewilderment as the boy's entire demeanor underwent a complete change.

"It's been a few years, Thanatos," Merlin said. "I'm pleased to see you've done so well. However, we can reminisce about your student days another time. There's someone here who wants to meet you."

Modred came forward, looking at Thanatos intently.

"Modred," Thanatos said softly. "Or do you prefer another name these days?"

"How do you feel about Morpheus?" said Modred, watching him curiously.

"It's my duty to arrest him," Thanatos replied. He paused and smiled faintly. "But I don't think I've ever met the gentleman." He held out his hand. "Your mother told me a great deal about you."

Modred raised his eyebrows. "Whereas you come as a complete surprise to me," he said, taking the proffered hand. He noticed Thanatos looking at his chest and smiled. "Is this what you're looking for?" he said, opening his shirt. The ruby runestone was glowing dimly.

Thanatos gazed for a long moment at the stone embedded in Modred's chest, then he looked up at Modred and glanced at the others.

"You must be Wyrdrune," he said.

Wyrdrune took off his hat. The emerald runestone gleamed in his forehead.

"Of course," Thanatos said, nodding. "The green aura." They shook hands and then he turned to Kira.

"And Kira, the bearer of the sapphire," he said. He reached for her hand, then hesitated slightly as he saw the soft blue glow emanating from her palm. He took her hand, feeling the warm hardness of the stone against his palm.

"You were very foolish tonight," Modred. "You might have easily been killed."

"Then you know about what happened?"

"It was on the news," said Modred. "Even if we could have been there, I'm not sure we could have done anything. The police were everywhere and they were only in the way. This is not the way to handle the Dark Ones."

"It was a sorcerer known as Brother Khasim," said Thanatos. He sighed heavily. "I'm afraid he escaped. I'd hoped that if we could have captured him—"

"You would have died," said Modred. "He was not alone. The Dark Ones were with him."

Thanatos frowned. "Were? You're speaking in the plural."

"There are at least two of them here," said Modred. "Perhaps there are more. I saw them. They were in the alleyway when the police opened fire on my friends. I wasn't as quick to get out of the way and I caught a stray bullet." And then he added ironically, "You almost killed me, Stepfather."

"It was not my intention, I assure you of that. The police overreacted."

"I've noticed that they often do that when confronted with something that infuriates them," Modred replied wryly.

"Modred's right. Bringing the cops in is not the way to handle this," said Kira. "They're not qualified to deal with a situation like this. They'll only make things worse."

"How much have you told them?" Wyrdrune asked.

"The police? Hardly anything," said Thanatos. "A police captain named Rebecca Farrell knows as much as I do, as does a newspaperman named Ben Slater, but they can both be trusted. Except for them, all anyone knows is that a sorcerer named Brother Khasim, a charity worker and sometime special effects adept, has been discovered to be a psychopathic, murdering necromancer. Officially, no one knows anything about the Dark Ones. Nor about you."

"How much do the I.T.C. and the B.O.T. know?" Modred asked.

"Even less," Thanatos replied.

"Even less?" said Wyrdrune, not sure he heard right.

"Officially, I'm investigating the disappearance of one of our agents," Thanatos said. He glanced at Modred. "Although I know about what happened to Fay."

"You mean Morgana," Modred said.

"She was always Fay to me," Thanatos explained, a note of sadness in his voice. "I knew her as Fay Morgan for five years before she told me who she really was. She told me the night we were married."

Modred grimaced. "Mother always was one for surprises."

"Yes, well, you can imagine what my reaction was. I was staggered. In any case, her true identity always remained our secret, as did the marriage. No one else ever knew." He sighed again. "I found out how she died from Michael Blood."

"Talkative boy, young Michael," Modred said.

"Don't blame him, he had no choice," said Thanatos. "I gave him none. I had already deduced a great deal on my own. He simply filled in the blanks. Anyway, no one at the Bureau or the I.T.C. knows anything about the Dark Ones. And I could never go to them without sufficient proof."

"And just how do you expect to present them with sufficient proof?" said Merlin, taking out his pipe and pouch. "Did you think you could capture a Dark One? Or perhaps you'd hoped to arrest one of their acolytes? You could certainly make a case for a renegade sorcerer practicing necromancy, but you could never prove a thing beyond that, not about the existence of the Dark Ones. And none of their acolytes would ever dare to testify. Jail would afford them no protection whatsoever.''

"Yes, I know," said Thanatos. "I've already had a rather vivid demonstration of that. However, that was not what I intended. I'd hoped to capture Khasim alive because I thought that I could make him lead me to the power behind him.''

"And then what?" Kira said. "What would you do? You don't really think you could place a Dark One under arrest, do you?''

Thanatos met her challenging gaze. "I would have to try. I have my duty.''

"Oh, jeez," said Kira, rolling her eyes. "We've got a boy scout.''

"And what about me?" said Modred. "You know perfectly well who and what I am. Where is your sense of duty as regards arresting me?''

"At any other time, I would arrest you," Thanatos replied, "stepson or not. However, in the present circumstances, the Dark Ones are obviously a far greater threat.''

"Then why not inform your colleagues at the I.T.C.?" said Modred.

"Because I have no proof yet.''

"I see," Modred continued. "And you only report your findings when you have absolute proof, is that it?''

"No, that isn't it," Thanatos replied tensely.

"Then what?''

"I don't see why I have to explain myself to you. I don't—''

"Getting a bit defensive, aren't we?" Modred said with a mocking smile.

Thanatos bit off his reply and took a slow, deep breath, composing himself. "All right. What do you want from me?''

"To begin with, I'd like for you to be honest with yourself," Modred replied. "Before you can hope to deal with the Dark Ones, you first need to deal with your own internal conflicts.''

"What would you know about my 'internal conflicts'?"

"Perhaps more than you might think," said Modred. "I have been observing human nature for about two thousand years and in all that time, I think I might have learned a thing or two. That you are conflicted is obvious. And I don't need to be sensitive to auras to see that in you. As to the cause of your internal conflict, I think that can be traced back directly to your marriage with my mother."

Thanatos stiffened.

"Oh, for God's sake, don't get your back up," said Modred. "You're going to tell me that you loved her. Well, let me tell you that a great many people have loved Morgana over the centuries and it didn't benefit a single one of them."

"She was your mother," Thanatos said stiffly.

"Yes, and her own half brother was my father," Modred replied. "Please, let's not have any illusions about the sort of woman that she was. Morgana was a compulsively manipulative, thoroughly immoral, and totally unprincipled bitch." He quickly held up his hand before Thanatos could reply. "And before you manifest the appropriate outraged response of the loyal, grieving husband, let me tell you that I meant that without any rancor whatsoever. It's the simple truth."

"He's right, you know," said Merlin. "Morgana had her good qualities, to be sure. Believe me, I was in an excellent position to appreciate that. After all, I'm the one who taught her all she knew. About magic, anyway. But Morgana was also a very complex and tortured woman. She was all those things that Modred said, and more."

Thanatos glanced at Billy, sitting there and smoking his pipe, tapping it lightly against his teeth as Merlin always used to do. It seemed absurdly surreal to listen to a thirteen-year-old, pipe-smoking street urchin sitting there, calmly and paternally discoursing about his one-time relationship with the woman he had loved, the woman who had been his wife.

"Keeping your marriage a secret was Morgana's idea, wasn't it?" Modred continued.

"Yes," Thanatos admitted. "The I.T.C. has a policy against field agents being married to one another. It could compromise their effectiveness and—"

"Yes, yes, I know," said Modred. "But you were in love."

"*We* were in love," Thanatos said.

"I have no doubt of that," Modred said quietly. "Otherwise, she would not have given you that ring. Don't misunderstand me. I am not questioning your feelings for each other. But because of those feelings, because she wanted you, Morgana got you to break the rules. She never gave a damn about rules anyway. But you did, didn't you? True, it was a rather minor infraction, perhaps, but it was the first step. And when she got what she wanted, she told you who she really was. And after that first broken rule, the first secret kept from your superiors, this one was a little easier to keep, especially since it was such a momentous one. How *could* you tell anyone that you'd married a two-thousand-year-old sorceress?"

The expression on Thanatos's face told Modred he was right.

"I imagine she waited for some time after that before she told you about me," Modred continued, "about who Morpheus really was. And by then you had become more accustomed to keeping secrets, which was rather fortunate, because this one was a little more difficult to bear. One of the I.T.C.'s most wanted criminals turns out to be your stepson. And your wife, his mother, was the agent in charge of his case. Suddenly, without doing anything but falling in love, you had become corrupt. And perhaps you began to wonder if the only difference between you and someone like Al'Hassan was a difference of degree."

Thanatos turned pale.

"Modred . . ." Wyrdrune said, taking him by the arm.

"No," Thanatos said tensely. "Let him have his say."

"I'm almost finished," Modred said. "When Morgana died, you probably blamed yourself. Perhaps you believed that if you were forthcoming with the truth, you might have prevented it somehow. Well, you couldn't have. Nothing you could possibly have done would have changed a thing. The bitter irony is that for the first time in her life, she acted in an unselfish way and it resulted in her death. So now here you are, working with the Los Angeles police in your official position as an agent of the I.T.C., only the I.T.C. knows nothing of your actions. Technically, that makes you a renegade agent, but that isn't what concerns me. What concerns me is that I think you are a guilt-ridden man embarked on a crusade to right an entire plethora of wrongs, both real and imagined, to make up for your past mistakes, when in fact the only real mistake you made was falling in love with the wrong person. I frankly don't care about your emotional self-flagellation, but a guilt-ridden crusader might very well get us all killed and that's something I care about very much, indeed.''

"Are you finished?" Thanatos said tightly.

"Yes, I'm finished. How did I do?"

"Not badly," Thanatos said. "Not badly, at all." He smiled tightly. "Your mother was right about you. You really are a heartless bastard, aren't you?"

"Quite literally," said Modred.

"So, you've said your piece. Now I'll say mine. Whatever feelings of guilt I may or may not have are none of your business. The relationship I had with your mother is none of your business, either. After all, you two were hardly what one could call close. My internal conflicts regarding my duty as an agent of the I.T.C. are none of your business, either, although I can see where you may be concerned about them.''

"Look, this isn't getting us anywhere," said Wyrdrune.

"No, now you let *me* finish," Thanatos said. He turned back to Modred. "First of all, I do not see myself as a crusader, and though I grieve over Fay's death, believe me, I am not so filled with remorse that I would throw away my own life. However, I do find myself in a very difficult position, a position that, from the ethical standpoint, is very similar to the position in which I found myself when your mother told me about you. You were quite correct on that point; I commend you on your insight. It was one thing to keep our marriage a secret, because in spite of the department regulations, that was something that really didn't hurt anyone and I didn't think the department had any business regulating the personal lives of its agents.''

"How very naive of you," said Modred.

"Perhaps, but that is beside the point. The point is that

although it was a breach of regulations, it was something I could live with, even if it did require some rationalization. But you were quite right, it was the first crack, so to speak, in the foundation of my ethics. When I found out about you, that wasn't something I could live with very easily at all. And yet I did, for her sake. So the crack opened a lot wider. But the foundation did not break. I accept the responsibility for the decisions that I made. I may not be very happy about them, but I do not feel guilt-ridden. More fallible, perhaps, but not guilty. Which brings us to the crux of the situation.

"I've come to the conclusion that the existence of the Dark Ones must be kept a closely guarded secret," he continued. "Not only because knowledge of their existence would bring panic to the population of the world, but because it would also completely undermine most of the world's spiritual belief systems, as well. And I do not wish to see a repetition of the Spanish Inquisition or the Salem witch trials, where thousands of innocent people were condemned to death. Such a climate of fear would only serve to help the Dark Ones."

"That's a very sensible conclusion," Merlin said, blowing out a long stream of peppermint-scented smoke.

"But knowing what I know, I can't simply sit by and do nothing," Thanatos said. "So I would like to help you."

"You can help us best by not getting involved," said Modred.

"That isn't an option," Thanatos said curtly.

"We aren't giving you any options," Modred replied.

"Wait a minute," Wyrdrune said to him. "Don't we get a say in this too?"

"I'm against it," Modred stated.

"Why? We didn't know about Brother Khasim. He did."

"That's right," said Kira. "He was ahead of us on that one."

"We would have tracked him down," said Modred.

"Yes, but not as quickly," Wyrdrune said. "Modred, you're allowing your personal feelings to get in the way. We could use someone on the inside at the I.T.C. Someone who could obtain information for us, get cooperation from the police. Run interference with the B.O.T. if need be."

"I am perfectly willing to let him do those things," said Modred. "But I'm against his taking an active part in this."

"You let Michael Blood take part," protested Thanatos, "and he wasn't even an adept."

"The question is not open to discussion!" Modred said, raising his voice.

"I'm sorry," Wyrdrune said. "I don't recall our ever voting to place you in charge."

Modred spun around to face him, his eyes flashing with anger. For a moment, they simply stared at each other, then Modred said, "Fine. Have it your way. But I'll not be held responsible."

He flung his arms up and teleported.

Thanatos took a deep breath and let it out slowly. "I'm sorry," he said "I only wanted to help. It was not my intention to cause dissension."

"I don't think it's your fault," said Kira. "Not directly, anyway."

"I don't understand."

"Modred won't admit it," she said, "but I think he's carrying around some guilt himself. What do you know about that ring you're wearing?"

"Fay . . . that is, Morgana gave it to me. On our wedding night. It seemed important to her. She said she'd had it for a very long time."

"For at least two thousand years," said Kira. "Modred said it belonged to her mother, Igraine, who received it on her wedding night, from Gorlois, the Duke of Cornwall. He was the youngest member of the Council of the White. The last of the Old Ones."

"I had no idea," Thanatos said, looking at the ring.

"You should have seen his face when Michael Blood told him about the ring," said Kira.

"I still don't understand."

"Don't you?" she said. "For all the distance between them, he still loved her. And he himself never felt loved. Only used."

"Ah," said Thanatos. "I'm beginning to see. Her giving me this ring implies a depth of feeling that she never had for him. So he resents me."

"No, he doesn't resent you," Kira said with a wry smile. "He's jealous of you."

"May I see that ring?" said Merlin.

Thanatos walked over to the boy, took the ring off, and handed it to him. Billy turned the ring over in his hands several times examining the runes carved into the setting, gazing deep into the large fire opal stone.

"Curious," he said. "You mean you never felt it?"

Thanatos frowned. "Felt what?"

"The power," Merlin said. "The power in the ring."

"What?" said Thanatos, raising his eyebrows.

Merlin handed it back to him. "You don't sense anything now?"

Thanatos took the ring back and stared at it. "No. Nothing."

"And you're a sensitive, too," said Merlin. "That's very interesting."

"What is it?" Wyrdrune asked.

"The ring's enchanted," Merlin said.

"How?" Thanatos said. "What sort of an enchantment?"

The boy shrugged. "I haven't the faintest idea," Merlin said. "But whatever it is, it's a spell that's at least as old as the runestones. And now I suggest that you ring room service and have them send up some breakfast. We have a great deal to discuss."

CHAPTER
Eleven

Khasim did not know where he was. A palace of some sort, judging by the vaulted ceiling, the arched cross-wall, and the stone pillars. The walls were hung with ornate tapestries depicting scenes of savage, carnal degradation, demonic visions that would have shocked even a de Sade. He had appeared inside the torch-lit chamber, the incensed braziers reeking heavily of musk, and though his clothes were wet with blood, the bullet wounds were gone, as if they'd never even been there. As he slowly pushed himself up to his feet, an imperious female voice commanded him to turn around. He did so and his mouth fell open.

Before, she had always appeared to him as a shadowy, featureless specter, a darkly glowing manifestation whose voice he had come to know as well as his own, but whose face he'd never seen. He saw it now. And it was so beautiful it took his breath away.

Her oval, fine-boned face was framed by lush, flame-red hair that fell long and thick to a point below her waist. Her skin was a creamy, almost golden color, and her eyes were a fire storm of gold-flecked green. Her nose was straight as a blade, her chin slightly pointed, her mouth wide and sensual, the lips thin and delicately formed. She leaned back languorously on her throne, a thin circlet of hammered gold around her forehead, her tall, slender frame sheathed in a simple, form-fitting gown of raw black silk, cut low and slit deeply up the side to expose a long and shapely leg. She was barefoot, with a thin gold chain around one ankle. Her green eyes flashed at him and when she spoke, her voice was like a whip crack.

"You dare stand in my presence?"

Khasim's legs suddenly buckled, as if he'd been struck viciously across the knees with an iron bar. He actually heard his bones crack. He collapsed to his hands and knees in agony, pressing his forehead to the floor.

"Forgive me, Mistress! *Aaah! Please*, Mistress, *the pain . . .*"

"Pain? What is your pain to me?"

"For pity's sake . . . *aaah! God!*"

"God?" she said, raising an eyebrow. "What god has done for you as much as I have? It was I who healed your wounds. It was I who saved your worthless life and brought you here."

"Have pity, Mistress . . . *aaah!* I beg you, make it stop!"

"Beg then," she said. "Crawl to me, like the vile lizard that you are."

His entire body was wreathed in pain, as if his bones were being splintered. He started crawling toward her, every slightest movement a symphony of torture, every breath a sobbing gasp of agony. She sat, watching him implacably as he slowly dragged himself, whimpering, across the floor. He reached the dais, crawled up the throne, took her foot, and kissed it. It was cold. As cold as ice.

"Please, Mistress, I beg you. . . . Make it stop. . . ."

The pain abruptly went away. He collapsed at her feet, breathing hard, sobbing with relief.

"Thank you, Mistress, thank you. . . ."

He glanced up and his eyes opened wide in astonishment. A second earlier, she had been alone. Now there were two of them. A tall and youthful-looking man stood beside her, leaning against the back of the throne. His skin was a pale golden color and his hair a darker shade of red than hers, falling to his shoulders.

"What do you think, sister?" he asked. "What shall we do with it? Has it outlived its usefulness?"

Khasim turned pale. He opened his mouth to protest, but his throat felt suddenly constricted and only a soft, strangled gasp came out.

"Perhaps, Ashtar," she said. "Still, his life energy can be useful."

They looked down at him as if he were some curious beetle that had scuttled across their field of vision. Khasim began to tremble with dread at the thought that they might do to him as he had done to so many others.

"It is a wretched-looking creature, is it not?" said Ashtar. "Yet, I suppose it's possible it might be of some further use."

"Yes! Yes, I can be of use!" Khasim said desperately. "I've served you well! When have I ever failed you? Haven't I done everything you've asked? Tell me what more I can do! Name it! I'll do anything!"

They turned to one another and smiled.

"We do need a priest, Yasmine," Ashtar said.

Khasim wasn't sure he heard correctly. "A . . . a priest?" he said.

"A sorcerer priest," Yasmine said with a sly smile. And her next words chilled Khasim to the bone.

"For the Black Sabbath."

Jacqueline Marie-Lisette de Charboneau Monet, who insisted on her name being pronounced "Zha-kleen" and never "Jack-we-line," looked more like a French leading lady than a witch. She was in her late forties, but she had the figure of a woman in her twenties. She chain-smoked unfiltered French cigarettes and could drink a Cossack under the table. She favored neo-Edwardian-style brocade suits and wore her dark, gray-streaked hair shoulder-length. Her voice was a husky whiskey baritone, her manner was abrupt and frequently abrasive, and she spoke English with only a slight accent. Most of the police agencies of Europe had a long dossier on her, remarkable in that it listed a large number of arrests for an entire plethora of charges ranging from fraud to grand larceny, and yet not one single conviction.

In contrast, the ebullient Sebastian Makepeace was a bombastic giant of a man, standing six foot six and weighing about three hundred pounds. His flowing, shoulder-length white hair was topped off by a black beret and his out-of-style brown tweeds were covered by a full-length, black leather trench coat. His voice had as much volume as a bullhorn and the only record he had was one of complaints from his fellow faculty members at New York University, many of whom took exception to a professor who was rumored to have connections with government intelligence, taught most of his classes drunk, and claimed to be a fairy. It was not that the more staid members of the faculty objected to his sexual orientation. There was no question on that score. Makepeace was relentlessly, incorrigibly, irrepressibly heterosexual. What they objected to was Makepeace claiming that he was *literally* a fairy . . . a magical sprite, in other words, the sort of creature usually depicted as being of miniature size, with gauzy apparel and gossamer wings.

The fact that Makepeace did not come even remotely close to matching this image did not discommode him in the least. If anything, it made him even more vociferous in his insistence that he was a supernatural being, a fey creature of enchantment. And the fact that the words "fey" and "fairy" had taken on considerably different connotations since the days when they were universally understood to refer to things magical made Makepeace even more vociferous. On occasion, it even made him violent. And a violent, six foot six, three-hundred-pound fairy was a thing not to be trifled with.

Thanatos already had some knowledge of Jacqueline Monet from seeing her Interpol dossier and he had been somewhat prepared for Makepeace by Chief Inspector Michael Blood, who had experienced some of his "fairy magic" up close and personal.

"I never was able to decide if Makepeace was simply a very gifted, albeit seriously neurotic sorcerer or if he was actually a fairy, as he claims," Blood had told him. "Mind you, there's a damn good case to be made in favor of neurosis, but I've known a good many adepts in my time—including the unforgettable amalgam of Merlin and young Slade—and none of them made use of thaumaturgy in quite the same way Makepeace does. I'm well aware that the I.T.C. accepts only the most talented adepts, but just the same . . . when it comes to Makepeace, watch yourself."

Thanatos recalled that warning as he stood with Wyrdrune, Kira, and Billy, waiting for Makepeace and Monet to deplane. He also recalled that first and foremost, their allegiance was to Modred, as both had been clandestine contacts of Morpheus for years. Modred's days as Morpheus were over, or at least so they all claimed, yet just the same, Thanatos resolved to be very cautious around his new associates.

"There they are," said Kira as they came into the concourse, and Thanatos had no difficulty in recognizing them from their descriptions.

Makepeace looked even larger than he had expected, the effect bolstered by his wild hair and dramatic attire. He looked like a black leather dirigible moving through the crowd, which parted before him with alacrity. Jacqueline Monet walked beside him with a firm, athletic stride, yet she still took two steps for every one of his. They both carried shoulder bags.

Hers was a businesslike piece of brown leather hand luggage with a buckle strap; his was a voluminous carpetbag that seemed to have been made from a handwoven Persian rug, suspended from a wide band of woven cloth that resembled a cross between a Navajo belt and a cyberpunk's guitar strap.

Jacqueline spotted Thanatos and hesitated, checking Sebastian's juggernautlike stride with a firm grasp on his elbow. She spoke to him quickly and he frowned, then they resumed their approach.

"Every time I see the three of you," she said, "you appear to be fraternizing with policemen. Did you know this man was an agent of the I.T.C.?"

"Yes, Miss Monet, they knew," said Thanatos. "Didn't Chief Inspector Blood tell you about me?"

"Who?" Jacqueline said carefully, uncertain of her ground.

"Apparently he didn't tell you," Thanatos replied. "In which case, I'm curious as to how you knew me."

"I saw you testify in court once," she said.

Thanatos frowned. "In Paris? I don't recall testifying in a case involving you."

"I was not charged in that case," she replied evasively. "I was merely observing from the gallery."

"No doubt because you must have been involved," said Thanatos dryly.

"You expect me to implicate myself?"

"No, Miss Monet," he replied with a smile. "Your record indicates that you are far too competent for that. I've testified in a number of cases in Paris over the years. I won't try to guess which one might have involved you. And as for your friends fraternizing with 'policemen,' as you put it, it wasn't entirely their decision. At least one of them is doing so under protest."

"And who would that be?" Makepeace asked cautiously.

"That would be your old friend, Modred," Thanatos replied. "Alias Morpheus, alias John Roderick, Michael Cornwall, and an entire host of other names. You see, you need not be so circumspect. I'm very well informed."

"So it would seem," said Makepeace with a questioning glance at Wyrdrune.

"Thanatos is here to help us," Wyrdrune explained. "It's okay. He knows everything."

"Does he?" said Jacqueline with surprise. "And where is Modred now?"

"He's picking up our things and checking us out of the hotel," said Kira. "It's no longer safe there. Thanatos has arranged a place for us to stay. We'll be meeting Modred there, along with some other people. We've got a car waiting."

"It's probably best to avoid teleporting so we can conserve our energies," Wyrdrune explained.

"Especially the way you teleport," said Kira wryly.

Wrydrune gave her a sour look, then turned to the others. "Come on, I'll fill you in on the way."

With Thanatos handling the driving chores, they left the airport and took the freeway to a rented house nestled on a hillside in Laurel Canyon. As the car skimmed smoothly and quickly above the surface of the road, Wyrdrune brought them up-to-date.

"Things have escalated in the last twenty-four hours. The Dark Ones know we're here and too many people knew we were staying at the Beverly Hills Hotel. However, we still have an advantage in that they don't know about you two. At least, not yet."

"They?" said Makepeace. "You mean there's more than one of them?"

"At least two," said Kira. "Maybe more. At this point, we just don't know for sure.

"That's not encouraging news," said Makepeace with a grunt. "What about these other people you mentioned?"

"Rebecca Farrell, a captain in the Los Angeles Police Department, and Ben Slater, a reporter," said Wyrdrune. "They've been working independently with Thanatos 'til now."

"Just how many people have you got involved in this?" asked Jacqueline.

"There's also a local producer we've been using as a contact," Wyrdrune said, "a man named Ron Rydell, but he doesn't really know what's going on. He owed Modred a favor."

"An adept who's been casting the special effects illusions for his films turned out to be in the service of the Dark Ones," said Kira. "He goes by the name Brother Khasim. He was also operating a charity mission on the Sunset Strip as a cover for his necromancy. He's been preying on the street people he was pretending to help, runaways, derelicts, hookers, sacrificing them to the Dark Ones. But last night, the mission was burned down. The bodies of a B.O.T. agent named Gorman and several women were found in the ruins. Khasim killed them and then went on a wild rampage, murdering over a dozen people on the street. And he may not have been the only one."

"You mean there have been more mass killings?" asked Jacqueline.

"If you mean mass killings like Al'Hassan's, no," said Wyrdrune. "At least, not that we know about. Captain Farrell is checking police reports statewide, but the Dark Ones seem to have been specifically avoiding that so far. Any spell powerful enough to consume life energy in a mass sacrifice on the scale that Al'Hassan did would release trace emanations strong enough to be detected at a distance. And they're apparently not ready to come out into the open yet. But after last night, it could come at any time."

"I don't like this at all," Jacqueline said. "Too many people are involved. The police, the B.O.T., the I.T.C., and even a journalist?" She rolled her eyes and shook her head. "I cannot believe it. Why not just call a press conference and announce it to the world?"

"It wasn't their decision to involve the others, Miss Monet," Thanatos replied. "That was my doing. Captain Farrell and Mr. Slater are the only ones aside from us who really know what's going on and you have my personal assurance that they can be trusted to keep it to themselves."

"I'm afraid the personal assurance of an I.T.C. agent does not mean very much to me," Jacqueline said. "Al'Hassan was on the board of the I.T.C., as I recall."

"Then you should also recall that he was ousted," Thanatos replied testily. "But your point is well taken, Miss Monet. For your information, my involvement in this matter is completely off the record. So far as the I.T.C. knows, I'm investigating the disappearance of one of our agents."

"Fay Morgan?" Makepeace said.

"Yes, that's right."

Makepeace hesitated. "You know she's—"

"I know she's dead, yes," Thanatos said flatly. "She was my wife."

"Your *wife*?" Makepeace said incredulously. "But that's . . . that's. . ."

"Impossible?" said Thanatos without emotion. "Is that what you were going to say? Impossible that the enchantress, Morgan Le Fay, should marry a mere mortal? I'd think that you of all people, Doctor, considering your reputation with female undergraduates, would acknowledge that such attractions can occur."

"Is this true?" Jacqueline asked the others with astonishment. "Does Modred—"

"Yes, he knows," said Thanatos curtly, interrupting her. "And he's satisfied himself that it's the truth. Though it seems he doesn't like it very much."

"I think I'm beginning to understand," said Jacqueline slowly. "This is something very personal for you."

"Oh yes," said Thanatos in a soft voice. "It's very personal, indeed." He paused. "I loved her very much."

"I am glad you told us that," Jacqueline said.

Thanatos glanced at her in the rearview mirror. "Why do you say that?"

"Because that is something I can understand," she replied. "I would sooner trust someone who seeks revenge than to merely do his duty. Revenge is a much stronger motive."

She reached into her bag and took out a silver flask.

"To revenge, *mon ami*," she said, and took a gulp. She passed the flask to Thanatos.

"I'll drink to that," said Thanatos grimly.

They turned off the freeway onto Laurel Canyon Boulevard and headed south. Once they reached the canyon itself, with its steeply curving roads, they took a side road that climbed up the hillside and bent back upon itself though several switchbacks until they came to a short driveway leading to a small frame house nestled out of sight behind a grove of trees and some rock outcroppings. Several vehicles were parked in the small open carport and in front of the house.

"What is this place?" asked Makepeace.

"A police safehouse," Thanatos replied. "Captain Farrell arranged for us to stay here indefinitely. We'll even have police protection. Two officers will be stationed outside at all times, though of course they're not aware of the exact nature of this case."

"What have they been told?" Jacqueline asked.

"Something fairly close to the truth, actually," said Thanatos. "They've been told that several 'expert witnesses' and an investigating team will be using the house as a base of operations in a case involving serial murder and necromancy. Needless to say, after last night, they all know about Brother Khasim. The media's been playing it up big all day, especially since he managed to escape. However, officially this is still a case involving one renegade sorcerer and nothing more. No one else knows about the Dark Ones."

Modred had already arrived, as had Rebecca Farrell and Ben Slater. While they were all being introduced to one another, the broom came swishing in, carrying a tray with coffee and doughnuts.

"So *there* you are!" it said, in an affronted tone. "You'd think maybe *somebody* would tell me what was going on, but noooo. . . . There I am, stuck in the hotel, nobody calls, nobody tells me where anybody is, I've swept the room for the twenty-second time and the maids are starting to give *me* tips—"

"I'm sorry, Broom, we've been very busy," Wyrdrune said.

"Busy, shmizzy! Well, excuse *me*, Mr. Man-about-town! It takes so much effort to pick up a telephone? It takes so much time to say 'Never mind with dinner, we'll be working late'? And then I have to run around and do all the packing for you when I suddenly find out that we're moving? It's too much trouble to call and say what's going on, so a person doesn't worry?"

Wyrdrune sighed. "I'm sorry, Broom, you're absolutely right; it won't happen again."

The broom sniffed, which was mildly interesting, since

without a nose, it really had nothing to sniff with. "Hmpf! I've heard *that* before!"

It finished pouring the coffee, then swept out of the room in a huff.

"Every time I see that thing, it makes me feel guilty that I haven't called my mother," Makepeace said.

"Phone's over there," Rebecca said.

"My mother's been dead for thirty years," said Makepeace with a sad shake of his head. "Guilt lingers."

"I've had a couple of calls from some of my old sources," said Slater, getting down to business. "I picked up the messages at the paper and got back to some of them from here. They'll call the paper in case they come up with anything else and I've arranged for the calls to be forwarded here."

Thanatos nodded with approval. "That's good. What have you heard?"

"You were right," said Slater. "There have been other disappearances among the street people, most notably the homeless and the addict population. And I don't think Brother Khasim's responsible for all of them, not unless he's been moving around an awful lot. There've been a number of unexplained disappearances in Venice, at least nine that my source knew of, people who had established patterns of behavior who suddenly broke the pattern and simply weren't seen by anybody anymore. I've also learned of similar cases in Burbank, Watts, and Maywood, as well as Pico Rivera, El Monte, and Covina."

As he spoke, he indicated the various areas on a map spread out on the coffee table. Rebecca took over when he was finished.

"I called the station shortly after we got here and spoke with the detectives I had checking with various local police agencies," she said. "And once again, Thanatos, you were absolutely right. There *were* patterns. Six ritual murders in Huntington Beach, same m.o. as Khasim's, only several of them occurred at times when Khasim's whereabouts were accounted for. There were also five murders in Newport Beach, six in Santa Ana, four in Buena Park, and seven in Placentia. All the same m.o.; all with the same peculiar runes carved into the bodies.

"We've also got a pattern of disappearances," she continued. "Three apparent abductions in Fullerton, high school girls who never made it home. No ransom demands were ever received. No leads; no clues. Nothing. They were all seen heading home, but none of them ever made it. We've got nine missing persons reports in Orange; similar circumstances. Only this time, four of the missing young people were male. Similar reports out of Garden Grove, Irvine, and Costa Mesa, as well as La Mirada, La Habra, Brea, Villa Park, and Tustin. You noticing anything here?"

She too had been indicating the areas on the map as she spoke.

"It all seems to be radiating out from an approximate center," Makepeace said.

"That's right, Doc," said Rebecca, indicating a spot on the map with her index finger. "About right here."

"Anaheim?" said Thanatos.

Wyrdrune and Kira exchanged surprised glances.

"What?" said Thanatos, looking up at them. "What's in Anaheim?"

"The Magic Kingdom," Wyrdrune said in a hushed tone.

Once, years before the time of the Collapse, a man named Disney had a vision of a special, magical place for children of all ages, a fairyland of entertainment that would appeal to the innocent in everyone. Located about thirty miles southeast of Los Angeles in Anaheim, the original park had been called Disneyland and it covered close to a hundred acres. The Magic Kingdom, as it came to be known to millions of enchanted visitors the world over, had something for the dreamer in everyone.

Originally, the Magic Kingdom was divided into different lands—"Adventureland," "Frontierland," "Tomorrowland," "Fantasyland" and so on, each with its own special atmosphere and attractions. In addition to spectacular rides such as the Matterhorn bobsled ride, the Space Mountain, the Pirates of the Caribbean, and the Mississippi riverboat, there were lifelike figures created by an almost magical technology known as "audio-animatronics," as well as real people costumed as fantastic characters from the live-action and animated films the Disney studios produced. It was a clean, well-maintained, and ever-changing world of wonder where everyone who came could forget their troubles for a while and become a child once again.

But sadly, the Magic Kingdom was forgotten in the time of the Collapse. There was no time for magic dreams when everyone was trapped within a living nightmare. And as corporations and governments alike collapsed the world over, so did the Magic Kingdom. There was no one left to wear the brightly colored costumes of Snow White and Mickey Mouse and no children came to wonder at these characters. With all the power gone, the incredible animatronic figures froze into silent immobility. The wonderful rides ground to a halt and slowly fell into disrepair. The Haunted Mansion became truly haunted, empty save for the ghosts of all the children who had once tramped through it to scream in delighted terror at the playful apparitions it contained.

After the Collapse had ended and magic had returned, there was a time of rebuilding and realignment with the natural forces that were once abused so cruelly. For a long while, with the memory so recent and so painful, no one wanted to remember the Collapse or the time that came before, when greed and irresponsibility had almost destroyed the world. It took many more years before people could accept that in addition to the bad things, there were good things about the old days prior to the Collapse. And one of those good things had been the Magic Kingdom.

A small, devoted group of antiquarians and scholars, comprised of both magic-users and lay people, joined together and acquired some of the land where the remains of the Magic Kingdom stood. There was not much left of it. Most of the buildings had long since been leveled and those that had been left standing were in ruins. But the new owners of the property did not give up. They formed an organization called ''Knights of the Magic Kingdom'' and, for a small fee that constituted annual dues plus whatever people wanted to contribute in addition, opened its membership to anyone who wished to join them in restoring the Magic Kingdom to its former glory.

There was a monthly newsletter that detailed their work and issued periodic calls for volunteers to come and spend some time in the laborious restoration project. There was a quarterly magazine that featured articles painstakingly researched and illustrated, depicting the Magic Kingdom as it once had been and telling anew the wonderful stories that had once issued from its creators. There were membership kits including an I.D., a "mousca-pin" and "mousca-patch," as well as a ranking system (from "Subject" to "Page" to "Squire" to "Knight" and even "Lord" or "Lady") based upon volunteer work and amounts donated, which also entitled members to free visits to the Kingdom and various other privileges and prizes. And when the craze for pre-Collapse nostalgia hit, membership in the Knights of the Magic Kingdom grew by leaps and bounds.

Soon, the new Kingdom was completed, this time with *real* magic powering its rides, attractions, and illusions. And adopting the slogan, "Earth is a Magic Kingdom," the Knights continued to support the Kingdom and work toward awareness of the magic energy inherent in all things.

As a boy, Wyrdrune had been a proud member of the Knights of the Magic Kingdom and had held the rank of "Page." Ben Slater somewhat wistfully confessed that he had also been a member, making it as far as "Squire," and Rebecca said she was a full-fledged "Knight" in her late teens, having often spent summers doing volunteer work at the Kingdom. Makepeace, as it turned out, was still a member with the rank of "Lord" and while Billy, due to his harsh life in the London slums, had never before heard of the Magic Kingdom, Merlin surprised all of them when he revealed that he had been one of the founders who began the restoration project. The thought that the Dark Ones might actually be hiding in the Magic Kingdom was a profound shock to each and every one of them.

"You know, I've always wanted to go there," Thanatos said, "but somehow I never found the time."

"My mom took me there once when I was thirteen," said Wyrdrune. "I've never forgotten it."

"One summer I got to be Cinderella," Rebecca recalled. "I still have a picture of myself wearing the costume."

"I always wanted to be Peter Pan and fly away to NeverNeverland," said Kira.

"Well, you've got Tinkerbell right here," said Modred, grinning at Makepeace.

"If that's Tinkerbell, then I'm Pinocchio," said Wyrdrune.

"How'd you like your nose to grow about a foot?" growled Makepeace.

"Enough!" Jacqueline said. "Before we go jumping to conclusions, first of all, how do we know that the Dark Ones are somewhere in the Magic Kingdom?"

"We don't know for certain," admitted Thanatos, "but it does seem as if it would provide the ideal hiding place for them. With all the thaumaturgic energy it must take to power the Magic Kingdom, the trace emanations from their spells could easily go unnoticed unless one were specially looking for them."

"But surely the staff adepts there would have become aware of necromantic spells being cast within their midst!" Jacqueline said. "The trace emanations would be greater! Surely someone would have seen or felt something!"

"Perhaps not," said Makepeace thoughtfully. "Thanatos does have a point. True, the thaumaturgic energy already present in the Magic Kingdom might not be enough to mask the far more powerful trace emanations of necromancy, but it might easily help hide the existence of a spell maintaining a dimensional portal such as the one we encountered in London."

"That's true," said Merlin. "The energy used to maintain a dimensional portal wouldn't have to be any more powerful than the spells used to maintain many of the illusions in the Magic Kingdom."

He used Billy's left hand to slap at his right, which was in the process of reaching for a jelly doughnut.

"Ey!" protested Billy. "Wot's the idea?"

"I can't speak with you stuffing your mouth full."

"But I'm bloody famished!"

"You've already eaten six of those damn things!" said Merlin. "You'll give us an upset stomach!"

"Yeah, an' you should talk with all that rotten swamp moss you go stuffin' in your pipe all the bleedin' time!"

"Look, can you two settle this some other time?" said

Kira. "We've got more important things to worry about right now."

Wyrdrune grimaced. "Yeah. Such as how to find a magic doorway hidden somewhere in the middle of a place that's full of spells."

CHAPTER
Twelve

Jessica Blaine gasped as she opened the door. "What are *you* doing here?"

"You don't sound very pleased to see me, Jessie," said Khasim, pushing past her into the luxurious apartment. "The last time we spoke, I got the distinct impression you thought we should get to know each other better."

"That was before the police were looking for you," she said, then put her hand up to her mouth in her patented theatrical gesture, performed so often it had apparently become natural to her. She stood by the open door and clutched her white silk robe around her.

"Oh? Were the police looking for me?"

He glanced around at her apartment. The living room was decorated all in white. White carpeting, white walls, white furniture, white marble on the bar and coffee tables. A large oil painting of Jessica hung over the mantelpiece, showing her nearly naked, strategically wrapped in a white fur, head back, lips pouting invitation. He smiled.

"You must be crazy, coming here," she said behind him. "What do you want?"

He turned around to face her. "You," he said.

She drew herself up indignantly. "Get out."

Khasim made a languid gesture and the door to the apartment slammed shut with a bang.

"In good time," he said softly.

"Jessica?" said a man's voice from the bedroom. "Who was that?"

By the accent and the drink-slurred speech, Khasim easily recognized the voice of Burton Clive.

"Really, Jessie," he said, turning back to her and frowning disapprovingly. "You disappoint me. I might have thought you would have better taste than that."

"Get out, Khasim," she said, picking up the phone. "Get out right now, before I call security."

Khasim chuckled. "Go ahead and call them."

"You don't think I will?"

"I couldn't care less, Jessie. If you really believe that the security guards can help you, then by all means, call them. They weren't very helpful in keeping me out."

She hesitated, still holding the phone.

"Jessica, who was that at the door?" said Burton Clive, coming out of the bedroom, belting one of her spare robes around himself. It was pink silk with a fur ruff around the collar and wide, fur-trimmed bell sleeves. He saw Khasim and stopped abruptly. "Good Lord!"

"Good evening, Burton," Khasim said. "I must say, that looks rather becoming on you. The color matches your eyes."

"Bertie, throw him out!" said Jessica. "I'm calling building security." She began to dial.

"Now . . . eh, let's not be too hasty, darling," said Clive uncertainly, finding it difficult to maintain his Shakespearian poise in a fuzzy pink lounging robe. "After all, we're responsible, civilized adults. . . ."

"Civilized, my ass," said Jessica. "This man's a murderer! Hello? Security?"

Khasim sauntered over to the bar, picked up a bottle of expensive Scotch, and poured himself a drink. "She's right, you know," he said. "Haven't you seen the news?"

"Security, this is Jessica Blaine. A man's just broken into my apartment. He's wanted by the police for murder. He's a lunatic! Get up here right away!"

Khasim poured another glass for Clive and offered it to him. "Join me?"

Clive swallowed hard and nervously ran a hand through his thick, graying hair. "Uh . . . don't mind if I do," he said, taking the glass and tossing it back quickly. "Now see here, Khasim . . . I . . . I won't pretend to know just what's going on here, but . . . well, there's no reason why we can't be civil about this, is there?"

"Another?" said Khasim, picking up the bottle.

Clive took a deep breath and held out his glass while Khasim filled it to the brim.

"Look, what Jessica said just now . . . I mean, that is . . . I . . . I'm sure there must have been some kind of unfortunate mistake. No doubt it's all some sort of terrible misunderstanding."

"No," said Khasim, shaking his head. "There's been no mistake. The police are looking for me because I *am* a murderer. A necromancer, to be exact. I've sacrificed dozens of people to the Dark Powers. One more?"

"Dear God." Clive's hand shook as he held the glass while Khasim poured.

"Oh, God has very little to do with it, I'm afraid," Khasim said.

"Bertie, for God's sake, *do* something!" Jessica shouted.

"What would you have me do?" Clive said helplessly. "The man's a sorcerer." He slam-dunked the Scotch and took a deep breath. "Look," he told Khasim, "I don't know anything. Honestly I haven't seen the news, so I really don't know what you're talking about. In any case, I swear, I won't tell anyone a thing. . . ."

"How can you, if you don't know anything?" Khasim said, refilling Clive's glass yet again.

"Yes . . . yes, of course. . . ."

Someone started hammering on the outside of the door.

"Miss Blaine? Security! Open up, Miss Blaine!"

"Come, Jessie, it's time to go," Khasim said.

"You must be out of your mind," she said. "I'm not going anywhere with you!"

"Miss Blaine! Miss Blaine, open the door!"

She turned to get the door. Khasim gestured at her.

And she vanished.

"Oh, my God. . . ." whimpered Clive.

"Drink up, Burton," Khasim said, clinking the bottle against Clive's glass.

"Okay, break the door down!"

The bottle of Scotch crashed to the floor. Khasim was gone.

The door splintered and flew open as the security guards burst in with their guns drawn.

"All right, freeze! Don't make a move!"

Burton Clive stood there, swaying drunkenly, naked beneath a diaphanous pink silk lounging robe with pink fur trim around the sleeves and collar.

His eyes rolled up and he fainted dead away.

Detective Sergeant Harlan Bates stood at the head of the muster room, facing the uniformed and plainclothes police officers assembled before him.

"All right, now I'm going to go over this one more time to make sure that everybody's clear on this. All uniformed units will take up their positions near all entrances and exits to the Magic Kingdom. Plainclothes units will circulate inside the park within their respective assigned areas. Keep a low profile. Remember, we don't want to cause a panic. Captain Farrell wishes me to stress that we still don't know for sure the suspect's in there, but if he is, there's a good chance he may not be alone. He may have accomplices. In that event, when the signal comes, we're going to have to move in very quickly."

He slowly looked around at all their faces.

"None of you need to be reminded of what happened on the Strip the other night. Brother Khasim is an accomplished sorcerer who won't stop at killing police officers or innocent bystanders. He is insane and extremely dangerous. He is to be shot on sight. Those orders come straight from the I.T.C. agent in charge of this investigation, in case any of you might have concerns about your legal standing in this. And once again, any of you who might have such concerns need only think about what happened to Officers Paterno, Andruschak, and Levy on the Strip the other night. We never even found the remains of Andruschak and Levy. All we found were the charred pieces of their patrol car.''

He looked around at everyone significantly.

"I want you to think about everything you've heard about this case," he said, maintaining eye contact with them. "I want you to think about the body of Sarah Tracy. You all saw the photographs and the coroner's report. I want you to think about what happened to Victor Cameron, who was literally torn apart while in police custody. I want you to think about those bodies that were discovered in the Lost Souls Mission after the fire that destroyed it. I want you to think about those hookers Khasim murdered and your brother officers who were slain and all the other victims whose bodies we haven't even found yet.''

The room was utterly silent save for the sound of Bates slowly pacing back and forth.

"We know there is at least one sorcerer—Brother Khasim—who's gone renegade and has become a necromancer. Evidence strongly suggests there may be others and that they might have non-adept confederates. The layout of the Magic Kingdom and the diverse number of spells active throughout the park will make them difficult to find, but that's not your job. Captain Farrell and the I.T.C. investigating team will be taking care of that. I don't want any heroics. Your job is to move in when Captain Farrell gives the word and clear the people out of there as quickly and efficiently as possible.

"When the order comes," he continued, "I want everyone to follow instructions implicitly. I don't want any sirens. I don't want anyone running around with their weapons out. I don't want any panic. I don't want any accidents and I don't want any mistakes. I want the citizens moved out of the way and I want it done *fast*. Our number one priority is to keep the people safe. At all times, keep in mind that thaumaturgy draws its power from life energy, only a necromancer can utilize that power much faster and much more efficiently by drawing it from outside sources. . . . In other words, by killing people. Lives are ammunition for the necromancer's spells. And it's the height of the tourist season. The Magic Kingdom will be full of lives.''

* * *

"They're here," said Modred, bringing his hand up to his chest and touching the runestone through his shirt. "I can feel it."

Kira took off her black glove and gazed down at the sapphire runestone in her palm. It was glowing brightly.

"Right," she said. "Only how do we find them in this crowd?"

All around them, people surged in currents and eddies, standing in lines, buying snacks and souvenirs, jostling one another, pushing strollers and tugging small children behind them.

"We're simply going to have to let the runestones lead us to them," Modred said.

"How are you going to do that?" asked Thanatos.

"We'll head in one direction and see if the reaction of the stones is stronger. If it turns out to be weaker, we go back the way we came until their pulsations become stronger once again."

"But that could take all day," protested Slater.

"It could," Modred admitted as they started walking. "However, we have no alternatives. The number of spells that are active in the park already complicate the situation. It would not surprise me if there were decoy spells in place, as well."

"Decoy spells?" Rebecca said with a frown. "What do you mean?"

"The Dark Ones may have cast spells specifically designed to throw us off at different locations in the park," Jacqueline explained.

"Necromantic spells intended to confuse the runestones," Wyrdrune added. "And probably to act as booby traps, as well. The spells could be cast in such a way as to be triggered by the power of the runestones."

Rebecca gave a small snort of exasperation. "Terrific. You're telling me they've sprinkled magical booby traps throughout the park?"

"It's very possible," said Modred, pausing and looking around uncertainly.

"Then why don't you just have the park closed down right now?" Slater said. "Get everyone evacuated."

"Because that will undoubtedly alert them that we're coming," Modred said. "And if they have enough advance warning, they can devise a spell that would endanger the lives of all these people. Timing is everything. We have to get in close enough before they can divert us by striking at the people."

"Fortunately, the same thing that's helping to mask their presence from us works against them, as well," said Wyrdrune. "With any luck, they won't be able to detect our presence until it's too late."

"Assuming we don't stumble into any of these magical booby traps," said Slater.

"We may not have to stumble into them, Mr. Slater," Modred said, looking around. "Some of them might well be ambulatory."

"What?" said Slater.

"They could be moving around the park," Modred said.

"You're sensing something?" Rebecca said, looking around uneasily.

"Perhaps not," said Modred. "I'm not sure. The feeling's not as strong as what I experienced when Khasim was close. There could be something near, but I don't have the sense that it's anyone living."

"Jesus, what the hell does *that* mean?" Slater said. "On second thought, I'm not sure I really want to know."

"Well, I do," Rebecca said. "I want to know what we're going up against. What are you saying, we might have some sort of zombie on our trail?"

"No, that wasn't what I meant," said Modred, "although it's an interesting possibility."

"Interesting isn't exactly the adjective I think I'd use," said Slater apprehensively.

"What I was thinking of was more like a sort of . . . well, a sort of mine, for lack of a better way of describing it," said Modred. "I've encountered spells used in that way once before, as part of a security grid for a—" He caught himself and glanced at Rebecca and Thanatos. "On second thought, it might be best if I did not elaborate on that point. Suffice it to say that it's possible to place a spell on something in such a way that its activation would be delayed and achieved only by a specific stimulus. For example, if a spell of this sort were to be placed upon an object you wanted to protect, then it could be cast so that merely touching the object would trigger it. Or perhaps the spell could be activated by picking the object up or trying to move it, or even by coming into the same room with it.''

"And what would happen?" Slater said.

Modred shrugged. "It would depend entirely on the nature of the spell."

"What about the one you encountered?" asked Rebecca. "The one that was part of this security setup you mentioned. What would have happened if you'd triggered it?"

"Unfortunately, I did trigger it," said Modred. "I managed to escape, but two of my associates were not so fortunate. They died quite unpleasantly."

"Great," said Slater sourly.

"You don't have to come with us, you know," said Wyrdrune. "In fact, it would be better if you didn't. We may not be able to protect you. No one will think you're afraid if you elect to stay behind with the police."

"Are you kidding?" Slater said. "I'm not ashamed to admit that I'm afraid, but if Rebecca's coming with you, there's no way I'm staying behind."

"You don't have to protect me, Ben," she said. "I'm a police officer. This is my job."

"I'm not going to argue about it," he said. "I'm coming with you and that's final."

"Perhaps it might be better if we were to split up," said Makepeace.

"I agree," said Modred. "We could cover more ground that way and we're much too vulnerable bunched together like this."

"But I'm the only one who has a radio," Rebecca said. "How will we keep in touch?"

"We can communicate telepathically," Modred said. "The runestones can forge a mind link between Wyrdrune, Kira, and myself. It will mean expending a greater amount of energy, but it can't be helped. Wyrdrune, why don't you take Sebastian and Rebecca? Kira, you go with Ben and Thanatos. Billy and Jacqueline can come with me. That way we can teleport to whoever finds them first. But whatever you do, wait for the others. Don't go in alone. All right, let's go.''

She awoke to find herself stretched out on something cold and hard. She was in a small, dark room, dimly illuminated by torchlight. She was chained down to a stone slab and she was completely naked. Two pretty teenaged girls stood over her, also naked, their eyes expressionless. One was fingering a string of beads and the other held a small ceramic bowl into which she kept dipping her fingers and then smearing the oily contents on Jessica's skin. Whatever it was, it smelled awful and it made her flesh tingle.

"What . . . what are you doing?'' she stammered at the girl. "Stop that! Let me go! Leave me alone!''

The girl paid no attention to her. Slowly, methodically, she continued to spread the oily balm all over Jessica while her companion stood close beside her, fingering the beads and slowly swaying back and forth while making a tuneless sound somewhere between a hum and a groan.

"Don't touch me! Stop it, I said!''

"I'm afraid they can't do that, Jessie,'' said a familiar voice out of the darkness.

"Khasim?''

He stepped into her field of vision and looked down at her. "It's unguent, Jessie,'' he explained. "A very special sort of unguent, made from the blood of the lapwing and the bat, the raspings of necromantic bells, soot, and a few somewhat less appetizing ingredients. It's ground up by hand with a mortar and pestle, boiled over a fire of vervain and applied over every inch of flesh while it's still warm. It's known as 'witch's unguent,' and it's necessary to be anointed with it prior to the mass, so as to properly prepare the flesh. It nullifies the effects of Christian baptism, you see, allowing you to attend the Sabbath in the same state of nakedness and purity as Adam and Eve.''

"What in God's name are you talking about?'' she said, staring at him with fear.

"Not in God's name," said Khasim with a sinister smile. He held up his right hand with the thumb and two middle fingers bent in toward the palm, little finger and index finger extended. "In the name of Satan."

"You're crazy," Jessica whispered, shaking her head, refusing to believe that this was happening to her.

"Am I?" said Khasim, taking the string of beads from the second girl and holding them over Jessica's face, so she could see them. "Do you know what this is, Jessie?" he asked.

It looked like a small necklace strung with amber-colored beads that alternated with obsidian, as well as dice in various shapes and sizes, tiny bells of gold and silver, a broken crucifix, and what appeared to be a miniature skull.

"It is Satan's Rosary," said Khasim, handing the horrid thing back to the girl, who immediately started fingering it once again, counting the beads and swaying back and forth, groaning unintelligible words in some unspeakable, guttural tongue.

"And these," Khasim continued, holding up a large bowl filled with what looked like old brown sticks, "are the bones of a murderer buried in unhallowed ground. Crazy men imagine things that are not there, Jessie. Yet there is nothing imaginary here. It is all absolutely real and authentic."

He put down the bowl and picked up two black, leather-bound books, one in each hand.

"*La Clavicule de Salomon*," he said, showing her the one in his right hand. "And *Le Grimoire du Pape Honorius*." He held up the other book. "Both dating back to the seventeenth century. The Church declared these to be abominations and ordered them all burned, but a few were hidden away by the sorcerers of those dim, dark days, who only groped blindly toward the powers I serve now."

Jessica began to cry. "Khasim, please . . . please, I'm begging you, please let me go. I'll do anything, anything you want. . . ."

Somewhere above them, a giant gong was struck.

"It's time," Khasim said, his eyes glittering with madness.

The two ensorcelled girls, one holding the dish of bones, the other the bowl of witch's unguent and the Satan's Rosary, stepped up onto the platform on which stood the stone altar that Jessica was chained to. One of them stood on either side of her, their expressions vacant, their eyes glazed. Khasim also stepped up on the platform and stood at the foot of the stone slab, the two black books held clasped against his chest.

"Khasim," sobbed Jessica, "please . . . please. . . ."

The gong rang out again and two trapdoors opened in the ceiling. With a low, scraping sound, the stone platform slowly began to rise.

"Mommy, Mommy, that man's got a rock in his head!" shouted the little five-year-old, tugging on his mother's hand and pointing at Wyrdrune.

They had stopped to make way for a small parade of fantastic-looking mythical creatures, little two-foot-high gargoyles with scaled, batlike wings and goat's horns, capering around for the amusement of the onlookers, led by a piper in a dark, hooded cloak. Wyrdrune scowled and pulled the brim of his hat down farther to cover the bright green emerald runestone.

"Come on, dear, it's not polite to point," said the boy's mother. She tried to pull him along, but he stubbornly dug in his heels and pulled back against her.

"Mommy, *I* want a rock in my head, too!"

The tired-looking woman glanced at Wyrdrune and gave him a strained, apologetic smile. "Come along now, Michael."

"Mommy, buy me a rock for my head!"

"Michael. . . ."

"I want a rock in my head, too!"

"Come *on*, Michael. . . ." She tugged sharply on her son's arm.

Wyrdrune brought his hand up to his forehead.

"Are you all right?" asked Rebecca.

"I don't know," said Wyrdrune. "There's something—"

"Mommy, *look*!"

The little gargoyles suddenly took flight, their metallic wings making clicking sounds as they swarmed toward Wyrdrune.

"Look out!" shouted Makepeace, shoving Wyrdrune aside as one of the creatures came diving down at him, raking the air with its sharp talons. It caught Wyrdrune's hat as he fell and the brown fedora started smoking as the caustic acid from the creature's talons ate into the cloth. Rebecca pulled out her gun, but there were too many people around to risk a shot.

The gem in Wyrdrune's forehead blazed and a bright green bolt of thaumaturgic energy shot out from it, striking one of the dive-bombing gargoyles as it plummeted toward Rebecca. The creature shrieked loudly and broke apart in an explosion of bright, gleaming shards that rained lightly to the ground like pieces of cut glass.

Makepeace whipped off his beret and threw it up into the air. It stiffened and started whirling like a discus, then began darting among the flying creatures with astonishing speed. As it struck them, they broke apart and fell to the ground, shattering into tiny fragments, the pieces melting away into small puddles of steaming ooze. Wyrdrune's energy bolts knocked the remaining few creatures out of the air and the onlookers broke into delighted applause at the display, thinking it was all part of the show. The beret returned to Makepeace like a boomerang and softly fell back into his outstretched hand.

"Mommy, Mommy, I want a frisbee hat, too!" the little boy named Michael shouted.

The hooded piper who had led the creatures took off running, his cloak billowing out behind him.

"Don't lose him!" Wyrdrune cried.

They shoved through the crowd, running after the hooded figure, who pushed through a line of people waiting to get into The Enchanted Grotto. He vaulted the gate, hopped into a cart, and disappeared inside.

"Hey, wait your turn!" one of the parents shouted as they pushed past the people on line in pursuit of the hooded figure.

"Wait a minute, lady," the attendant at the gate protested, grabbing at Rebecca's sleeve. "Get to the end of the line."

"Police officer!" she said, shoving the man away and leaping into a waiting rail cart. Wyrdrune and Makepeace piled in beside her as the cart shuddered off down the track, into the darkness. As they passed through an arched gateway made to look like the entrance to a cave, they were greeted by a cacophony of sounds, like the wailing of spirits echoing throughout the artificial cavern. They could barely see several feet ahead of them.

"I'm not sure this was such a good idea," said Rebecca, nervously holding her gun.

With a bloodcurdling howl, a grinning troll suddenly came scuttling out at them from a crevice in the wall. Rebecca fired and the magically animated troll burst apart in a shower of plaster dust.

"You'd better put that thing away," said Wyrdrune as their cart lurched around a sharp bend in the tunnel. The gem in his forehead glowed brightly in the darkness.

"That's it. I'm calling in the order to evacuate the park before somebody gets hurt," Rebecca said.

She reached for the radio she had clipped to her belt, but it wasn't there anymore.

"*Damn!* The radio's gone! I must have dropped it somewhere back there!"

"It's too late, we can't go back for it," said Wyrdrune. "We've got to catch that piper before he can warn the Dark Ones."

"We'll never do it at this rate," Makepeace said. "Hold on."

He took a deep breath, grabbed onto the edges of the cart and it suddenly started to pick up speed.

Kira heard Wyrdrune's voice in her mind and came to a sudden stop. "Wait," she said.

"What is it?" Merlin asked. "You sense something?"

"It's Wyrdrune," she said. "Come on, he's after someone!" She sent a telepathic call to Modred.

"I heard. We'll meet you there."

The cart was gathering speed as they hurtled through the tunnel, past screaming apparitions that popped up on either side of them.

"Slow down, Sebastian!" shouted Wyrdrune. "We're liable to run into something!"

Rebecca recoiled with a gasp as a flock of gibbering bats

came swooping down at them from the ceiling, but it was only a magical illusion. They passed harmlessly right through the insubstantial flock of bats and lurched around another sharp bend in the tunnel, into a chamber that widened out around them in a garishly illuminated diorama scene depicting little dwarves at work with picks and shovels, digging glittering diamonds out of the rock wall. They sang in high-pitched voices as they worked and some of them paused to wave as the cart went by. They made another turn and the cart swung wildly around, almost overbalancing as they hurtled down another tunnel.

"Sebastian, we're going way too fast!" said Wyrdrune.

Suddenly there was another cart ahead of them. Sebastian tried to slow them down, but they collided and the impact knocked both carts off the rails. Their cart overturned and they came tumbling out onto the floor of the tunnel.

After a few moments, Wyrdrune slowly picked himself up off the ground, groaning and rubbing his shoulder. "Damn it, Sebastian! I *told* you we were going too fast!"

A dancing skeleton knocked into him as it came prancing out from a niche in the wall. Wyrdrune cried out, startled, then angrily batted it away. It fell rattling to the floor, then scuttled back into its niche. Wyrdrune glanced toward the other cart, lying on its side in the middle of the tunnel. It was empty.

"Terrific," he said. "Looks like we've lost him." He looked toward Makepeace. "Are you all right?"

"A little bruised, perhaps," said Makepeace, dusting himself off, "but nothing seems to be broken." He sighed. "I'm sorry. I should have listened to you, but I was afraid we wouldn't catch him."

"Never mind," said Wyrdrune sourly. "Rebecca, are you okay?"

He turned around.

"Rebecca?"

There was no sign of her.

"There's something wrong," said the attendant at the exit gate. "One of the carts must've gotten stuck or something."

"Shut down this ride at once," said Thanatos.

"It shuts down by itself," said the attendant. "It does that automatically if there's any kind of stoppage. Don't worry, sir, it's perfectly safe. I'm sure it's only a minor problem. Kids, you know. Teenagers. Sometimes they get out of the carts and . . . hey, wait a minute, mister, you can't go in there!"

Modred pushed past the attendant and started into the tunnel. Kira, Ben, Jacqueline, and Billy hurried after him.

"Hey, you people can't go in there!"

"Let them go," said Thanatos, showing the attendant his identification. "You stay right here. Under no circumstances are you to let anyone else inside, you understand?"

"Look, mister, what's this all about?"

A plainclothes officer came up to them and flashed his badge. "Police officer," he said. "What's going on here?"

"I.T.C.," said Thanatos, showing his I.D. "You're part of the task force?"

"Yes, sir. Detective Foster."

"Task force?" said the attendant. "What task force? What the hell is going on here?"

Thanatos ignored him. "Captain Farrell's in there," he said. "Something's gone wrong. Get on your radio and have your people move in. I want this park closed down right now. Get everybody out, as quietly and as quickly as possible."

"Yes, sir!"

Thanatos ran into the tunnel after the others.

The stone slab came rising up through the floor into a large, torch-lit, vaulted chamber with walls of mortared blocks of stone and fluted columns supporting arched stone cross braces. It looked like the throne room of some ancient castle. And, in fact, there was a throne, on a high dais at the far end of the room. It glittered in the flickering light of the large bronze braziers placed on either side of it. It was made entirely of gold and encrusted with precious stones. For the moment, it was empty.

To the left of the dais hung a giant gong and it was ringing out steadily, despite the fact that no one was there to strike it. Its sound was deafening. Jessica wanted to cover her ears, but her arms were chained down at the wrists. Drawn on the stone floor around the altar was a large cabalistic circle, with strange signs painted within it. The circle itself was inside a larger drawing on the floor, that of two interlaced triangles forming the Seal of Solomon. Jessica recognized the satanic paraphernalia from the necromancer films that she had starred in. Placed on the floor at various points inside the circle were a human skull, cracked and brown with age; a severed human hand, known as a "hand of glory"; a lamp burning scented oil; a violin and bow; and a turnip painted black that was used in the satanic mass in place of the Host.

It was both ludicrous and terrifying at the same time. It was just like a scene from one of Rydell's films. It had to be a set. None of this could possibly be real. And then Jessica recalled what had happened the last time they filmed a scene that was almost identical to this and she began to tremble uncontrollably.

Khasim stepped off the dais and carefully laid the two black books down inside the circle, opening each of them to a specific place marked with a raven's feather. The two enchanted girls stepped back away from her as well, to the outermost points of the circle. In the darkness at the far sides of the cavernous room, Jessica thought she could see shadowy shapes moving.

The ringing of the gong ceased abruptly, its echoes reverberating off the walls. Khasim raised his arms up to the ceiling and the violin and bow suddenly floated up into the air, as if borne up by some invisible musician. The bow moved as if of its own volition across the strings and Jessica recognized the opening notes of "Night on Bald Mountain" by Saint-Saens. Death playing his violin at midnight while the evil spirits come out of their graves to dance.

The Black Sabbath had begun.

CHAPTER
Thirteen

"*Rebecca!*" Wyrdrune shouted.

His call echoed in the dark tunnel. There was no answer.

"We'd better split up and look for her," Makepeace said.

"No way," Wyrdrune said. "One of us has already disappeared. Let's not try for two, all right? We stick together."

They heard running footsteps.

"Be careful, someone's coming." Makepeace said.

"It's all right," Wyrdrune said, hearing Modred's voice in his mind. "It's only Modred and the others."

Slater came running around a bend in the tunnel. He was breathing hard. "What's happened?" he said, gasping for breath. "Where's Rebecca?"

Modred and the others were right behind him.

"Rebecca's disappeared," said Wyrdrune.

"What the hell do you mean, she's disappeared?" Slater said.

"I mean she's gone," said Wyrdrune. "We were chasing a man in a dark, hooded cloak through this tunnel and our cart collided with one that was ahead of it. We overturned and were thrown clear. When we got up, Rebecca had disappeared."

"You were supposed to be protecting her!" cried Slater.

Modred put a hand on his shoulder. "Take it easy, Slater. Both you and Captain Farrell were advised to stay behind. You were told we couldn't guarantee protection, yet you both insisted on coming along. Now recriminations are not going to help us find her. She might still be around here somewhere, lying unconscious—"

"No," said Wyrdrune, shaking his head. "We've already looked all around here."

"Then she's either been carried away or she somehow passed through a dimensional portal," Modred said.

"If she passed through a portal, then it must be around here somewhere," Kira said.

"Unless it was closed after she passed through it," said Jacqueline.

"God, then what do we do?" asked Slater anxiously.

"What we started out to do," said Modred. "Find the lair of the Dark Ones. This is probably nothing more than a diversion intended to draw us away from our objective."

"You're not going to just leave her!" Slater said.

"We have no choice," said Modred. "We must find the Dark Ones at all costs."

"No!" shouted Slater. "I'm not going! Somebody's got to look for Rebecca! She could be in danger!"

Modred paused, hesitating. "Very well. Jacqueline?"

She nodded. "I will stay and help look for her."

"I'll stay, too," said Makepeace. "It's my fault she's been taken. We'll try to catch up with you."

"How will we know where you'll be?" Jacqueline asked.

"If we find the Dark Ones," Wyrdrune said, "I have a feeling you'll know."

"Good luck," said Makepeace.

"You, too," said Kira.

They split up and Wyrdrune, Kira, Modred, Billy, and Thanatos went back out through the exit while Slater, Makepeace, and Jacqueline headed in the opposite direction, retracing the route the cart had taken.

"How will we know if we find one of these dimensional portals?" Slater asked. "What do they look like?"

"You cannot see them," said Jacqueline. "They are invisible."

"Well, that's just great," said Slater. "How the hell are we supposed to find it, then?"

"If you come in contact with one, it will be very cold," Jacqueline explained. "It will feel like freezing water."

"But you can't see it," Slater said.

"Correct."

"So by the time I get this feeling like I'm touching freezing water, I'm already going through the damn thing."

"All the more reason to proceed with caution," Jacqueline replied. "If you pay close attention to your surroundings, then if you pass through a dimensional portal, you will be able to get back the same way."

"Wait a moment," Makepece said, pulling up short.

"What's wrong?" said Slater.

They had come around a bend and Makepeace stood in the center of the tunnel, between the rail tracks the carts traveled on. He stood frowning, staring at a place where the tunnel opened out into a garishly illuminated diorama.

"The dwarves," he said.

"What dwarves?" asked Jacqueline. "I see no dwarves."

"Precisely," Makepeace said. "What the hell happened to the dwarves?"

Rebecca couldn't move. She was being taken down a narrow corridor by two ranks of tiny dwarves, who carried her between them on their shoulders while they swung their free arms in exaggerated motions and sang, "Hi-ho, hi-ho, it's off to work we go . . ."

She had struck her head and lost consciousness when she was thrown clear of the cart and when she came to, she was being tightly bound and gagged. The magically animated dwarves had dragged her from the spot where she had fallen and pulled her through a narrow maintenance door in the tunnel before Wyrdrune and Makepeace had recovered. By the time Rebecca realized what was happening, it was too late. They had her legs tied together and her arms bound tightly to her sides. She couldn't move a muscle.

The little dwarves reached the end of the maintenance corridor and came out into a fenced-in work area around the back of the ride. They dumped Rebecca into the back of a small cart with a fringed canvas top, piled in themselves, and drove off through the gate. Down in the bottom of the cart, Rebecca couldn't see a thing. All she could see were the grinning little dwarves all around it, swaying happily from side to side as they sat in the cart and sang in their high-pitched voices.

* * *

"Watch it!" said Thanatos, pulling Billy back by the arm as the little cart whizzed by, almost running him over. The cart swung around wildly with a screech of its small tires and continued weaving its way down the walk while the dwarves inside it swayed back and forth like beer buddies and sang their little work song. .

"Ey! Watch where the bloody 'ell yer goin'!" Billy shouted. He turned to Wyrdrune. "Blasted little morphodites," he said in Merlin's voice. "They shouldn't let them drive!"

"Why *are* the dwarves driving?" Wyrdrune said, thoughtfully staring after the cart.

"*Ladies and gentlemen, the park is being closed,*" a police officer announced through a bullhorn. "*Please proceed immediately to the nearest exit. Thank you for your cooperation. Ladies and gentlemen, the park is being closed. . . .*"

"What did you say?" asked Modred.

"The dwarves!" said Wyrdrune. "The dwarves from The Enchanted Grotto!"

"What?" said Thanatos.

"Come on!" shouted Wyrdrune. "Run!"

Jessica could not believe her eyes. It was a scene wilder than anything she'd ever seen and she was trapped right in the middle of it. Musical instruments were whirling around in midair and playing by themselves while fantastic-looking creatures danced and capered all around her. It was like a surrealistic scene by Breughel, with little bird-legged, furry creatures with short horns and long tongues leaping all about, whistling teapots and steaming cauldrons waddling around her on stubby little legs, herds of great horned toads and white mice hopping about in time to the music while the torches blazed up on the walls, revealing nude figures standing there, entranced, naked teenaged girls and boys waiting in stiff, ensorcelled postures, eyes blank, jaws slack, oblivious to their surroundings.

The torches blazed up once again and several niches opened in the walls, through which a number of somber figures stepped into the room. They were sorcerers, like Khasim, dressed in their ceremonial robes. Adepts in the service of the Dark Ones. They came toward the cabalistic circle and stood around its circumference, their hands clasped in front of them. They looked up at Khasim, the high priest, and bowed respectfully.

Jessica gasped when Khasim turned back to face her. She almost didn't recognize him. His long, sleek, jet-black hair had turned completely gray and his handsome face had aged. It was lined and wrinkled, pale, and his lips trembled like an old man's.

The sorcerers around the circle shrugged off their robes and stood naked in the torchlight as the music peaked and the surrealistic creatures spun around in their wild dance. And as Jessica watched in disbelief, the sorcerers started changing. Matted fur started to sprout from their bodies and horns pushed up through the skin of their foreheads. Their feet seemed to wither and gnarl, then harden into bone as they turned into tufted hooves. Their knees bent sharply and their thighs grew larger and more muscular. They were turning into satyrs right before her eyes.

And then Jessica saw other strange creatures, elves and skeletons and little pigs in human clothing walking up on their hind legs, all leading little children by the hand, bringing them into the room where they stood watching, fascinated, not realizing the danger they were in. Now other people started coming in, groups of men and women dressed in pirate costumes, Indian loincloths and headdresses, cowboy clothing, the fringed buckskins of frontiersmen, and each small group carried a person, either bound and struggling or unconscious.

Jessica realized with horror that there was going to be an act of mass sacrifice—and she would be the main offering.

"Look!" said Slater, bending down to pick up something from the ground. "Rebecca's gun!"

He tucked it into his waistband as the others came to join him.

"Yes, she was unquestionably brought this way," said Makepeace. He pointed at the ground, where there were long tracks in the dust. "Looks like she was dragged."

They followed the trail to a narrow door made to look like

part of the artificial rock wall. Makepeace found the handle
and opened it.

"Be careful," Jacqueline said.

Makepeace felt around inside. "Nothing so exotic as a
dimensional portal," he said. "Just a plain, ordinary doorway. The dwarves took her this way. Come on."

"You're telling me Rebecca was carried off by a bunch
of magically animated dwarves?" said Slater.

"It certainly seems that way," said Makepeace, moving
down the narrow maintenance corridor. He bent down quickly
and picked up something off the floor.

"What is it?" Slater said.

"A piece of rope," said Makepeace. "They must have
tied her up."

They proceeded quickly down the corridor and came outside into an open, fenced-in work area. There were two little
maintenance carts with fringed canvas tops parked against
the fence and the gate was open.

"They must have loaded her up in one of the carts and
driven off," said Makepeace.

"Now what?" asked Slater.

"We'll have to try and find them somehow," Makepeace
said. "There's nothing else to do. Come on."

They climbed into one of the other carts and drove out
through the gate.

"*Attention, ladies and gentlemen, attention! The park is
being closed. Pleased proceed immediately to the nearest
exit. Thank you for your cooperation. Attention. . . .*"

"They've started to evacuate the park," said Makepeace
as he drove, looking all around for a sign of any cart similar
to theirs.

"We're never going to find her," Slater said.

"We'll find her, Ben," Jacqueline said. "We'll find her."

"My baby!" screamed a woman. "What happened to my
baby?"

"Michael?" another woman cried. As they drove by,
Makepeace recognized the mother of the obnoxious five-year-
old. "Michael, where *are* you?"

"Jennie?" called a young man as they passed him. "Jennie?"

"There's going to be a panic," Slater said tensely. "The cops are going to lose control. People are getting separated from their kids, it's all going wrong. It isn't going to work."

"Sheila? Sheila, where *are* you?" someone called as they drove by.

"My God," said Makepeace, weaving through clumps of people running around and streaming toward the exits. "They've started snatching people!"

"What?" said Slater.

"That's why Rebecca was abducted," Makepeace said. "They've started grabbing people, children . . . victims for a mass sacrifice."

"A mass sacrifice?" said Slater, alarmed. "What are you talking about?"

"A Sabbath," Jacqueline said softly. "They're celebrating a Black Sabbath."

They ran hard, trying to keep the crazily weaving cart in sight. All around them, people were moving toward the exits, some proceeding in an orderly fashion, others running. People were calling for their children, boyfriends were calling for their girlfriends, husbands seeking wives they had suddenly become separated from. Nobody knew why the amusement park was being evacuated and everyone had their own suspicions. The police were moving through the crowd, trying to keep order and keep everybody moving, but the people who had become separated from members of their families were refusing to be herded out. The crowd was on the verge of panic.

"Do you feel it?" Modred called out as they ran.

"It's all around us," Kira said. "What the hell is happening?"

"It's much worse than I thought," said Modred. "They've taken over. They've overwhelmed the spells controlling all the attractions and illusions. They have the entire park under their control."

"There's an incredible amount of energy being gathered," Wyrdrune said, gasping as he ran. "I can sense the focus somewhere just up ahead."

They passed a sign that said, "Sleeping Beauty Castle

closed for repairs.'' The castle was just ahead of them, its graceful towers and turrets rising up into the sky. The drawbridge had been lowered and the cart driven by the dwarves turned and drove across it.

''There!'' said Modred, stopping to catch his breath. ''The Dark Ones are in there! I can *feel* it!''

''No,'' said Wyrdrune, aghast as he stared at the beautiful castle, the famous symbol of the Magic Kingdom. ''Not in there!''

As they stood there, the drawbridge slowly started to rise.

''We'll never make it,'' Thanatos said.

''Yes, we will,'' said Modred. ''We'll teleport.''

''Kira, quick, give me your hand,'' said Wyrdrune.

''Not this time, warlock,'' she said. ''I'm not ending up in that damn moat! Modred?''

He took her hand. ''Thanatos?''

''I can make it.''

''All right. Now!''

The drawbridge was already up at a forty-five-degree angle. They teleported. Modred, Billy, and Kira reappeared inside the courtyard of the castle. Thanatos popped in a second later, right behind them.

''Where's Wyrdrune?'' Kira said.

''Shiiiiiiiiiiiiit!''

They turned around in time to see him sliding down the inside of the rising drawbridge, rolling end over end until he hit the ground and came to a tumbling halt at their feet.

''Well, that certainly was graceful,'' said Modred wryly.

''Get any splinters?'' Kira added.

''Very funny,'' Wyrdrune said sourly.

''Modred, look!'' said Thanatos. He held up his hand. The fire opal on his ring was glowing brightly.

Modred stared at it and frowned.

''What does it mean?'' asked Thanatos.

''I haven't the faintest idea,'' Modred said. ''I didn't even know it was enchanted.''

''Don't look at me,'' said Merlin. ''Morgana did not always confide in me, you know. For that matter, even she might not have known. The ring belonged to Gorlois. It's as old as the runestones themselves.''

Thanatos tugged at the ring. "It won't come off!"

"Well, then I guess you're about to find out what the spell is," said Modred as they went through the castle doors. "Let's hope it isn't too unpleasant. This is not a good time for surprises."

Jessica watched in frozen fascination as the last of the captives were brought in. Rebecca was among them. The dwarves set her down and joined in the whirling dance as the sorcerers-turned-satyrs moved among the captured victims, making passes at them and putting each into a deep trance. The ropes holding Rebecca magically fell away, along with her clothing, and she had time only for a brief gasp as a leering satyr stepped before her and then her vision blurred and everything went numb as she retreated somewhere deep inside herself, still able to see and feel, but no longer able to control herself.

Khasim stood on the altar beside Jessica, his arms thrown wide, his chest rising and falling as he gasped for breath. He was a doddering old man now, aging rapidly before her eyes. His hair had turned pure white. His pale skin now translucent, the flesh hanging in slack folds. His dark eyes were glazed and deeply sunken, his hands were liver-spotted, gnarled, and palsied, the fingernails as long as talons. His right hand held the ritual dagger and Jessica could not tear her eyes away from it. She writhed panic-stricken on the altar, pulling against the chains, but they held her fast. The music was reaching a crescendo and the dancing figures whirled faster and faster and faster.

Suddenly there was a mist in the shadows over the throne, an area of deeper darkness that slowly formed into the brightly glowing outline of a man. A moment later, the dark shadow with the glowing border resolved into a handsome, golden-skinned young man with dark red hair and a crimson robe thrown over his well-muscled shoulders. Except for the long robe, he was naked. He had the body of a Greek god. But below the waist, he was a goat with cloven hooves and a forked tail. Ram horns sprouted from his forehead. He held a pitchfork in his hand. Jessica cried out and shook her head. No, she thought, it couldn't be, it couldn't possibly be. . . .

A strong voice suddenly rang out in the torch-lit chamber, rising above the music and echoing off the walls.

"Khasim!"

The music stopped abruptly. The skeletal sorcerer jerked as if struck. His hair had all fallen out and the bones showed through his face. He was barely able to stand. He looked up toward the sound of the voice. He was astonished when he saw that it was only a young boy.

"Drop the knife!" called Merlin, extending his arm toward the high priest. "Drop the knife or die!"

Khasim looked down at Jessica, his face a grinning death's head. She screamed as the knife started to descend.

A searing, bright blue bolt of thaumaturgic energy shot out from Billy's outstretched hand, lancing across the torch-lit chamber and striking Khasim in the chest. It blasted him right off the altar platform and he flew backward to land on the stone floor, lifeless, his skin shriveling away to nothing, his bones collapsing, turning into dust.

With a snarl, Ashtar threw off his robe and leapt from the throne. Large, batlike wings unfolded from his back, spreading as he launched himself into a long glide across the chamber, swooping down over the altar. Jessica screamed hysterically as he raised his hands, claws extended, intending to rip her open as he swept on past her in his dive toward Billy, but in that moment, three bright beams flashed out across the chamber. Modred had torn open his shirt and a scarlet beam lanced from his chest to strike Kira's upraised hand, where she stood against the wall, near the center of the chamber. A bright sapphire beam shot forth from Kira's palm and struck the stone in Wyrdrune's forehead, which in turn sent its emerald beam across the chamber to strike the stone in Modred's chest. The living triangle was formed and it extended up and out from them in a pyramid shape, trapping the Dark One and all the shape-changed sorcerers beneath it. With a cry of agony, Ashtar fell, his wings collapsing and shrinking away as he reverted to his normal form under the combined power of the runestones. The satyrs started bellowing as they reverted to their human shapes and sank down to the floor, clutching at their throats. Billy ran up to the platform and climbed up to the altar. His eyes sizzled with blue fire and twin beams of thaumaturgic energy shot out from them, burning through the chains holding Jessica. He picked her up in his arms and carried her through the archway and down the corridor, which led out to the courtyard, calling to the others to follow him. In a daze, Rebecca and the other captives stumbled after him. Behind them, Ashtar fought to struggle to his feet, but he collapsed at the foot of the altar, gasping as he tried in vain to draw air into his lungs. He clawed at his throat and thrashed upon the ground, his movements growing weaker and weaker as the living triangle leeched his life force from him.

Halfway down the corridor, Billy came to a sudden stop. A strikingly beautiful, golden-skinned young woman with a thick mane of fiery red hair stood at the far end of the corridor, blocking their way. She was wearing a long black robe and her green eyes glowed with thaumaturgic fire.

"*No!*" she snarled in a voice that was laced with venom. "You'll all die for this!"

"No, Yasmine," said Thanatos, stepping out from a side corridor to stand between her and the others. His voice sounded much different, deeper and more resonant. "You have killed enough. This time, you shall be the one to die."

The fire opal on his ring burned like a star, glowing brighter and brighter and brighter, its blinding light enveloping him entirely and when it died away, Thanatos was gone and in his place stood a knight in full, gleaming armor, a twisting, ivory horn rising from his helmet, his shield bearing the device of a unicorn rampant.

Yasmine stared at him with disbelief. "*You!*" she said.

The knight unsheathed his sword and started walking toward her.

She opened her mouth and a deafening screech issued forth that sounded like the trumpeting bellow of some prehistoric beast. She spread her robe out and scaled wings began to form. Her face lengthened and her back arched. She began to grow, looming larger and larger as the metamorphosis progressed with amazing speed. Her long tail whipped back and forth, her giant wings beat at the air, her long, curving teeth snapped as she hissed and bellowed at the knight who continued to approach her resolutely. She grew until her scaled bulk filled the entire corridor and her wings scraped against the ceiling. And then the dragon opened up its mouth and a stream of fire shot forth.

"'Gor'blimey!" Billy said, staring slack-jawed as the knight took the fire full upon his shield and continued to advance.

The dragon flapped its wings furiously and pieces of the ceiling started to rain down.

"Get back!" Billy shouted. "Everyone get back!"

The dragon's tail whipped around and the knight jumped over it, then he dropped his shield and caught it as it whipped around again. The dragon bellowed and started to rise up into the air as the knight climbed up along its tail, clinging stubbornly despite all her efforts to dislodge him. Debris rained down as she broke through the ceiling and rose up high into the air, screeching with fury and pain as the knight clung to her back, his sword rising and falling as he hacked away at her repeatedly.

The little cart swerved wildly as Makepeace nearly lost control and almost crashed. Around them, people ran screaming toward the exits, the police no longer able to control them.

"Sebastian, look!" Jacqueline said.

"I see it," Makepeace said, braking sharply and staring at the apparition ahead of them.

"My God," said Slater, staring wide-eyed at the sight. "What the *hell* is that?"

A dragon was rising up high over the fairy-tale castle, its huge wings beating at the air, its bellowing screams echoing throughout the park. There was a tiny figure perched upon its back, an armored knight who kept plunging his sword down between the dragon's shoulder blades again and again and again. The creature threw back its head and screeched in agony, then fell, pinwheeling to the ground. They felt the force of its impact as it struck.

"Come on!" Jacqueline urged Makepeace. "Drive on!"

The cart lurched forward, toward the castle.

Billy stood over the dead woman's broken body. Her back was covered with raw stab wounds and blood trickled from her mouth and nose. Her neck was at a strange angle and her legs were splayed out beneath her. As Billy watched, she slowly began to fade away like a mirage until there was nothing left of her at all.

Thanatos lay on his back in a pool of blood a short distance away, his glazed eyes staring sightlessly up at the sky. Billy bent down and closed them. He heard a clinking sound as the ring fell from the dead sorcerer's finger and rolled toward him, coming to a stop at his feet. Billy picked it up and put it in his pocket.

A crowd was gathering around him. The dazed captives from the castle stood around, confused, some embarrassed by their nakedness, others too disoriented to fully realize their state. The small maintenance cart pulled up and Slater leapt out and ran over to Rebecca, taking off his coat and wrapping it around her protectively. Modred, Wyrdrune, and Kira came through the crowd to stand behind Billy. They looked utterly exhausted.

Makepeace took off his long black leather coat and was about to offer it to Jessica, but she didn't even see him. Heedless of her nakedness and the crowd around her, she came up to Billy and put her arms around him.

"You saved my life," she said, and kissed him deeply.

"Please, madam," Merlin said in an embarrassed voice, extricating himself awkwardly. "Go get some clothes on."

EPILOGUE

They sat drinking coffee in the kitchen of Rebecca Farrell's small apartment. It was late and she had just come off duty after the busiest and longest day of her career.

"Officially, the story is that Khasim went completely off

the deep end at some point during his involvement in Rydell's necromancer films and started taking it for real,'' she said. ''He supposedly 'discovered' a sub-basement underneath the mission, a relic from the days of the Collapse when an older building had stood there, and he used it as a meeting place for a satanic cult he organized. The department called in Gorman to help with the investigation of the murders and Gorman asked the I.T.C. for help when he realized that necromancy was involved. Gorman uncovered what Khasim was doing at the mission and Khasim killed him, then holed up in the Magic Kingdom after subduing the wizards on the staff, which allowed him to assume control of the spells used to maintain the attractions and illusions in the park. That part of it, at least, is true, except it was the Dark Ones who overpowered the wizards at the Magic Kingdom and not Khasim.

''As for what happened in the castle,'' she continued, ''the official word on that is that the whole thing was an elaborate special effects illusion executed by Khasim. He had become obsessed with Jessica Blaine and intended to murder her in a reenactment of the climactic scene from the last necromancer film. A team of non-adept special effects technicians who worked with Khasim on that film have testified that he was a gifted illusionist who could easily have pulled off such a sophisticated series of effects, especially if he was able to tap into already existing spells devised by the wizards of the Magic Kingdom. Thanatos had managed to put it all together and he stopped him with the aid of a special department task force, but both Khasim and Thanatos died in the confrontation. Fortunately, the people who were kidnapped by the Dark Ones and their acolytes were sufficiently dazed and confused by everything that happened and none of them can really contradict the official version of the events that transpired in the castle. The Bureau has brought in a team of therapist adepts to debrief the victims and provide counseling. So far as the official version of the story goes, none of you were even there, although both the Bureau and the I.T.C. are very anxious to find out what *really* happened. In particular, they're anxious to speak with the staff of Warlock Productions, but luckily, I was able to get to Ron Rydell before they could question him.''

"How did Rydell respond?" asked Modred. "What did you work out with him?"

"Rydell's story is that Warlock Productions decided to back out of the film deal due to adverse publicity and he doesn't know what happened to them. He told the investigators that the Warlock people closed down their L.A. office and left town, leaving him holding the bag, and he made a lot of noise about how he'd like to find them himself because he intends to sue. He conveniently neglected to mention the twenty-five million dollars that you gave him but assured me that he intends to pay it back as soon as the heat's died down.''

She smiled at Modred. "He seemed extremely anxious not to antagonize you. Anyway, he was very convincing. In the meantime, the so-called adverse publicity has given Jessica Blaine's career a tremendous boost and there's apparently a deal in the works to adapt *Ambrosius!* as a Broadway musical, starring both her and Burton Clive.''

"Oh God!" said Merlin with dismay.

"Serves you bloody right," said Billy, still angry with him for not having allowed him to take full advantage of Jessica Blaine's gratitude. "'Gor', I ain't never 'ad anyone kiss me like that before an' you 'ad to go an' ruin it!''

"That will be enough of that," said Merlin sternly. "You're much too young for that sort of thing and as for me, I'm much too old. As far as I'm concerned, the sooner we leave Los Angles, the better.''

"That's a very good idea, said Rebecca. "There's an I.T.C. investigator by the name of Graywand who's been asking a lot of very pointed questions about the four of you. And he's particularly interested in 'Michael Cornwall.' I had a pretty close call with him.''

"I know of him," said Modred. "He's the I.T.C.'s senior field agent. I've had a couple of close calls with him myself over the years. He's very sharp and extremely competent.''

"That was my impression, too," said Rebecca. "He's convinced I know a lot more than I'm telling. He wanted to interrogate me under a spell of compulsion, but the police commissioner and the chief put a stop to that idea. They said that I'd already answered all his questions and the fact that I'd been abducted and almost killed entitled me to some consideration, so he decided not to push it. But he's not the sort to let it go. He'll keep after it, you can be sure of that. So if I were you, I wouldn't stay around too long.''

"No, I think we'll be leaving right away," said Modred.

"What, *again* we're moving?" said the broom, swishing in with a fresh pot of coffee. "Nice of somebody to tell me. How do you expect me to keep things organized if nobody ever tells me anything? Always everything at the last minute! Rush, rush, rush! *Gevalt!* I'm going to get permanent jet lag at this rate!''

"Since when does a stick get jet leg?" Kira said.

"You hear this?" said the broom, turning to Rebecca. "You see the kind of respect I get? What it is with young people these days, I'm asking you? They're spoiled, that's what they are. Spoiled rotten.''

"There's still one thing that I don't understand," said Slater. "Not that understanding it will do me much good. It's really ironic. The greatest story of my career and I can't even write it. But I still can't help being curious.'' He turned to Billy. "That spell on the ring Thanatos wore. When he changed into that knight, you said he called the Dark One by name. Yasmine. And from what you said, she seemed to know him, too. So if he wasn't Thanatos, who was he?''

"No, he was Thanatos," said Modred. "But for a short time, the spell of the ring changed him into someone else. And it explains why my mother always wore that ring and why she gave it to him after they were married. She wanted to protect him.'' He paused. "The unicorn device on the knight's shield means that it could only have been my grandfather. The last survivor of the Council of the White. Gorlois, the Duke of Cornwall.''

"Of course!" said Merlin. "I, of all people, should have realized that. Only it was so very long ago . . . I had forgotten.''

"But . . . I thought you said that Arthur killed him," Kira said.

"He did," said Modred. "But my grandfather was as powerful a mage as the ones who fused their life forces with the runestones. He must have prepared a similar spell to guard against his physical death, one that would preserve his spirit." He paused and sighed heavily. "I looked for the ring when Thanatos died, but he was no longer wearing it. The only explanation I can think of is the spell must have worn off."

"No, wait!" said Billy, reaching into the pocket of his coat. "You should 'ave told me! I've got the ring!"

"*What?*" said Modred, sitting bolt upright. "*Where is it?*"

"Just a minute," Billy said, rummaging through all his pockets. "Wait, I know I've got the bloody thing 'ere somewhere. . . ."

"Billy," Kira said. "It's on your hand!"

"It's what?" said Billy. He looked at his hands. The fire opal was gleaming on the ring finger of his left hand. "'Gor'blimey!" he exclaimed. "So it is! But it wasn't . . . I didn't put it on! I swear I didn't! I 'ad it right 'ere in me pocket!"

He tried to take it off.

"I think it's stuck," he said, grimacing. "I can't understand it, it was way too big before. . . ." He kept pulling on it, but it wouldn't budge. "Bloody 'ell, now it won't come off!"

"I don't think it's meant to, Billy," Modred said softly.

Billy stared at him. "What? No, g'wan, it's only stuck, see. . . ."

He put his finger in his mouth and moistened it, then redoubled his efforts to pull it off, but it remained stuck firmly on his finger.

"It looks like Modred's right, lad," Makepeace said. "It seems as if the spirit of Gorlois has chosen to remain with you."

Billy looked up at them with alarm. "No," he said. "No, it can't be!"

"I'm afraid it is, Billy," Modred said. He smiled. "It's the supreme irony, in a way. Arthur killed Gorlois with Merlin's help, and now both their spirits are with you. It should prove rather interesting, to say the least."

"No!" said Billy, shaking his head with disbelief. "Aw, *no*! You mean now I'm stuck with *two* of 'em? *Oh, bloody 'ell*!"

"You can say that again," said Merlin, miserably. "Oh, bloody hell!"

As if in answer, the fire opal glowed brightly for a moment and Billy got a very strange smile on his face. Then he threw back his head and laughed. Only they knew it wasn't Billy laughing. And Merlin was not at all amused.